SHOW ME

SHOW ME

CELIA MAY HART

APHRODISIA

KENSINGTON BOOKS

http://www.kensingtonbooks.com

KENSINGTON BOOKS are published by

Kensington Publishing Corp.
850 Third Avenue
New York, NY 10022

All Kensington Titles, Imprints, and Distributed Lines are available at special quantity discounts for bulk purchases for sales promotions, premiums, fund-raising, and educational or institutional use.

Special book excerpts or customized printings can also be created to fit specific needs. For details, write or phone the office of the Kensington special sales manager: Kensington Publishing Corp., 850 Third Avenue, New York, NY 10022, attn: Special Sales Department, Phone: 1-800-221-2647.

Aphrodisia and the A logo are trademarks of Kensington Publishing Corp.
Kensington and the K logo Reg. U.S. Pat & TM Off

ISBN: 0-7582-1464-2

First Kensington Trade Paperback Printing: June 2006

10 9 8 7 6 5 4 3 2

Printed in the United States of America

1

The Honorable Mark Knightson lounged on the divan, the red silk cushions shifting beneath him. Utterly free of all traces of gentlemanly attire, even his cravat, he focused on pretty Miss Adeline's pert form.

She rose from kneeling by his feet and sat at her tiny vanity, patting her mouth and reapplying her make-up, casting many a flirtatious look at his sprawling form via her cheap mirror.

Mark's gaze traversed the golden falls of her loose hair, which ended right above the perfect round peaches of her buttocks.

Miss Adeline was no innocent miss but one of Madame Garbadine's finest girls. Madame catered to his every need and he made it worth her while on the rare occasions he visited her establishment.

Adeline had done an excellent job, working him into the necessary frenzy before he spent himself into her wide, willing mouth. He'd almost failed her, the thoughts of his latest coil, of how nearly Lady Cecily Lambeth had snared him, almost undoing his erection.

Marriage.

That one word alone made his cock go limp. If it hadn't been for the arrival of a second girl, a stunning redhead, who posed so prettily while playing with her gorgeous tits, it would have been absolute disaster.

Alas, the sex had not sated him, only a temporary distraction from his problems. He cursed under his breath. There had to be a way out of his dilemma. He reviewed the situation.

He'd taken Lady Cecily for a bored widow, a woman no doubt consumed by dullness since the early days of her marriage to a senile lord who had vainly hoped for an heir, and who had finally done her the favor of dying.

Even dressed in the black crepe of mourning, he watched her flirt with one handsome young man after another. He came to the rapid conclusion that Lady Cecily shared her charms freely and he joined the pack. He knew he'd be successful in claiming her, although he'd no desire to catch another man's syphilis.

And Lady Cecily had hung upon him, in public and in private, and dismissed her other playmates.

The idiot girl had more naiveté than he had dreamed, thinking his determined pursuit was to result in a leg-shackling.

Marry her? He'd disabused her of that notion and quit her company, coming here to drown out such a near catastrophe.

He couldn't lurk inside a brothel forever. Some solution to Lady Cecily's expectations must be found.

He rose and dressed, restoring his cravat to almost neat precision. At this late hour, nobody would care about a wrinkled cravat, except perhaps for Beau Brummel and his set, and they he avoided.

So. What to do?

His time honored solution of fleeing to the Continent had been soured by war, although Italy was not out of the question.

To the countryside, then, he must go.

* * *

Miss Portia Carew slipped into the library, closing the door behind her. Not even a full day at Willowhill Hall and she'd already had enough of Mama browbeating her about marriage. Worse, she'd noticed the other guests looking at her and whispering behind their hands. Whispering about her.

Society agreed she'd been wronged, but still the circulating rumors and accumulating doubts continued.

Portia ran her gloveless fingertips along the book spines, her fingernails making a satisfying snap each time it caught the edge of a book. The staccato sounds pleased her, soothed her.

A title caught her eye: *Clarissa* by Richardson. Her lip curled. She wouldn't end up like that silly ninny. Dying over being compromised? Not she!

She stomped her foot, her slippered feet almost silent against the soft rug beneath her. Her irritation built again. No, not irritation. Anger.

Never mind that all the rumors were true—she'd fought hard to keep her parents' trust and bamboozle the rest of her social circle.

It mostly worked.

She scanned the book titles, noting the uniformity of the golden bindings. Was this a show library, or a real one? If she pulled out a book, would any of the pages be cut showing they had been read? The book bindings varied in color: red moroccan leather encompassed an entire set of encyclopedias, and farther down she spotted olive-green spines.

She looked at other shelves. Dull geography, duller politics and mind-numbing encyclopedia entries. Wasn't there anything of interest?

She circled, taking in the small room.

A series of bay windows brought in filtered light, filtered for the translucent curtains were drawn. Fitted bookshelves of golden-hued wood covered the remaining walls from floor to ceiling. Two ladders stood affixed to a brass rail, making them steadier and easier to move along the shelves.

She scanned them, her head tilting back as she took in those book spines out of reach. All were volumes of tedious likeness, no sign of any romantic novel, or stirring adventure. Unless . . .

On the upper shelves, the books were a riot of sizes and bindings. Some, she noticed, were little more than cheap paper. That's where the good reading lay.

Gathering her skirts of her high-waisted gown, she ascended the ladder. No titles were written on any of the spines. On the thicker books, initials had been imprinted, but nothing more.

Curiosity piqued, Portia pulled out a volume. *The Seduction of Julia.*

She almost put it back. She didn't care for another rendition of *Clarissa*. Resting the bottom of the book on the shelf, she paused. If it was another variation on that abysmal story her mother had forced her to read, why had she not heard of this book, if it were meant to be "improving"?

Portia flipped to the first page, staying atop the ladder. If it were no good, she'd put it back and find another.

Lord Darkmoor groaned. The tongues of three different lovelies flicked over his hard nipples, his flat belly, his burgeoning cock—

Portia shut the book with a snap. Breathing hard, she shoved it back into its place on the shelf. She steadied herself on the ladder. *Imagine! Such things in writing!*

Her hand visibly trembling, she reached for another. Were they all like that? She read the next title. *Lady Godown and Miss Bottom.* Her brows rose and she opened the book at a random page.

Miss Bottom lay spread before her, white limbs wide and begging for her lady's embrace. Her skin was like milk and soft to the touch.

Lady Godown trailed a finger along the girl's ribs, watching with pleasure as the girl shuddered. With one touch, the girl's tits hardened, ready for sucking.

The lady accepted the invitation, fastening her ruby-red lips upon the girl's taut tit, sucking and licking . . .

Portia shivered, gripped in some undefinable emotion and held the ladder tighter. How would that feel? Her breasts knew the touch of a man's hands, but a mouth?

She squeezed her legs together, feeling desire rise. Lust. Such feelings ought not come from books.

She should put this back and see if the shelves contained anything less lascivious.

Instead, she kept reading. The ladder had a built-in narrow seat, so she turned and sat on it, hooking one arm around the ladder's stile for safety.

She read on, lifting a hand to cover her breast. If a woman could do this to another woman, could she not do it to herself? Dare she?

Portia slipped a hand into her bodice, letting her fingertips be the lady's tongue and mouth, plucking and flicking her nipple. What would be more like a mouth? She experimented using the tips of all her fingers, and then just her thumb and forefinger. Perhaps if she wet them—ah, but then there might be a mark on her bodice when she left. Better not risk it.

The lady in the book lavished attention on both breasts and Portia's hand followed her path.

Heat washed over her. Her nipples hardened into pebbles, swelling to double their size. An urgency welled in her belly, and Portia knew these feelings would soon fade and end. They usually did.

The lady kissed down the girl's belly and to the cleft between the girl's legs, already spread for her. Squeezing her legs together tightly, Portia read of the girl's private parts glistening in the candlelight. She assumed that's what the author meant by "cunt." What else would be down there?

Portia's hand slipped to the vee at the top of her thighs. She glanced toward the library door. She dare not lift her skirt. What if someone came in?

Perhaps it would be better to sneak the book back to her room. . . . But no, she had the library to herself.

She pressed her fingers against herself, feeling the top of her slit. Oh, how she wanted to! But no. She returned to playing with her breasts. So hot and sensitive, they almost couldn't stand to be touched.

She moaned, almost under her breath, and with one hand unfastened her bodice. If she were to be damned, she might as well enjoy it. Her bodice had come all askew anyway.

She released her breasts from their linen prison and the cool air of the library felt like a balm upon them. She sighed with relief and resumed her reading, twirling her exposed nipples and feeling a darker heat build within her groin.

Something sparked and ached and demanded more attention than the squeezing of her slender thighs. She wriggled in her narrow seat, her breath coming in short pants.

Someone cleared his throat.

Portia's book slipped between nerveless fingers and plunged to the floor. The loud smack of the book against the wooden floor made her jump. She clung to the ladder, avoiding a nasty fall.

No one was at the door. In the opposite direction to the entrance, a man gazed up at her, twisted around the edge of a high-backed wing chair in order to see. Beneath his hooded eyes gleamed a look like a hawk finding its prey.

Shivering, she covered herself, refastening her bodice with

lightning fingers. She hastened down the ladder to make her escape.

You're beyond ruined now, girl.

"Not so fast." Mark Knightson stood behind the wanton chit. He laid a hand on her half-bared shoulder, aroused as all hell and in a dilemma.

Clearly one of the guests, this girl should be untouchable. He hadn't known that when he'd first heard her sighs and muffled moans.

Concealed by the back of the chair he'd meant for his refuge, he listened to her until he could bear it no more. His cock strained at his breeches, wanting to join in the fun, wanting to make her scream.

And so, he revealed himself, discovering that his target was not some young widow, but a fresh-faced—correction, pink-faced—miss.

Ravishing her on the library floor was no longer an option. He took another deep breath, regaining control of his enflamed nerves.

The girl hung her head. "Please go away," she murmured.

His fingers stroked a luscious dark curl. So much for being under control. "Why?"

Her head turned to the side, much of her face still concealed, so he heard her more clearly. He wouldn't forget that face in a hurry, pink with desire, delicious lips parted. She'd been approaching the pinnacle of release. She must be awfully disappointed.

He released her and stooped to pick up the book. "An interesting choice of reading."

The girl must have realized he wasn't about to let her escape, for she turned and faced him. "It . . . It was unexpected."

He handed the book to her. "I am sorry to have interrupted your pleasure."

She pinked further but delivered a careless shrug. "I was done."

Done? The girl hadn't even reached boiling point.

"I would appreciate it if you said nothing of this."

"You may be assured of my discretion." He paused. *It was really none of his business.* "May I ask why you say you had, er, finished?"

"There is nowhere higher to go."

Poor, frustrated thing. "But there is."

Her eyes widened. "Not in my experience. You mustn't fib to me."

He raised his hand. "On my honor, I would not tell a lie." He worried that he leered. "In fact, I was on my way to assist you to that conclusion."

Her face remained pink, but her brows rose in an attempt at coolness. "To help me, or satisfy yourself?"

"That has been your experience too, I warrant."

She bit her lip, not replying. No doubt she had realized too late what she had revealed about herself. He wondered if she planned on packing her bags as soon as she left the room. He didn't want that.

"I swear, not a word about what has happened or been said in this room will leave my lips."

The girl stepped back from him, as if considering flight. Fear and uncertainty consumed her fair features, giving her a peaked expression.

"But you are wrong when you say you were done. There are much higher heights to climb. I could show you."

Apparently, his brain had no part in this conversation, except to provide grease to his still-aching cock.

She shrank back against the ladder. "Show me?"

"There is an art to touching yourself, to arousing yourself, to bringing yourself to completion." He kept his voice low in an effort to keep it steady. He might demonstrate the art here and now. At any moment, his cock might burst its constrictions in his eagerness to possess her. "I am very familiar with a woman's body."

Her eyes narrowed. "I am sure you are. What sort of a woman do you think me?"

He chuckled. "You ask that after what I saw?"

"It was—I was just following what was in the book." She'd turned a delightful shade of pink again.

His right eyebrow rose. He was inclined to believe her on this, actually. Oh, she was no green miss. She'd had experience of some sort, she'd as much as confessed it. But whoever her previous amours had been, they hadn't been at all proficient in pleasing her.

"Indeed," he said at last. "You have a natural sensuality . . . that I would hate to see go to waste."

The fire rose in her eyes and she clenched her fists. "And who says it will go to waste? How dare you, sir!"

He stepped back to deliver a short bow. "My apologies," he murmured. He closed in again, succumbing to the urge to stroke her flushed cheek. So smooth. "But think on it. I will look forward to your answer."

She stared at him for a long moment, her pretty little mouth gaping. "Oh!" she exclaimed in an indignant huff, and stormed out of the library.

Mark grinned. He'd noticed she still clutched the book to her not inconsiderable chest. She might pretend she's some innocent, outraged miss, but he knew better, even on such short acquaintance.

He sobered, marking out paces across the small library's floor. To tease the girl about bringing her to sexual fruition did little more than whet his appetite where it should not be whetted. To consummate his plan was quite another matter.

Oh, not that he would have any trouble in doing it. He imagined the chit laid out before him, naked and begging him to make her come.

He smirked. Of course, he'd have to teach her those words.

His smirk widened. Teach a sweet Society miss how to talk dirty? Oh, wouldn't her future husband get the surprise of his life?

Rubbing his hair, Mark sighed. Why indulge in this daydream? If the girl were even halfway respectable, she'd not even speak to him for the remainder of this house party.

Halfway respectable and the girl may already be screaming to Mama about how she's been compromised. Especially if the chit had some half-baked plan to trap him in wedlock. In fact, perhaps it would be best if he took himself off—

He halted. Run away? A Knightson? Without proof, the girl would ruin herself in making such a foolhardy declaration. No, he remained quite safe for the time being.

Besides, what if she said *yes*?

Portia hurried upstairs, and down the shadowy wood-paneled hallway to her allotted room. She prided herself on never getting lost. Even though she'd been here at Willowhill Hall for only a few hours, she knew her way.

She burst into her room to find her mother waiting for her and groaned inwardly. Mrs. Carew was a graying, stout woman and a bundle of eiderdown fluff when it came to managing her children.

"Oh Portia! I do wish you wouldn't disappear like that! You have a reputation to recover." Her mother wrung her hands.

Portia ducked her head in seeming contriteness. "I'm sorry, Mama. I went to visit the library for something to read." She choked on a gasp. She still had that explicit book in her hands, for all to see! Trembling, she restrained the urge to hide it behind her back.

Mama seemed mollified by her answer. "What did you find?"

"A penny dreadful novel." The answer came quick to her lips. "Lady Barrington has quite the collection."

"Those were her father-in-law's, dear."

Portia had the sudden longing to know more about old Lord Barrington. Was he incredibly masculine like the fellow she met in the library? Was he the shade of old Lord Barrington? But no, he seemed far too real, and far too modern. There must be a portrait somewhere. She would seek it out.

"Portia?"

"Yes, Mama?" She had not been attending her mother's conversation. She blinked away the blurred cream walls of her room and focused on her mother.

"Do sit down. I will do your hair for dinner tonight, and then you may do mine. There is no time to dawdle, for we must be introduced to everyone beforehand."

Portia obeyed, sitting at the small cherrywood table and mirror in her room. They had not received the best rooms in the house, hers being quite small, but at least she didn't have to share with her mother.

Mama stood behind her, unpinning her hair. Portia closed her eyes. Any minute now, the tirade would start. "Do this . . ." "Don't do that . . ." At twenty-one, Portia had heard it all.

Repeatedly.

"Portia, my dear, you must be your sweetest self tonight." Mama started combing out Portia's hair. "Lady Barrington has invited a number of eligible young gentlemen. One is a viscount—the son of a duke! You must aim for him, my dear, how nice it would be to see you well settled and with a title. Your dear father will be so proud of you if you achieved such a thing.

"Although, Lady Barrington's son is also of age to marry and Lady Barrington confided to me that he would be looking for a match during this little house party. Surely she would not have intimated that to me if she did not think, did not hope as I do, that our friendship could be bound by the bliss of matrimony. You and Freddy! Just imagine it! Lady Barrington and I can see each other so much more often and it will be—"

"Mama." Portia had received the message. "You don't need a marriage to see Lady Barrington more often. You can see her whenever you like."

"Not until you are married, my dearest pet. I will not eschew my duty to you for some frivolous friendship."

Portia sighed. She didn't dare remind her mother she really didn't care for the idea of marriage. Not any more. Not when soon she would have the skills to satisfy herself without the brutish inconvenience of a man.

That is, if she dared to accept the stranger's offer.

She sighed again. Mama and Lady Barrington had been close since a brief stint in finishing school. "Your friendship is not frivolous," she soothed. "Are you sure she wants me to marry Freddy? After all that horrid gossip . . ."

Not even that could dissuade Mama. "Nonsense, child. Lady Barrington knows as well as I that you were utterly innocent of that charge. That man is a libertine and a rake and I only wish I'd known that before I allowed him to court you. Who knew he would be so horrid about breaking your engagement? Wretched, wretched man. I wish you'd never laid eyes on him."

"So do I, Mama." Portia's heartfelt response held no duplicity this time.

"But, my dear, you do see the importance of becoming the absolute epitome of girlish innocence. You must be proper in all things. Never allow a gentleman to take even the smallest advantage of you. And they might try, given those dreadful, horrid rumors."

"Mama," Portia warned, but it went unheard.

"Not even the tiniest kiss, Portia. Not even a flirt with a fan, or whispered conversations that nobody can hear, and above all else, Portia, you must never be alone with a gentleman, for Lady Barrington and all the other guests will think the worst."

"If I cannot flirt, Mama, how am I supposed to attract them?"

"By your sweet, biddable nature, my dear," Mama replied, blithely.

Portia jerked her head forward, trying to conceal a laugh. Her? Biddable?

"Keep still, dear, or your curls will be all askew."

"Yes, Mama." Portia straightened and stared at her reflection in the mirror. Her eyes still danced with suppressed amusement, bright with unshed tears of laughter.

Her mother caught her looking. "There, there, dear. It will all turn out well in the end, you shall see. We shall find you a nice husband and you will be able to face London Society without a mote of shame."

Portia doubted that, but said nothing, giving her mother a small smile before schooling her features into something that approximated sweet biddability.

"Good girl," Mama cooed. She twisted Portia's black hair into more ringlets. "Now let us review the gentlemen who will be there tonight. You will express interest in everything they say, but it helps to say something of mild intelligence back. Not too smart, my pet, else they will think you smarter than they and that will not do. I will not have you lose a husband because you have been given free rein in your father's library."

"Yes, Mama." Portia forbore rolling her eyes, but at least she now had a technique for scaring off any suitors who might decide to pursue her seriously, ill gossip or no.

"First, there's Lord Freddy Barrington. I am sure I don't need to describe him or his interests to you. You have met him a number of times."

Indeed, she had. Freddy seemed perfectly agreeable: to someone who was horse-mad, hunting-mad and drinking-mad, which she was not.

"Then we have Viscount Winterton. He's the youngest son of the Duke of Winterton—"

"Mama, how do you know all this?"

"Why Lady Barrington and I had a little coze about it this afternoon, after we arrived, and of course I consulted my copy of Debrett's Peerage."

Which had probably taken up at least half of one of Mama's bags. Portia groaned inwardly.

"In any case, my dearest pet, that is not important. Viscount Winterton is."

"He is?" Portia had lost the thread of conversation. What did Mama mean?

"Yes, my dear, you may be thinking that he is out of your league because he is the son of a duke, but he is the youngest son, with three older brothers to succeed to his father's title before him, so there is little hope of him ever achieving that title. Which makes him, and his family, a little less particular about who he should wed. Money, if we may talk about such a vulgar thing for a moment, is the last thing they need, the Duke being so rich."

"Not too rich for us?"

"No. Lady Barrington tells me that the young viscount will have a small estate upon his marriage, which will set up him and his future bride, which might be you, quite comfortably."

"If that's true."

"Of course it is true, why would Lady Barrington lie to me?"

In some ways, her naive mother excelled at manipulation. "I don't know." Portia could think of at least one reason: to keep her away from Lord Freddy and not have her precious son tainted by scandal.

Mama slipped silk flowers into Portia's hair. "Do try not to lose these, Portia dear. They are expensive to replace."

"Yes, Mama," Portia replied meekly. "Is that all of the eligible men?" She hoped so. Was her mysterious stranger in the library the Duke's youngest son?

"There is the Honorable Mark Knightson. His father is a viscount, and he will inherit the estate. He's older than the others, but shows no sign of settling down into marriage."

"Why not?" A chill settled on Portia's shoulders. The man she had encountered had been no young whippersnapper like Freddy. Could he be Knightson?

"Who can say?" Mama examined Portia's hair in the mirror. "Yes, that will do you. I do not know why Lady Barrington asked him to come. No doubt he will keep Lord Barrington company, he is quite the man's man, I hear."

Portia stood to give her mother the chair and proceeded to do her hair.

That sounded like her stranger. Tall, broad shoulders, a look in his face that said he had seen much, although perhaps not so much as a young lady touching herself in the library. That dark, saturnine face, wavy black hair and blue eyes, eyes that burned both hot and cold. He had to be Knightson.

"Portia! Stop daydreaming. There is much to do."

Lady Barrington's guests gathered in the drawing room, waiting for the call to dinner. A riot of royal blue papered walls greeted Portia, the walls heavily decorated with faded gold curlicues. Gold echoed again in the edgings of the delicate furniture scattered almost negligently throughout the room.

"Mr. Knightson, may I introduce Miss Portia Carew?" Lady Barrington's words faded into Knightson's incredible blue eyes twinkling with what Portia suspected as secret amusement.

He murmured something over her hand. His heat soaked into her skin from that light touch, and she muttered something in reply, disconcerted.

She let Lady Barrington move her on to the next person, without dropping into a faint or becoming confused. Portia straightened her shoulders. She refused to let that man's laughing gaze cow her.

At last she met the remaining ladies of the party: sharp-faced Mrs. Chalcroft and her two daughters, who blessedly, did not take after her.

Portia calculated they were two men short for dinner, which with the rankings of precedence, left her trailing in alone, or arm in arm with one of the Chalcroft females, whoever was the younger. Not a good start to finding a husband.

She suppressed a victorious grin.

Lady Barrington must have noticed her compressed lips. "Do not fret, my dear. Not all our guests have arrived. Freddy has some friends coming up from Town in the next few days. I do hope you will bear the imbalance."

Portia shot her a genuine smile. "It is of no concern at all, my lady. I shall enjoy getting to know the Misses Chalcrofts better."

Miss Sophia Chalcroft turned out to be the younger.

"I shouldn't go in with you," Sophia muttered to Portia. "I'm the one Mother is marrying off. Lucy's well past it."

Portia clucked in sympathy, filing away the tidbit of knowledge. Lucy may become an ally later if the pursuit of suitors became too hot.

They took their seats and Portia glanced down the table at where Knightson took his place.

He sat, seemingly oblivious to her, conversing to the elder Miss Chalcroft, Lucy.

Now that she had the chance to have a proper look at him, Portia saw that her first impressions in the library had been accurate, except that his expression had thawed.

His boyish smile seemed at odds with the dark arousal she'd faced in the library. Had she, in her impassioned haze, imagined it?

Knightson glanced at her, his expression freezing. For an instant, his hungry gaze drank her in, his parted lips caught on an intake of breath.

Portia gasped. His burning eyes asked the question again: would she let him become her teacher of self-pleasure? She hadn't imagined either his lustful gaze or his offer. Should she take it?

2

What should she do? With a certainty, Portia knew allowing the Honorable Mark Knightson to teach her this intimate activity made her vulnerable to either further scandal, or in being used by him.

She didn't know him. How could she trust him?

Yet, if she didn't agree to be taught, what would she miss? He'd said that she should reach greater heights in her arousal.

How did he know she hadn't? What if he'd lied to her? She'd always thought that something felt just out of reach, but time after time, she never touched it. Yearning formed part of the experience, making her want to come back and do it again and again.

Her mind turned it over and over, undisturbed by the sulking Miss Sophia on her left and Mrs. Chalcroft on her right. For once, being snubbed had its benefits.

Portia glanced down the table at Knightson. She'd have to tread warily. Mama had given her notice to be on her best behavior and another scandal would end her place in Society forever.

Portia's plans for her future did not include absolute exile.

After dessert, the ladies returned to the drawing room for tea. Portia settled herself on the edge of the feminine group, not entirely by choice. Her mother had left a place open for her, but Portia had no intention of being trapped next to her all night.

She accepted a cup of tea from the maid and sipped at the hot brew. When would the men come in? She burned to ask Mr. Knightson questions, to discover any treachery that may lie beneath his offer before she dared to accept it.

She ignored the conversation, mostly soothing Sophia's complaints.

"Sophia is very young for her age."

Portia almost spilled the remains of her tea onto her pale blue gown. She glanced aside.

Miss Lucy Chalcroft sat beside her, sipping her cup of tea. "My pardon, I did not mean to startle you," Lucy said, her voice husky.

"No, not at all. I'm afraid I was daydreaming."

Lucy's blue eyes sparkled, bringing life to her previously dull visage. Of course, the dull gray gown and her blond hair pulled back into a tight bun had given no hint of her mischief. "Of the man you might marry?"

Portia examined her and risked a less than ladylike snort. "Hardly."

Lucy's face creased into a smile. "Then why are you here?"

"Mother." Portia nodded in her parent's direction.

"Ah. At least you're still being given the chance to dream of a future husband."

Portia's gaze narrowed. "You're not?"

"I am past my prime, my mother says," Lucy said, keeping her voice low. Like a conspirator, her head bowed toward Portia's. "It is Sophia who must have first chance at the men. I am to stay a wallflower, she says, and keep her company." Lucy darted a glance at the older women, cooing over Sophia's future. "Not that she needs me."

Platitudes burst into Portia's head but she said none of them, patting Lucy's gloved hand with her own. "Do you wish for a husband?"

"No more than you, it's true. I wanted it once, no longer."

Portia smiled at her. "Then we shall become bosom friends and allies. You will help me avoid catching a husband, won't you?"

Lucy returned her smile. "Even at the danger of catching one myself!"

The two girls chuckled.

Portia asked, "Do you know any of these gentlemen?"

"Not a soul," Lucy confessed, "although young Barrington seems a bit wet behind the ears to be looking for a wife."

"There's nothing wrong with young and eager." Portia smirked. "He's an only child. I'll wager his father wants heirs and spares before the estate falls out of the family."

"You gamble, Miss Carew?" Lucy's warm voice cooled and the dull, prim version of Miss Lucy Chalcroft reappeared.

Portia flushed a little. "Only on sure things, Miss Chalcroft. Forgive me. I am afraid Mama has thrust me at some very young suitors indeed, and I have picked up some of their language."

"She's that desperate?"

"I have a younger sister who will be coming out next year. She doesn't want to be bothered with me."

"I am sure that is not true."

Portia sighed. "True enough. She wants to see me well-placed before my prettier sister—"

Lucy withdrew, retreating from Portia.

"Oh! I didn't mean to offend!" How careless of her to forget Lucy's situation.

"None taken."

"But you did!" Portia insisted, leaning forward and taking Lucy's hand. "Do forgive me. It seems we really are in the same boat and I know how much it stings. I forgot myself in my complaining. Forgive me?"

"Forgiven." Lucy's smile and the squeeze of her hand sealed it. She looked up. "Here come the gentlemen."

They entered in a riot of laughter, sobering at the sight of all the expectant females. Lord Freddy Barrington made a beeline for Miss Sophia and soon drew her away from her chaperones. With much giggling, Sophia settled at the pianoforte and played the opening bars to a popular duet. Freddy joined her in song.

"This is going to be a long night," Lucy whispered to Portia.

"Better her than I," Portia replied. She saw Mrs. Chalcroft flutter her handkerchief. "I think Mrs. Chalcroft is trying to get your attention."

Lucy looked and sighed. "Please excuse me." She rose and crossed to her mother's side, bending over to listen.

Mark Knightson took her place. He kept a respectable distance, close enough for quiet conversation. Too close, Portia thought. He overwhelmed her—his trim exterior hid a voracious sexual hunger underneath. Portia practically smelled it. "Good evening, Miss Carew." His voice, like dark, rich chocolate, did little to revise Portia's opinion of him.

She started to squirm, her thighs rubbing together, before realizing Knightson had noticed even this subtle movement. "Evening, Mr. Knightson. Were the port and cigars to your satisfaction?"

"Frankly, no."

Portia's eyebrows rose.

"I hardly tasted them." He drew closer, his low voice a delicious burr that resonated in her crotch. "I wanted to talk with you, to allay your fears."

Portia kept very still, very cool. She couldn't allow him to see how he affected her. She couldn't let anyone else in the room see either. "What do I have to be afraid of?"

"Me."

At least he was honest. She swallowed. "I am aware of the dangers."

"Then let me assure you that I am a man of my word. I will not take more than is agreed upon and I am the epitome of discretion."

He wouldn't plunge inside her? Fill her until she screamed? Portia suppressed the disappointment. "You seem eager to teach me," Portia mused. "I wonder why that is."

The duets sung by Sophia and Freddy masked his murmur. "You have a raw sensuality, Miss Carew. One that needs taming—"

"I have no wish to be tamed, Mr. Knightson," Portia hurled at him in soft outrage, her back stiffening.

"I meant in the sense that if you satisfy yourself, you do not need to proceed into dangerous liaisons with other gentlemen."

Cold washed over her. Had he heard the gossip too? Or did he just warn her? "Mr. Knightson, you have been listening to nasty rumors."

The corner of his mouth twitched upward. "You forget, I have seen how unbridled your desire is, Miss Carew. It will get you into trouble."

"If I were a man, nobody would talk to me of 'getting into trouble' if I chose to have affairs." She put down her teacup, the china making a dreadful clatter.

Knightson shifted in his seat, a worried frown scarring his forehead for a moment. "Not unless the man in question was known to cause trouble. Women tend to steer clear of such types."

"But *he* would still be accepted into Society, still be able to marry into Society, and still be able to carry on with mistresses afterward!"

To her astonishment, Knightson chuckled, concealing his laughter with a large hand. "Miss Carew, you are not supposed to know such things."

"Mr. Knightson, we women are not so blind as you'd like to think!"

A silence fell between them. Portia pretended to listen to yet another duet from Freddy and Sophia. Lucy had not been joking when she said it would be a long night.

Mr. Knightson spoke again, the humor gone from his voice. Instead, Portia heard patience and understanding. "I agree, it is unfair for women, but that's the way things are, and you have to learn to live within those boundaries. If you'd let me teach you how to pleasure yourself, you may be less inclined to seek fulfilment elsewhere. It would also be helpful if your husband didn't come up to snuff."

Portia sniffed. "I don't intend to marry." She glanced sidelong to gauge his reaction.

His eyes widened. "Then why are you here?"

"Why are *you* here?"

"I needed a break from the City."

Portia's brows arched. "Don't you have a home to go to?"

"I do." Knightson's shoulders hunched. "It also contains a father who insists I marry and sire him more heirs. I am not interested in matrimony either, I assure you."

A wave of relief washed through her. "Then there would be no attachment, no commitment between us if I choose to accept your offer."

His father dismissed, Knightson resumed his purring charm. "None whatsoever. Believe me, I never bed a woman more than five times before I tire of her." His black brows lowered. "Fair warning."

How many women? Portia wanted to ask, but dared not. It made him a greater danger, not merely experienced but a rake.

"It should take but a lesson or two," he prompted. He seemed to hold his breath.

"Two lessons." She nodded, bowing her head. "I agree."

"Excellent."

Her mother trilled from her place on the sofa. "Oh, Portia dear! They're forming up sets for whist. Why don't you join in?"

Portia rose, trying to ignore the trembling in her limbs. "Duty calls."

He delivered a roguish grin. "Meet me in the library tomorrow morning at nine."

She nodded again, and hastened to join the whist table. She sat across from Freddy Barrington, who had thankfully tired of singing with Sophia, still banging away on the piano, and played against his parents.

She lost dreadfully, her mind not on the game at all, to Freddy's disgust. Her mind filled with the possibilities of meeting Knightson in the library the next morning.

Even now, she grew aware of his gaze burning into her back. She wondered what he did. Did he flirt with Sophia or Lucy? Or heaven forbid, talk to her mother? She didn't dare turn and look, didn't dare show that he affected her so deeply.

She played another wrong card and winced an apology to Freddy. His father, Lord Barrington crowed in triumph.

How would Knightson teach her? She chewed on her lip. Did he have a book, complete with diagrams, or did he plan a more intimate approach?

Portia wagered it would be the latter.

Unable to drink more than a cup of chocolate for breakfast, Portia hurried to the library. Why had Knightson insisted on such an early hour?

She drank in the early morning sounds of a house just waking up: the quiet steps of the servants going about their morning tasks.

She slipped into the library, the door snicking shut behind her.

Mark Knightson stood at one of the bay windows, gazing out at the morning. "There is a key in the lock. Turn it."

Portia obeyed. It trapped her in there with him, and she had no desire to be caught in whatever Knightson had planned for her.

"You are a foolhardy girl, Miss Carew." He still stood with his back to her.

She admired the broad shoulders. "You made the offer too tempting to refuse, Mr. Knightson."

"Indeed. Curiosity killed the cat."

The first frission of fear shot through her but she faced it head on. "How are we to start?"

He faced her, clasping his hands behind his back. "What excites you?"

"Excuse me?" To unsettled to sit, Portia strolled, placing a sofa between them.

"What arouses you, what drives you to touch yourself?"

"I—I don't know." She hated that she blushed. Heat radiated from her cheeks.

"The book you borrowed yesterday afternoon . . . that excited you." His hands now clasped in the front. "What was it?"

"It was called *Lady Godown and Miss Bottom*."

His brows rose. "Lesbian erotica? Interesting. No wonder you don't want to marry."

Portia flared. "I am not interested in women that way. It just happened to be the book I found. The other was too—too shocking."

"Shocking?" Knightson grinned. Portia wondered if that first book was mild compared to what Knightson had in mind. "Very well," he said, walking toward her. "We shall see what else whets your appetite."

He climbed the ladder to the very spot Portia had perused the previous day. "Words, you see, heighten arousal and with a good imagination can satisfy."

Portia hardly heard. Knightson wore a short coat and his breeches clung to his buttocks like a second skin. She watched his rear muscles clench and release as he ascended, stilling while he browsed the shelves.

What would it be like to cover his buttocks with her hands, dig her fingernails in while she rubbed her body against his? What a shame that their agreement excluded such things.

He descended and Portia averted her face to compose herself. Her breathing seemed much faster, as if she had done the climbing.

"Here, read this." He thrust the book under her nose.

The heat of him behind her almost threatened. She read the title: *The Erotic Adventures of Julia.* Why was the heroine always named Julia? Portia considered, for a moment, changing her name.

Opening the book, she glanced at the chapter headings. "Do you want me to start at the beginning?"

"Here, let me." Knightson retrieved the book. "You will learn to skim until you reach the sections that arouse you. Here is one."

He handed her the open book.

Portia scanned the words, already feeling her insides warm.

"Not to yourself."

"What?" Her gaze shot up to his face, startled.

"How can I tell what arouses you, if you read silently? I want to hear it. I want to hear the lust, the desire in your voice."

"Oh." She gestured to the sofa. "May I sit down?"

"Of course." He sat next to her, their legs touching. He put an arm around her and peered over her shoulder. "Begin. Here." His thick finger marked the passage for her.

How could she read with him so close to her? She took one steadying breath, and then another. She could do it. She would show him.

"Vauxhall Gardens were crowded," Portia read. "Groups dined in private booths, and couples danced to the energetic, lighthearted music. Along lighted paths, people strolled, some-times in groups, sometimes just two of them. It was a joyful spring night and spirits were high.

"In the midst of all this, Julia strolled alone, her folded para-sol a weapon against any who might accost her.

"'Miss Julia! Miss Julia! Is that you?'

"Julia turned and all her senses came startlingly aware. 'Joshua Raven! How long as it been?'

"'Too long.' Raven slipped her arm into his. 'Walk with me.'" Portia looked up at Knightson, finding his piercing blue eyes close, sharp and watching. "Why did you have me start so far ahead?"

Knightson growled. "Keep reading."

Portia returned to the story. "Julia had yet to learn how to refuse Raven a single thing that he wanted, that he needed."

She paused. Would that be what it was like with Knightson? Drifting in and out of her life, her succumbing to a single word from him. Nonsense. After this house party, she would never see him again. Why think otherwise?

She resumed reading. "Her insides churned with excitement when she saw that he guided her to the private walks, paths lined with tall hedges and secret paths where trysting lovers would vanish.

"Almost at once, Julia was confronted with a couple kissing, sitting on a cozy wooden bench. The man had his hand down the woman's bodice.

"Julia's breath caught. Just the sight of this couple made her clutch Raven's arm. Is this what he planned? She couldn't wait."

Knightson leaned even closer, his breath hot on her neck. Portia felt his lips brush her neck.

"Mr. Knightson, what do you think you are doing?" she snapped, staring down at the book, frozen by his touch.

"Adding atmosphere," came his low-burred reply.

She twisted away to face him. "Is that absolutely necessary?"

"Absolutely," he agreed, his features solemn, although his blue eyes burned.

Her heart plummeted, pounding excitedly all the way. He wanted her. This had all been a big mistake.

"Part of bringing yourself to full pleasure is to imagine it. Can you not imagine Raven's breath hot on Julia's neck? Wanting her?"

"We agreed . . ." Portia began shakily.

"Miss Carew, your virginity will remain intact. You need not have any fear on that score. However, memories of ecstasy help in reaching that place a second time."

Portia thought Knightson protested a bit too much, but relented, reclining against him to continue reading.

"That's my girl," Knightson breathed.

"Julia realized that Raven had not moved either, arrested by the sight of this passionate couple. She shifted closer to him, and his arm slipped around her waist. Beneath that coat, Julia felt the familiar hardness of his body and gave a delicious shiver.

"Becoming entranced in the pair's intimacy, Julia watched as their bodies moved together, clothing shoved aside in an eagerness to merge and combine. She pressed her thighs together, hiding and heightening her arousal. Raven's hand slid up from her waist to cup her breast."

Without a word, Knightson shifted, slipping along her high-waisted bodice, mimicking Raven's action. Portia half expected he might do something like that, but still it surprised her.

His hand flexed, just the slightest bit, before relaxing. In her next breath, he smoothed over her nipple.

Portia sucked in her breath and expelled it to continue to read. "Julia closed her eyes for a moment, reveling in the sensation. Her nipples hardened under his touch." Portia swallowed. How did her own body copy something she read in a book?

"Raven persisted in his sensual assault, teasing the hard little point of her nipple poking against the fine silk fabric of her gown—Knightson!"

He did not relent. Portia's head fell back against his shoulder, letting sensation wash over her. Knightson didn't mash her bosom in his hand like her traitorous fiancé had. His firm strokes knew just how to rouse her.

"Yes, my dear?" he whispered in her ear, his breath tickling her.

Portia flushed. "What you did—what you do," she corrected herself. "It is not seemly. I want you to—to stop."

"Do you? Do you really? Are you so ready to abandon your lessons so soon? I had not thought you a coward."

"I am not." Portia straightened, moving away a little. Knightson did not relinquish his hold on her bosom. "It is just . . . just . . ." She grew breathless. How was she ever supposed to think when he did *that* to her?

"Julia's breathing deepened. Raven raised his other hand, exploring both her pert breasts at the same time." Knightson shifted beneath her, covering Portia's bosom with both hands.

Portia swallowed her sounds of pleasure. Her whole body afire, she yearned for Knightson to ravish her. She didn't want him to know, but feared her body had already betrayed her.

Such large hands, Portia thought, not for the first time, and kept reading, quailing at her incipient submission to this man. "Raven caressed and teased her until both her breasts felt afire. Julia didn't want the fires to subside, writhing against Raven's turgid cock which pressed against her lower back.

"Before them, the woman tore open her partner's breeches. The man, his head half-buried in the woman's bosom, hitched up her skirts and dragged her under him. The woman's stockinged legs kicked delightedly in the air.

"Raven slid one hand down her stomach, until it rested over her—" Portia paused. Knightson wouldn't, would he?

"Until it rested where?" Knightson prompted, his large hand splayed over her lower belly.

Portia took a shaky breath. "Over her mound of Venus."

Knightson's hand dipped lower. Through her thin skirts, Portia felt his middle finger press against the top of her slit.

"Raven pressed his hand against her. 'You are mine,' he growled in Julia's ear, and Julia knew herself to be lost.

"Pressing her against him, he gathered up her skirts until he bared her to any who cared to watch. His hand covered her pubic curls, his middle finger working its way into her damp slit. Julia's heartbeat sped up, a throbbing echoed in her moist quim."

Reclining even farther, Knightson guided her to lie on top of him, her legs falling to either side of his, their bodies lying at an angle on the sofa. It felt oddly safer to Portia, even though she felt pressure at the base of her spine from his swelling groin. He hauled her skirts to her waist. Both of them panted, and not with the effort of shifting position.

"Raven found the tip of her clit, already peeking out in eagerness. His fingertip grazed it and Julia parted her legs, wanting him with unabashed shame. His light teasing—" Portia's breath caught. Knightson's feather-light touch aroused her more than even touching herself had.

"Raven's gentleness did not last long, nor did Julia want it to, being so eager for him. Raven increased pressure against her clit, massaging the swelling nub in circles and back and forth—"

Knightson didn't hesitate, his expert touch sending molten fire through her. Oh, she could roll over and take him inside her. He had to be as hot as she was. Surely, he couldn't remain unaffected by this? Wasn't that his cock hard at her hip?

The hell with the lessons: this was far, far better.

Sighs escaped her lips. She would not moan aloud. What if

someone heard her and interrupted them? Knightson increased the intensity of his fondling in a silent urging for her to continue.

Portia moaned, unable to stop it from escaping her lips. She took a hopefully steadying breath and continued:

"Julia's hips shifted with his movements, increasing the pressure on her clit, wanting more, much much more. She played with her nipples—" Knightson took care of that for her. "Through half-closed eyes, she saw the man thrust hard into the woman. She burned for Raven to take her like that. Hard and with no thought of their surroundings. Right here and right now. Her hips jerked in time with the man's thrusts."

Portia blushed, discovering that her hips already pulsed under Knightson's touch.

"Over his shoulder, the woman looked at them, a smile on her lips to see her performance to be so appreciated. Julia didn't mind the stares. It gave her a connection to the woman. They both wanted their men and would have them, anywhere, any time.

"Raven ended the intensity, barely touching her eager flesh." Knightson lifted his hand from her crotch. Portia whimpered. "Julia cried out, her body aching. How could he stop now?

"Raven delved deeper—"

Knightson's fingers parted her slit, her juices easing his way. For she was wet, Portia realized. This was as far as it ever went for her. Would Knightson take her further?

"His fingers plunged, along her juicy quim—"

"Juicy quim," Knightson murmured. Did she imagine the strain in his voice? "Go on."

Portia squirmed. The base of Knightson's thumb rubbed along her clit while he explored her crevice. ". . . and slid up, flicking at her clit. Julia moaned, gasping for air." Portia knew how Julia felt. Portia punctuated each phrase with a gasping breath. How could she keep reading?

"Around her clit and down, gathering Julia's juices from her—" Portia paused. Dare she say such a word? "—cunt hole and coating her clit over and over again."

Portia moaned, helpless against his incessant, arousing touch. "Oh, please," she begged.

"Do you want to stop reading?" He kissed her collarbone, his teeth nipping.

"Yes!—No, ohh, no." Heat blossomed through her. She arched her back, pressing her bottom against his groin, straining, searching for something. The words blurred on the page.

"You're lovely," Knightson almost groaned his words.

If she stopped reading, would Knightson stop touching her? Did she dare? "Julia plucked at her nipples."

Knightson squeezed a tender nipple. Portia whimpered.

"Julia's cunt was on display, sleek, velvety and wet. Raven's frotting touch danced at the upper edge, before diving between her lips. He repeated the process, with no rhyme or reason until Julia couldn't tell where he'd touch her next."

Portia punctuated every third or fourth word with gasps. She had to finish, she had to.

3

Portia continued to read. "Not once did he dip into Julia's eager hole.

"His thumb massaged her clit—" Portia uttered a sobbing moan. She'd traveled higher than she ever had either alone or with a man. She felt ready to fly apart from the hunger, the tension and the blaze scorching through her that threatened to consume her utterly.

"At last, Raven dipped into her cunt hole. Julia . . . Julia lifted her hips to meet him."

Knightson's digit slid inside her. Portia wanted to scream with pleasure, but pressed her lips shut tight, muffling her moan.

"Raven twisted his finger inside—oh, sweet mercy!" Portia sobbed. What was he doing to her? ". . . pressing in deeper."

Portia met each of Knightson's thrusts, her hips beyond her command. Somehow, she held on to the book. With sobbing breath and unable to get more than a word out between pants, she continued:

"Raven responded to Julia's eagerness by thrusting his finger in harder and deeper—Oh!" Portia cried out. "Knight—Mark!"

What words had she to beg him for mercy, when she wanted none?

"Again and again his finger fucked her. Julia met each thrust with gusto."

Portia's body had divorced from her mind. She *was* Julia. "Oh, Knightson, please!" She didn't know what she begged for, she just wanted it. Wanted it now.

"Julia's cunt clutched at his finger. She writhed, reaching behind her to drag him against her. Aah!"

Portia moaned, beyond gasping silence. Something wonderful swelled inside her, threatened to drown all her senses. She wanted to give in, but what would happen if she did? Would he stop? Would he fuck her?

"Julia cried out. Her head squirmed against his chest, her begging sobs expelled with each thrust." Portia expelled almost every word spoken with a dazed moan. It amazed her Knightson even followed her breathless reading.

"Her desperate spasmodic move . . . movements—" Portia cried out in frustration. Even an entire word was lost to her now.

"Enough." Knightson snatched the book from her and tossed it onto the carpeted floor.

"But—" Portia protested, feeling his hand still half-buried in her wet slit.

"Let me tell you what happens next," he murmured into her ear. "I know the story well."

Portia relaxed against him, closing her eyes.

"Raven's hand dripped with her juices." Knightson's low voice burned every word into all her fiery senses. "One finger wasn't enough for Julia and he knew it. He slid free of Julia's eager cunt and returned with two." Knightson thrust hard inside her. "All the way up to the knuckle."

Portia moaned, a soft cry of expectation. Something incredible was about to happen and soon.

"Thrashing about, sweet tension exploded inside Julia, setting her afire. Her thrilled cry became lost in the screaming fireworks overhead."

What bursting sweet tension? Portia strained to find it.

"That's the end of the scene." Knightson growled, sounding hoarse. He slipped his hand out of her and rose, striding to the window.

Left lying on the sofa, Portia attempted to restore order. She sat up, pulling down her skirts. She didn't dare broach the reason for his rapid retreat. "Knightson?"

Knightson returned to her, bending to pick up the discarded book. It failed to hide the massive bulge in his breeches. "The whole point of these lessons is to let yourself go, Portia."

She pouted. "I did."

"You tried too hard. A block of wood has less tension than you."

Did that mean self-pleasure would be denied to her? Was she defective in some way? She lowered her gaze, finding his crotch in the process. His cock bulged, straining against his breeches. She swallowed. He was huge. What would it be like to have that crammed up inside her? She couldn't help it; she squirmed at the thought, licking her lips.

"Knightson . . . I am sorry." Sorry that her throbbing parts would get no release, no relief.

"I am sure you are." He knelt at her feet. With his hands, he parted her knees. "Lie down and let us try again."

Portia obeyed, hoisting her skirts. She hooked one knee to lean against the sofa's back. The other leg dangled off the sofa's edge. It was utterly shameless of her, but it seemed natural with him. He had touched her so intimately already. Why should she deny him the sight of her most private self?

Her eyes on him, she saw his tongue flick over his lips. He reached for her, his fingers sliding into her wet hole, the thumb manipulating her swollen clit.

"Let it come," he murmured, his voice rough. "Portia, let it come."

The swirling of her clit, so sensitive, sparked a soft cry. Her head fell back and she gave in to sensation. Her parts were on fire, and each thrust of his fingers brought her closer, ever closer.

She trembled with it, her hips shaking as she met each thrust. Oh, what she wouldn't give to have Knightson's big cock inside her.

Her release hit her like a wall. She bit down on her finger, a muffled wail escaping her lips. There was no thought at all, just wave upon wave of delicious energy, energizing and draining her.

Portia opened her eyes to find Knightson gazing at her.

"Magnificent," he murmured.

"More." She sat up, reaching out to him.

He didn't move, kneeling between her legs. He bent to kiss her knee. "You don't need me. I have given you all that I can."

Portia sat up. "No, that is not all. I know you want me, I can see it." Indeed, his breeches stained dark where he had leaked a little already.

Knightson took a shaky breath. "No."

In one swift movement, she slid from the sofa and onto his lap, straddling him. "Yes," she breathed.

Her lips brushed his. How strange, to kiss him for the first time, when they'd already been more intimate. His hard lips compressed beneath hers.

He grabbed her arms and pushed her away. "I could remove you in an instant. You are no match for me."

Portia leaned in and his arms relaxed, letting her. "Then do it," she breathed.

He didn't move. She stared into his eyes, seeing resolve fight with lust. Only his eyes showed life, the rest of him remained still, like granite, solid stone, hard and immobile.

She drew closer. Her lips brushed his freshly shaven cheek. He smelled good, the clean of soap softening under his manly heat, darker notes of his natural fragrance coming to the fore. "Make me, Knightson."

Still, he remained motionless. Her hands went to his lap, unfastening the top of his breeches. She raised up on her knees, undoing the remaining buttons.

She felt, rather than saw, his cock spring free. It slapped against her lowered thighs and nudged against her wet cunt.

Knightson let out a long breath, his granite facade melting in a flow of lava. His hands shot to her waist, gripping her hard. "You want it?" he growled.

"Yes," she breathed, wriggling against him. His cock slipped, fitted against her hole.

He managed in strangled tones, "You want me to fuck you."

She gasped at the word and at the same time it filled her with a delicious thrill. "Yes."

"Here it is."

In one swift movement, he shoved his bulk inside her. She fell against him, pressing her mouth against his shoulder, biting down on the heavy material of his coat to muffle her scream.

He stretched her. Both awful and wonderful, his cock plunged so deep, giving the sensation of penetrating her belly. He held her, until her shuddering ceased.

She dared to move, wrapping her legs around his waist, feeling him shift inside her. He pushed her back against the sofa, the seat cushions sinking beneath her shoulders.

He held her by the hips, fucking her in short, sharp thrusts. She jolted with each inward incursion. Never had she been fucked with such abandon and yet, such control.

Portia remained aware enough to sense Knightson's wild fury remained under his restraint. His tight grip had her totally in his power. She should feel helpless and frustrated by it, but she had asked for it. And oh God, he made her feel incredible.

He urged her legs higher about his back and plunged deeper. She didn't think it possible he could cram any more of himself into her, but the change in angle did it, piercing her and stretching her even deeper.

Low groans emanated from his throat, his head bowed in concentration. Sweat gleamed in his hair.

Portia's head fell back against the sofa. That sweet crescent of pleasure rose within her again. She didn't expect to experience that exquisite release again. It did not deny her.

She jerked, her body shuddering as it clamped down around Knightson's cock, writhing to get every last moment of climax from him.

He uttered a low groan and stiffened, his buttocks flexing in rapid bursts.

They sunk down onto the floor, Knightson still holding Portia in a seated position. She felt his cock slip from her, leaving a large sticky trail. Her gown, dampened by perspiration, stuck to her body.

"Damn it," he growled in a low breath.

Not exactly the response Portia had expected. "What?" she asked, smoothing back his wavy dark hair from his sweaty forehead.

Knightson looked up at her, his blue eyes uncharacteristically dark. "I came inside you." She stared at him. "That's how babies are made, Miss Carew."

"I know, Mr. Knightson." Portia kept her voice steady. Such consequences would be worth living with, if they came with more of this fantastic sex. "This was scarcely planned, was it?"

His lips twisted ruefully. "Hardly." He took a deep breath. "I broke my promise to you, I apologize."

"I goaded you," she consoled. "I wanted you." Her voice dropped. "Still do." She shut her mouth around the risky pronouncement. What kind of fool was she to offer herself to him so? Once was bad enough. It didn't stop her from aching for him.

He inhaled a sharp breath. "You are no virgin, are you?"

His accusation slapped her across the face. She stiffened, hiding it under fluttering eyelashes. "I felt like it." She stopped teasing him. After everything they had shared, he deserved the truth. Or close enough to it. "I was engaged, almost married. So almost married, that waiting no longer mattered. So we didn't. And then he called it off."

"The idiot."

"Yes, my sentiments exactly." She flashed him a quick grin. "However, he didn't—I never—"

"Is it like you to be lost for words?" Knightson wondered aloud, stroking her cheek, his eyes alive with pride.

"You shall have to find out, won't you," Portia replied, getting up. She stepped over his thighs, pulling down her skirts, annoyed that she had let slip even a little that he had pleasured her beyond her wildest imaginings.

She looked over her shoulder at him. "Are my lessons over?"

"Yes—no." Knightson shook his head. "There is more to learn, if you dare to trust me."

"I trust no one, Mr. Knightson." Portia gave up trying to put her gown back into some semblance of order. "But I want to know how to . . . to . . ."

"Bring yourself off," Knightson supplied in a quiet voice.

"Exactly, and to do it by myself, without any assistance."

Knightson regarded her for a long moment. Portia held up under his examination, knowing her bedraggled appearance had to be less than desirable.

He licked his lips, proving her doubts wrong. "You need to change."

Her gown did cling to her perspiring form. She turned to go. "My lessons?"

"Will be arranged."

Mark Knightson waited until the door closed behind her before uncurling his body from its kneeling position. He propped an elbow on a raised knee and started at the ornate wood door. "You were magnificent, Portia," he whispered.

He shook his head. He had not come to this house party to get entangled in another affair, and yet he'd already started down that path.

But to resist that charming girl, perched on the ladder and touching herself? Well nigh impossible. Resist her sultry demands to take him? What man would? Well, he should have and let her go. She'd been satisfied once, she hardly needed his cock.

She'd demanded it, though, with such boldness unlike a proper miss, that he had caved, wondering at this new seductress. He'd give her another lesson, perfectly clinical, scientific and safe and send her on her way.

He didn't need another woman getting her hooks into him. She ought to know, too, that if she conceived from this ill-thought incident, he would deny her. Not even the incipient birth of one of his blood would sway him from his course of avoiding matrimony at all costs.

Giving himself a shake, he rose, buttoning his breeches. He had quite ruined his cravat, or that Carew minx had, and he needed to change before someone saw him and started to wonder at his activities.

Willowhill Hall buzzed with unseen activity. Past the hour of rising for the household, Portia risked discovery. She made it back to her room without anyone seeing her. Stripping off her gown, she dipped a washcloth into last night's washing water, and sponged her breasts.

Her nipples tingled, still feeling hot, under the rough caress of the cool washcloth. Turning, Portia looked at herself in the mirror. Her mussed hair needed to be redone and her face was too flushed to make a public appearance just yet. Her nipples were dark, almost swollen, a far cry from their usual shell-pink color.

She swallowed. He had changed her. On some deep level, she wasn't the same girl who had gone to the library.

She ran the cloth over her face, hoping the cold water would banish the telltale signs of pleasure.

Portia lowered her gaze to the black hair at the top of her thighs, shining with their mingled sex juices. She parted her legs, washing thoroughly.

There, she was almost normal again.

Almost.

She picked out a fresh gown, stuffing the other into the bottom of the wardrobe. The muslin brushed over her sensitive breasts and Portia wondered if she would be in this exquisite agony all day.

She needed help with the tapes, but didn't want to call anyone. Not until she had calmed herself.

The door opened. Portia jumped.

"Not dressed yet?" Her mother bustled in. "Turn around and I'll do you up."

Portia obeyed, relieved to hide her high coloring from her mother, who hadn't seemed to notice in any case.

"We are to have breakfast with Lady Barrington this morning. I received the message just a little while ago." Mama paused. "It is rather an immediate summons. I fear she may be having second thoughts about having us here."

Portia's first thought centered around Mark Knightson. To leave now—well, it would be a fine memory to touch herself to. "Would she be that cruel? Lady Barrington knew before she invited us, didn't she?"

Her mother remained silent.

"Mama? Didn't she?"

"Of course she knows, dear. She believes you to be innocent as I do."

"But . . ." Portia prodded.

"I may have gilded the lily somewhat. It isn't done to talk of such horrid things, and you are innocent, my dear, and so—"

"Oh, Mama." Portia sighed. And now she had to face the old dragon with the flush of sex still on her cheeks? She checked the mirror and found that the color had faded somewhat. Thank goodness.

Portia towed behind her mother, across to Lady Barrington's salon adjoining her bedroom. Lady Barrington was still *en deshabille* in a riot of fine lawn and lace, blending in with the creams and gold of her salon.

Lady Barrington imperiously gestured for them to sit.

They did so, eyeing the spread which had been laid on the low table before them.

"Eat." Lady Barrington waved her hand again.

Neither woman dared to disobey. Portia made sure to keep the food to a minimum, in a show of maidenly modesty. Truth to tell, she wasn't hungry—not for food, at any rate.

After they had eaten, Lady Barrington lowered her cup to the end table by her elbow. "My dear Mrs. Carew, I have heard disturbing things."

"How terrible," Portia's mother murmured. "I am honored that you can confide in me."

"They concern your daughter." Lady Barrington's gaze shot to Portia, who bowed her head. "You were not wholly frank with me, Mrs. Carew."

"Oh not so!" Mama put down her plate and her hands fluttered in the air like captured moths. "I told you the essence of the nasty gossip. I couldn't bear to go into details, my dear Lady Barrington, how could I? It is bad enough to hear this calumny heaped upon my daughter, let alone to speak of it with my own lips."

Lady Barrington unbent, leaning over to pat Mrs. Carew's

hand. "I was sure that was all it was, my dear, but it leaves me in a somewhat sticky situation."

"That was not my intention," Mama protested, her voice faint. "It is so unfair to my girl."

"I agree, but Mrs. Chalcroft has complained to me already. She gave me *all* the details surrounding Miss Carew. I became additionally concerned when I realized that Miss Carew had spent much time in Mr. Knightson's company last night after dinner."

"He came and sat with me," muttered Portia.

"I suspect he knew of the rumors and wanted to try his luck. I had not wanted him here, but Freddy would insist on his coming."

"He's a bit old for Freddy, isn't he?"

"More of a family friend, in truth. Mr. Knightson and my husband get along famously as well. So I am outnumbered in this." Lady Barrington gave herself a shake. "Well! Enough of that." She pointed at Miss Carew. "I have decided to let you stay."

"Oh thank you!" trilled Mrs. Carew, clasping her hands together at her expansive bosom. "Thank you! You won't regret it, I swear!"

"I should hope not," Lady Barrington returned. She focused on Portia. "There are conditions. Should you break them, I shall ask you both to pack your bags and leave."

Mama switched from blissful relief to a shocked sob.

Portia regarded her hostess with equable calm. "I believe I am to behave perfectly, Mama, if not to stay, then to shrug off these terrible rumors forever. I hope I shall not always be proving myself."

"A husband would fix that, my dearest pet." Mama dabbed at her eyes. "And the sooner you find one, the sooner all this horridness will go away."

Lady Barrington agreed. "Are you fond of my Freddy?"

Was the old biddy matchmaking? "I have not known him long enough to be sure," Portia replied carefully. "He's young and handsome."

"That shows a care in contrast with the gossip." Lady Barrington's brows rose.

Portia remained steady under her examining gaze. Never mind that her heart pounded. The memory of her rashness with Mr. Knightson was all too clear in her mind. So long as Lady Barrington never found out about *that*, Portia had nothing to fear. Except for whatever Mr. Knightson had next in mind. She shivered at the thought.

"I think Freddy would make a wonderful husband for my Portia," Mama gushed. "Do you not think so, Lady B.?" Now that their eviction had been averted, her mother clearly felt at ease to return to her old familiarity with their hostess.

"I would not like to rush these things, my dear." Lady Barrington's brittle smile conveyed how little she wanted the match.

It didn't bother Portia. She didn't want the match either.

However, her mother remained undeterred. "Of course not. These matters need to be nurtured, supported. They will have plenty of time together in these next few weeks. Just think of it! You and I, grandmothers to the same children!"

"Mama likes to dream," Portia reassured Lady Barrington, who dabbed at her upper lip in some consternation. Lady Barrington managed a smile, exchanging an understanding glance with Portia.

"Now, I must leave you to dress." Lady Barrington rose. "Feel free to continue your breakfast, but I must prepare for our new guests. They should be here by luncheon."

"The Wintertons?" Mama leaned forward in eagerness.

Lady Barrington inclined a regal nod. "All the more reason

for you to be on your best behavior, Miss Carew. His Grace does not countenance scandal."

Portia rose and bobbed a curtsey. "Yes, my lady."

The Carews abandoned breakfast with Lady Barrington's departure. Portia's mother followed her into her room and collapsed into a sofa chair.

"Oh thank goodness!" Mama waved her fine lawn handkerchief before her face. "You did very well, my dear. I think that may be why Lady Barrington was lenient."

"It's more likely your friendship with her." Portia frowned. "Now we have to face that witch Chalcroft."

Mama waved airily, dismissing the problem. "Nonsense. We shall not sink to their level, my pet. We shall behave as if she had never gossiped. Leave it to Lady Barrington to smooth the waters there. Besides," and Mama took on an unholy smile, "if she decides to withdraw, that's all the more suitors for you."

Portia restrained a groan. That's the last thing she wanted.

"The ladies are gathering for a walk before luncheon," Mama continued, not noticing Portia's discomfort. "We shall see how badly the Chalcrofts will behave."

The Chalcrofts knew better than to behave badly, Portia noted, trailing behind the group of ladies strolling through Lady Barrington's extensive gardens. Sophia had actually scowled at her and Mrs. Chalcroft had cut her, hurrying forward to take Lady Barrington into whispered conversation.

Mama's smile had grown strained, but she looked about her as if she had not a care in the world.

Miss Lucy Chalcroft dropped back to walk alongside Portia. "Mother told me the terrible gossip about you," she began without preamble. "Is it true?"

For the briefest of moments, Portia thought of telling the truth. "No, none of it. Oh, I had allowed him to kiss me, but that was a terrible, terrible mistake." She lowered her voice. "He wanted more."

"And you refused him?"

"Naturally, and the villain has been blackening my name ever since."

"How terrible," Miss Chalcroft murmured.

Portia agreed.

"And that is why you've decided not to marry?"

Portia nodded, looking away and pretending to blink back tears. She'd long finished crying over him, unless it suited her purposes.

"But what if you found the right man, a good, honorable man?" Miss Chalcroft persisted.

"I wouldn't find him because I'd not be looking." Portia tried not to think about Mr. Knightson. He was wrong for her for all the right reasons, and yet, it had been good. She gnawed her lip. Would he do the honorable thing and keep quiet? But of course he would. He wouldn't offer to continue her lessons otherwise.

"What of you Miss Chalcroft?" Portia gathered the threads of their conversation. "Are you that dedicated to spinsterhood?"

"Please, call me Lucy. We lag far enough behind that Mama won't take offense."

Portia choked back a laugh at this show of defiance against Mrs. Chalcroft's sticking to propriety.

"As for spinsterhood, I am hardly given a choice, am I? But if no man will marry me because I'm not pretty enough, then I am better off without such men, I have decided." Lucy sighed. "And they all seem like that."

"Not all of us."

Both girls leaped and shrieked, almost striking Mr. Knightson with their parasols.

"Forgive me for startling you. I was just coming to tell Lady

Barrington that more guests have arrived when I overheard your remark."

Portia gazed up at him. "Beauty is not of interest to you?"

"Beauty is attractive," he admitted, "but what makes a man stay lies beneath."

"And if there isn't beauty, you'd never find out," Lucy retorted, her face reddening.

"So quick to take offense, Miss Chalcroft?" Knightson riposted. "You are pleasing in appearance."

Portia saw Lucy's cheeks flush a deeper red. "Th-thank you."

"There, I am glad you can take a compliment with grace, no matter what its source. Now if you'll excuse me . . ." He hurried on ahead of them, hailing Lady Barrington.

"He—he's nice," Lucy stuttered. "Nicer than I thought after hearing of his reputation."

Portia chuckled. "More than nice," she confessed, although she wouldn't dare say how. "Your head has been turned by him."

"Yes, but it will come to naught. Oh look, we're turning around."

Portia swallowed Lucy's interest in Knightson with difficulty, although she managed to keep her expression pleasant. It might have been nice to matchmake on Lucy's behalf. But not to Knightson.

He was hers.

The two women rejoined the rear of the procession. Mrs. Chalcroft called Lucy forward, sending her hurrying away on an errand.

Portia grimaced in sympathy.

"Poor thing," Knightson agreed, dropping back to walk alongside her. He tucked her hand under his arm.

Portia gave her parasol a desperate twirl, trying to regain her scattered thoughts from the sudden heat of his touch. "Yes, yes indeed."

He lowered his voice to a rumbling burr that made her insides fire up in anticipation. "I have been giving thought to your next lesson."

"You have?" Portia tried for nonchalance, but failed.

He didn't spare her his amusement, chuckling softly. "I have."

"Will we meet in the library again?" She knew she sounded eager, but she couldn't help it. Just the thought of being under his command made her wet.

"Early in the morning," he confirmed.

The others ahead made a turn around a hedge. Knightson pulled her up against the leafy divide. "A moment," he demanded.

She surrendered, letting the hedge prickle her back. His hand flattened against her mound, sliding down. She parted her legs, suppressing the urge to hitch up her skirts and reveal herself to him. What if they were seen?

No more than a hair's breadth apart, his body heat radiated and warmed her. His hand pressed in between her legs, probing. It took all her self-will not to throw herself at the man. She remained still, vibrating with tension.

"You are wet," he murmured against her brow, his fingertip tickling the top of her cleft.

"Yes," she whispered. Her lips quirked. "You seem to have that effect on me."

Knightson laughed under his breath. He toyed with her clit for a few moments longer before stepping back and releasing her. "You are most refreshing, Miss Carew."

"Thank you, Mr. Knightson. As you can see, I too can accept compliments. Shall we go meet our new fellow guests?"

4

The two Winterton men made a compelling pair. The younger had carrot-red hair, smoothed into order. His neat, dark blue traveling suit had not the tiniest speck of white fluff to mar it.

One saw why, when the elder gentleman, the Duke of Winterton, stepped out of the carriage. Slender like his son, the duke strove for perfection in tidy dress. His shining white hair gave him an air of austerity. He strolled forward, swinging a silver-topped cane he clearly didn't need to use.

He bowed his welcomes to Lady Barrington and cast his gaze upon the rest of the assembling guests. Portia saw his gaze fall upon her and his slender white brow twitched before moving on.

Portia exhaled a sigh of relief. With luck, that meant the duke had also heard the rumors about her and felt her too tainted to be pursued by his son. Everyone knew His Grace remained a strong force in his sons' lives, even as adults.

Lady Barrington did not make a distinction between Portia and the other girls, introducing both gentlemen to her as if scandal had not attached itself to her.

The duke lingered over her hand a moment longer than was polite. Portia sensed Knightson go tense beside her and smothered a smile, unaccountably pleased that Knightson seemed possessive. The younger Winterton mimicked his father, moving on to greet Knightson with a smirk.

Not so disinterested after all. Portia repressed a sigh of disappointment and went into luncheon with the rest.

Knightson managed to avoid her for the rest of the day. Easily done, for Lord Barrington had taken the men out to view his estate.

Portia ascended the stairs. It had been easy to escape the circle of women earlier. All of them ignored her, with the exception of Miss Chalcroft who shot her many a sympathetic look but remained by her mother's side. Yes, even Mama had refused to meet her gaze.

She heard someone come up the stairs behind her, but didn't pause, not caring to speak to anybody. The booted footsteps warned her that a man approached.

An arm swooped around her waist, dragging her against him. "Why are you in such a hurry?" Knightson's voice burred in her ear.

"I am changing for dinner." Portia didn't try fighting him, although she longed to. "If somebody sees . . ."

"Let them see." Knightson bent his head, nipping the skin on her neck. "You like to play it dangerous, don't you?"

"Do I?" she shot back, giving a token struggle.

"So I heard. You like to give a little more than the other girls do?"

Portia stiffened in his grasp. "Nonsense, sheer nonsense. Now let me go before somebody comes."

"You don't want me to fuck you the way your past lovers have? Where did you do it? In a rented hotel room?" He thrust against her with each question, his prominent, trapped cock rubbing against her rear. "Where? His rooms? Did you fuck him in public? At Vauxhall Gardens? On the Thames? Where? Tell me."

If only her fiancé had been quite that daring. Banking down a sudden thrust of fear, Portia replied, quite breathless, "Why should it be any of your business?"

"Not the wronged little innocent you pretended to be, are you?" His grip tightened on her arms. "Should I fuck you for the liar you are?"

Portia wrenched out of his grasp and whirled on him, eyes blazing. "I take it this means that my lessons have been canceled?"

"You want lessons?" He grabbed her again by the arms, hauling her against him. "I'll give you lessons."

Knightson hustled her up the stairs, past her room and up a farther set of stairs. These were narrower, less ornate, used by the servants to ascend to their sleeping quarters.

Portia twisted in his grasp, trying to loosen his hold, just a little. "Where are you taking me?"

"Right here."

He spun her until her back slammed against his chest. He bent her over the sturdy wooden railing. The breath left Portia in a whoosh and she gripped the banister, afraid of toppling over.

Knightson hiked up her skirts and tore her drawers apart. He forced his legs between hers. His hand plunged between her thighs, parting her cunt lips. "Why, you little bitch," he snarled in her ear. "You're soaking wet."

What could she tell him? That his voice alone made her go liquid? That even outraged, she still wanted him?

She made no answer. He pushed his cock against her, nestling against her opening. She let out a little moan.

"You want this, don't you?"

No point in denying it. She arched her back, pushing back against him.

"Witch." He grabbed her hips and thrust inside. All the way inside.

Portia let out a stunned groan. Knightson pounded into her cunt, his cock pistoning in and out of her. The sucking sound of their wet sexes moving apart and together drove her wild. She writhed against him, feeling his hairy thighs rub against her smooth bottom.

He stayed deep, rolling his pelvis, creating even newer sensations inside her. The sweet tension built, and Portia knew it was about to break. She squeezed her muscles around his cock, wanting to feel more of him against her throbbing walls.

He slid from her and thrust in, deep and hard. Her release shot through her in a single sword stroke. Her back arched and her body locked in place with the awesome rush.

Knightson fucked her in long hard bursts that had her sobbing her release to any who might hear below. He groaned, emptying his seed into her.

He hauled her upright, pulling her against him. His cock slipped free, leaving a wet trail, mingling with his escaping semen, down her inner thighs. His breath rasped heavy in his ear, but he said nothing, just holding her.

Portia waited until her vision cleared and her breathing returned to normal. "I told you the truth, Knightson. We were almost married."

"You weren't engaged." He sounded flat, exhausted.

"It was a secret engagement. Mama didn't exactly approve of him." Portia released a low, slow breath. "I should have listened to her. For once, she was right."

"There were others."

Nestled in his arms, Portia dared to feel safe, despite sensing Knightson's banked fury. Certainly safe from the ingrate who had almost ruined her life. "That wretched liar took my virginity. I had never gone so far before."

"But you had done more than kiss your beaus."

She trembled and whispered, "Yes." She took another breath. "I didn't fuck them."

At once, the anger had vanished. He spun her in his arms and tilted her head up. "Truth?"

"Truth," she affirmed, meeting his gaze steadily, and then hungrily. She swayed upward on her tiptoes and Knightson's mouth smothered hers.

He plundered her mouth, his tongue claiming her. She kissed him back, tangling her tongue against his, wrapping her arms around his neck. Her breasts rubbed against him and she moaned in the back of her throat.

His hand, buried in her hair, pulled her head back.

She gazed up at him, at his wet lips.

"I don't love you."

Her gaze widened for a moment. "Your point?"

"My point is, this is temporary, a need we both have and will soon be sated. I will move on to others, even if you fall pregnant. You will learn to pleasure yourself. This cannot, will not last."

"You think I care, Knightson? I hardly know you." She wriggled out of his loosened grasp and escaped.

She closed her door behind her, and stared at her immaculate room. She looked a mess, she knew it. He gown clung to her perspiring form. Knightson had wrinkled it beyond redemption. A lock of hair drifted over her forehead indicating further damage to her hairstyle.

Easy enough to repair her exterior. Inside, her heart pounded and her mind whirled with all that had just occurred. Hardly able to catch her breath, she sank onto the bed.

Knightson had been so harsh, so cruel. Had she imagined his brief softening? Was that the reason for his declaration, to warn her off?

She debated retiring for the night, pleading a headache. She wanted morning to come, and another lesson in the library. She flung herself off the bed. No, she wouldn't hide. He'd think he'd won and she wouldn't let him have that satisfaction.

Not yet, anyway.

She stripped off her gown and had a quick sponge bath, before dressing for dinner.

Knightson fastened his breeches, watching her go. He hadn't been far wrong when he called her a witch. He hadn't planned on fucking her like that again, but when the Duke of Winterton revealed the full scope of the gossip about Miss Carew, he'd been grateful his saddle concealed his hardening cock.

As a woman of easy virtue, Miss Carew became fair game, despite the duke joking it made her a great candidate for a willing, passionate wife.

Who needed a wife? Not he.

But he had to be careful. He wasn't about to break his rules over Miss Carew, and he had to ensure she would not jeopardize his freedom.

He descended the stairs, a smile tweaking the corner of his lips. He wondered what she would be like at dinner. All fresh and innocent again? Even at that thought, his loins tightened.

Portia made it just in time for dinner, slipping her arm beneath young Freddy Barrington's, who looked at her with some bewilderment.

She guessed that Freddy had heard the worst of the gossip. If she had been at all interested in landing the boy, she'd have teased him with the knowledge. She ran the imagined conversation through her head, the pretend flirting with Freddy driving Knightson into a jealous rage.

Instead, she remained meek and quiet, asking Freddy about the day's ride and making suitable small talk. She refused to look Knightson's way. Not even once! Pride filled her as the ladies retreated and left the men to their port and cigars.

Mrs. Chalcroft kept Lucy busy, preventing Miss Chalcroft from speaking to Portia altogether.

Portia determined she would not passively ride this one out, but sat, unasked, at the small pianoforte and began to play. She aimed for quiet, soothing music in the hopes to dull the sharp knives Mrs. Chalcroft had in mind for her.

She glanced over and saw Mrs. Chalcroft pinch the bridge of her nose. Any minute now, the woman would complain of a headache and bar Portia from playing, she just knew it.

The arrival of the men prevented that. They burst into the room, far earlier than their usual wont. Lord Barrington and the duke settled themselves by the older ladies, but the three younger men flocked around Portia at the piano.

She shot Knightson a curious glance, wondering what the gentlemen had up their collective sleeves. His face revealed nothing.

"You play the piano delightfully, Miss Carew." The viscount, Gareth Winterton, leaned forward, his red curls tumbling forward over his brow, escaping the restrictions of his hair oil. Had he imbibed too much before joining the women? His cheeks reddened.

"Thank you, my lord," Portia replied, her eyes downcast. She kept her fingers moving over the keyboard.

The young viscount didn't stop there. He sat beside her, perched on the very edge of the piano stool. She glanced askance at him.

"Play a love song," Winterton suggested.

Portia let the music trickle to an end. "A love song?"

"Perhaps a duet?" Winterton nudged closer.

Unthinking, Portia shot a look of appeal at Knightson, who merely smirked at her. She refocused on Winterton, who seemed even closer than a moment ago. She shifted away, realizing too late that it allowed Winterton equal possession of the stool.

"Do you know this?" She quickly fingered the introduction. He nodded and she launched into it.

As they sang, Winterton shifted even closer. This time Portia looked to Freddy for help, but he seemed to be watching the two of them as if they were flies racing up a window pane. What was going on?

The song told the story of two people looking for love, with the woman and the man taking alternate verses until toward the end. Portia completed the first verse, and Winterton launched into the second. He had a pleasing tenor voice.

Had the request been innocent? Portia started to think so until Winterton joggled her elbow. She missed a note, but kept playing. Nobody expected her playing to be perfect.

Winterton shuffled closer until his leg pressed against hers. Portia leaned away a little, but didn't surrender the piano. What was she supposed to do? Allow the contact?

His hand settled firmly over her ass.

This was beyond enough! She faked a coughing fit, doubling over and slipping off the stool. She braced herself against the piano with one arm and kept coughing. She looked up at the startled onlookers. "Water!" she rasped.

Lord Freddy Barrington hastened to the table holding refreshments and returned with a steaming cup of tea, handing it to her.

Portia accepted it with a grateful smile. She took long sips, while queries as to what happened came from those seated on the nearby sofas.

"I think I swallowed a bug." She managed a watery smile. "It flew right into my mouth." She turned to Winterton. "My apologies for ruining the duet."

Winterton had the grace to look a bit discomfited. "Not at all, Miss Carew. There is no blame to fall on you, but on nature." His uncomfortable expression transformed into a winking leer.

She gaped at him.

"You'll catch another bug, Miss Carew," Knightson murmured in an undertone.

Portia shut her mouth with a snap and surrendered the piano to Sophia, who wanted her turn to shine.

"I shall finish the duet with you," Sophia offered.

"Let's not risk another flying insect." Winterton declined with a bow and followed Portia.

Choosing a seat that would prevent Winterton sitting next to her without attracting undue notice, relief filled Portia to see the men disperse. Freddy Barrington sat by Miss Lucy and Knightson joined the older ladies in conversation.

Winterton stuck to her like glue. He pulled up an ottoman and sat with his back to the rest of the group, effectively blocking everyone's line of sight, except Miss Sophia's, who concentrated on her performance.

Portia shifted, uneasy. "Did you have an easy journey here, my lord?" she ventured.

Winterton grinned, rather at odds with the question. "Slow. His Grace doesn't like his frame rattled as he used to." He leaned forward. "You were very kind to excuse my forwardness earlier."

"I didn't excuse it, my lord. I removed myself from it."

"My attentions are unwelcome?"

"I don't know you." Unbidden, her gaze flashed to Knightson. She didn't know him either. Knightson acknowledged her glance with a brief nod. She returned her attention to young Winterton. "I fear you imbibed too quickly of the port tonight."

Winterton bristled. "I am more than capable of holding my liquor."

Portia groaned inwardly. "Forgive me. Like I said, I do not know you."

"Then you shall get to know me, Miss Carew. You quite intrigue me. The gossips say—"

She held up a hand, forestalling him. "I do not care what the gossips say, my lord. It is cruel and untrue, I'm sure."

His eyes narrowed. "Do you even know what they say?"

Portia lowered her voice. "That I am a woman of easy virtue." Which was probably true, given her behavior with Knightson of late. She met Winterton's predatory gaze. "I am very particular, believe me."

"Then I hope I will become worthy of your regard." Winterton reached out and gave her nipple a quick twist.

Portia didn't think. She slapped him hard across his face, leaping to her feet. "You, sir, must decidedly be unable to hold your drink. How dare you?"

"Miss Carew?" Lord Barrington's booming bass rose above the concerned hubbub of the group. "Explain yourself."

"I am sure he didn't mean it." Portia pinned the wilting Winterton with a glare. "I am sure he will apologize for his thoughtless, hurtful act."

"Gareth?" The duke's soft voice cut through the following silence like a knife through butter. "Apologize to Miss Carew and withdraw for the evening."

Young Winterton shot his father a sulky glare and mumbled his apologies. He stalked from the room, slamming the door behind him.

Lady Barrington's collection of porcelain figures rattled on their shelves.

"I apologize for my son's temper, Lady Barrington," the duke soothed. He patted a space by him. "Come, join us, Miss Carew."

Portia thanked him, joining him with alacrity. His invitation had forestalled her own banishment by Lady Barrington.

"We shall not quiz you, Miss Carew, as to what sin my son committed. Quite severe judging from your response."

"Thank you." Portia winced. "I am afraid I acted without thought. I should not have slapped him so hard."

The duke chuckled, smoothing his thick white hair over his scalp. "I don't doubt he deserved it, Miss Carew. Please set your mind at rest."

"Thank you." Would she be ever thanking this august gentleman?

"I want to know the cause of this outburst," Mrs. Chalcroft burst out, her face purpled. "I have never seen such unmannerly behavior. You will explain yourself."

Portia shot a glance at the duke. His lips had thinned in displeasure, but he chose not to speak. "I would not wish to embarrass His Grace with the particulars."

"Speak, child." Mrs. Chalcroft insisted.

Portia surveyed the group. Lady Barrington gave a slight nod. They all expected her to speak. "He was in his cups. He . . . He touched me inappropriately." She added in an undertone to the duke, "Forgive me, your Grace."

"I had hoped you wouldn't speak of it," the duke responded, loud enough for the assembly to hear. "But as you have—" He paused and Portia felt a chill go down her spine. Had she just made an enemy of the duke? He rose and bowed to the ladies. "Lady Barrington, I will remove my son and myself in the morning."

"Oh no!" Lady Barrington trilled. "Do not be so hasty! If you can make assurances it won't happen again. . . ."

"It won't," the duke growled. "I will speak to my son at once and inform him of his reprieve. If you would excuse me. . . ." He bowed again.

At the door, he turned and smiled at Portia. "Miss Carew, please be assured you are forgiven. Young Gareth has not been taken to task by a female for a long time. It is past time someone reined him in. I hope your actions will do him good."

He departed.

No further accusations or punishments fell upon Portia's head, although once more the other guests excluded her from their conversation. After a time, she begged her excuses and retired for the evening.

At least, she thought, she would have one more lesson before Lady Barrington banished her from the house, and from Knightson.

Once again, Mr. Knightson had reached the library before she had. An array of large books were scattered across a low table. He saw her hesitate. "Come," he said. "Sit down."

Portia did as he bid. "These are anatomy texts." It came out like an accusation. She flushed. What was she expecting? A more intimate lesson? *Yes, and oh, yes.*

Mr. Knightson pointed to one. "This is a sketch of a woman's parts." He paused. "Her cunt or quim."

Portia bit down on her lip. The forbidden words alone made her wet with desire, with need.

"See here. This is the clitoris, or clit. When teased, it gives a woman great pleasure."

"Like you did last time." Why did she sound so breathless?

Knightson shot her a glance. "Exactly so." He didn't do as she hoped and shift closer. He kept a small space between them on the sofa.

"And here," he continued, "is your cunt-hole. The technical term for that well is your vagina."

"Isn't that a place in the Americas?" she asked.

He snorted. "That's Virginia, Portia."

She knew that. She grinned at him, and he shook her head at her.

"There is a place within the vagina that, when stimulated, gives a woman even greater pleasure. Indeed, to the point where the woman ejaculates, much like a man."

Not a stranger to semen, this news puzzled Portia. "The same? Thick and white?"

"The liquid is clear," he amended. He smiled, his expression darkening. "Shall I show you?"

His request made her breathless. "Yes," she breathed. "Show me."

He gestured to a blanket spread on the floor. She hadn't noticed that when she came in, her eyes all for him alone. "Remove your clothes, and lie there."

Portia surveyed the room. Knightson had drawn the curtains, and even now, he moved to the door to lock it. She loosened the tapes to her gown and shimmied out of it, picking it up to drape over the sofa.

"My stays," she prompted, turning her back to him. He came to her aid, unthreading the cord.

Naked, she lay on the blanket, feeling the rough nubby wool scratch her skin. It felt awkward, being so naked, so vulnerable, while Knightson stood above her, fully dressed.

And aroused. The outline of his cock was plain against the fine weave of his breeches. He wanted her. She moistened her lips and reached up for him.

He ignored her, settling by her side, propped up by one arm. "Lie back," he commanded, "and relax."

Relax? Impossible?

He touched the swell of her breast and she stiffened. Knightson quirked an eyebrow. "What did he do last night? Young Winterton?"

Portia grimaced. "He pinched me. Hard. Here." She pointed to the affected nipple.

"Clumsy oaf," Knightson commiserated. "Allow me to kiss it better." He bent his head over her, his tongue skimming her flesh.

She bit back a moan. He hadn't done that before. What had taken him so long? The heavenly sensations spun a web of need across her bosom and beyond. The heat from his mouth seeped into her, flaring awake quiescent synapses and sparking in her belly.

Resisting the urge to bury her hands in his hair, to keep him at her breast, Portia's fingers curled into the blanket. Heavenly torture!

Knightson looked up at her for a moment. "You must remember this, Portia. What I do with my mouth, you will do yourself to bring pleasure."

Portia mewed in disappointment. She didn't want that. It became crystal clear to her that she wanted more of him. She squeezed her eyes shut. No. She had made a deal and there could be no more from Knightson except these few lessons.

What about that fuck on the stairs? Her cunt tightened at the memory. If it were nothing more than payment for his tutelage, she'd gladly pay it.

But nothing had been said of payment. What did Knightson want?

His mouth trailed a path down her belly, and he shifted to lie between her parted legs. His tongue tip brushed her—what did he call it?—ahh, clit. She spasmed. Such a featherlight touch! How would she reproduce something so light and wet touching her?

Conscious thought fled, nothing else existed but his lapping tongue and sucking lips upon her clit. She vibrated beneath him, straining, straining to capture the incredible release that Knightson had already delivered to her once. Perversely, she wanted him both to never stop and to gather him in her arms, to have his cock inside her while she found release. She choked back a cry.

Oh, God, she was close, so close. . . .

"Portia."

She raised her head to look down at him between her legs. The lower half of his face shone with her wet.

"Portia, I need you to trust me. Whatever happens, whatever you feel. Don't fight it, let it go."

Her head sunk back onto the blanket, wondering what he meant by that.

He slid his fingers inside her, smoothing along the upper wall of her cunt. "Here," he said, massaging one place. "Remember this."

"Oh, God!" Portia gasped.

Knightson chuckled and resumed his teasing on her clit.

Portia writhed. Release lurked just out of reach. Enough of her senses remained to realize Knightson extended her level of arousal, keeping her strung, on the brink, but refusing to let her topple over.

"Mark, please!" she gasped hoarsely. Her parts burned, driven to a high pitch of sensitivity.

He paused. "You need to make it last, Portia. Don't go for the quick come. Waiting makes for a bigger finish."

Bigger? "I don't care, Mark. Please, please, let me come."

"Remember, let go, relax your muscles."

She struggled to obey, to undo all the straining for release. His tongue flicked rapidly over her clit, his finger sliding inside. She whimpered, she sobbed.

And then the wall hit her, drowning her in gold. She let out a guttural cry and felt something gush between her legs. He kept her there in that golden state, milking her with his finger as she gushed and gushed again.

His fingers slid from her at last, and he lay beside her once more. "Beautiful, that was beautiful," he murmured.

She glanced at him. Liquid dripped from his face. Portia felt a hollow horror. "I—I wet myself."

Knightson swiped his chin and licked his hand. "No, you came. Women can come too, my dear. How did it feel?"

"I—I thought I couldn't come any harder. . . . But you were right, it was bigger."

He grinned. "When you do it to yourself, you will find it

easiest if you perch on the very end of a chair. It gives you a better reach."

Portia shuddered. Do this to herself? She understood at last, the precious gift that Knightson had given her.

Freedom. Freedom from relying on a man to satisfy her. She didn't need a man anymore.

She gazed sidelong at Knightson. But she wanted him. "Thank you," she said, still breathless.

His smile turned strange with a sudden uncertainty. He got to his feet, dusting off the knees of his breeches. "We'll be late for breakfast," he muttered. "I'll let you dress."

Knightson left, leaving her lying sprawled naked on the blanket. The breath caught in her throat. How could he leave like that?

She rose, her legs wobbling. Dulled, empty, she dressed, shrugging into her stays and pocketing the cords. Her attire would appear slightly amiss to the casual observer, but Portia had no intention of being seen by anyone.

She folded up the blanket. She closed the anatomy books, stacking them neatly in the middle of the table.

5

At luncheon, Mrs. Chalcroft asked if there were any plans to view the folly. "I hear it is a most charming walk."

"The day is fine," Lady Barrington agreed. "Shall we go?"

Portia shifted the food around her plate. Knightson's abrupt departure had deflated her, and it bothered her even more because she didn't know why.

The company assembled for the long walk. Pairing off, Portia walked in the middle of the orderly line with Miss Chalcroft.

"Are you well?" Miss Chalcroft peered at her under the deep poke of her bonnet.

Portia managed a smile. "Quite well, I assure you."

"Forgive me, but you seem . . . subdued. Has it to do with last night?"

She wanted to tell Miss Chalcroft it had nothing to do with the previous night, but with certain actions of a certain man in the morning, but that would reveal her as a fraud. "Perhaps. I woke up out of sorts this morning. I did not sleep easily." She glared into the back of Mark Knightson who walked some distance ahead with Lord Barrington.

"Bearing the burden of such cruel, unfair gossip must be difficult," Miss Chalcroft commiserated.

"You do not know the half of it." Portia gave her parasol an angry twirl. "I am opportuned at every turn because of it. Sometimes I wonder if I might give in and be damned."

Miss Chalcroft audibly sucked in air and expelled it in a laugh. "You would prove them right."

"Yes, but then I wouldn't have to worry about defending my reputation and being snubbed. I would be free of it all."

Miss Chalcroft examined her. "You're serious about this, aren't you. I beg you, do not destroy your life. These rumors will pass."

Portia doubted it, but patted her friend's arm. "Yes, you are quite right. I am a bit overwrought today, forgive me."

They wandered through a pretty wood, artistically rendered by the Barrington gardeners into a tamed wilderness. The path, now covered in slippery leaf mulch, wound around a small pond and over a bridge under which the overflow cascaded in a gurgling rivulet.

The sound did more to calm Portia than Miss Chalcroft's chitchat. She inhaled deeply, smelling the dark green of the woods, both alive and decaying.

They left the wood behind them and ascended a long hill, their goal in sight. A white-columned building awaited them. By now, the order of their expeditionary column had changed, the older women falling back to the rear of the line, the young men striding far ahead. Portia saw Sophia among them.

Knightson stopped and waved on Lord Barrington. He fell into step next to Portia and grunted a greeting at Miss Chalcroft. "Miss Carew, may I have a private word?"

Portia shot a startled glance at Miss Chalcroft. "I do not believe that is appropriate, Mr. Knightson."

Knightson swore under his breath. Portia's eyes widened.

He glared over her head at Miss Chalcroft, who met him with a steadfast, sunny expression.

Wanting to laugh at Knightson's frustration, Portia shot an appreciative grin at Miss Chalcroft. Truth be known, she wanted Miss Chalcroft to take Knightson's rude hint and leave them alone. She wanted some explanation for his actions that morning. No, not *those* actions, but his abrupt departure.

"Lucy!" The shrill voice of Mrs. Chalcroft pierced the women's amusement at thwarting Mr. Knightson. "Lucy! I need you."

Shooting a look of apology, Lucy dropped back to join her mother.

"Poor girl," muttered Portia.

"That could be you," Knightson said.

She shot him a sharp look. "Me? I think not. I will never marry, but I shall not be a toady to my mother, either."

"Brave words," Knightson murmured. "Remember the pond?"

Portia blinked up at him, startled by the change of subject. "What of it?"

"Meet me there before breakfast tomorrow morning." He grinned. "You will have to get up earlier to be there at our usual time."

"Another lesson?"

But Knightson had stepped off the path, dropping to a knee to adjust his boot in some manner.

Portia gave her parasol a jubilant twirl. She had thought their lessons were over. After this morning, what more could he teach her? The pond seemed an unusual location. Perhaps it was not another lesson. . . . Perhaps he wanted her for herself.

Her smile had not dimmed by the time she reached the folly. The younger gentlemen already lay sprawled on the grass, watching the approach of the remainder of the party. Miss Sophia appeared to be exploring the folly on her own.

Winterton hailed her. "Miss Carew, what a delightful smile!"

It vanished at once. She glanced back to see how far away everyone else was and remained where she stood, keeping distance between her and the men. She remembered to resume her smile. "My lord." She gave a brief curtsey in thanks for the compliment.

"The walk has given a healthy glow to your cheeks, Miss Carew." Winterton ignored Freddy's warning groan.

"Are you saying I appear sickly at other times, my lord?" Portia asked sweetly.

"No, no, of course not!" spluttered Winterton, scowling at Freddy Barrington's low laughter. "Must my every step seem wrong to you?"

Portia regarded him archly. "That remains to be seen."

The remainder of the group caught up with them, and the servants served tea in the shelter of the Ionic-columned folly.

Refreshed, the company prepared to make the return trip, leaving the servants to remove the debris. Laughing at something Freddy Barrington said, Miss Sophia leapt up and dashed to the edge of the small plateau.

Beside Portia, Lucy sucked in her breath.

Before anyone moved, Knightson rose and took Miss Sophia's arm. "Miss Sophia, would you do me the honor of allowing me to escort you down this steep hill?"

For a brief moment, Portia thought Sophia would refuse and carry out whatever dare Freddy Barrington had whispered in her ear.

Miss Sophia stiffened at his unspoken reproach. Knightson said nothing, only delivered a most winning smile. Miss Sophia's sulks collapsed at having won Mr. Knightson's attention.

Lucy let out her breath. "Thank goodness," she murmured. "Mr. Knightson reacted quickly, did he not?"

"Indeed he did," Portia replied, watching the couple descend the green hill.

"Lucy!" With muttered excuses, Lucy went to join her demanding mother.

Portia prepared to make the walk home alone. To her surprise, the Duke of Winterton fell in beside her. "Miss Carew, may I walk with you?"

"Of course." The man had come to her defense last night, after all. She modified her pace to suit his.

He tucked her arm under his. "We need not go quite this slow. I am not an invalid yet."

Portia blushed. "I shall allow you to set the pace."

"Indeed?" The duke raised a white, quizzical eyebrow. "How do you find my son today?"

"Not much improved from yesternight," she told him bluntly. "He has not affronted my person. . . ."

"I am very glad to hear it," the duke replied with asperity. "But?"

"He is not displaying the polish of a viscount, your Grace."

"You do not pull any punches, do you, Miss Carew?" He chuckled, easing Portia's fears that she'd offended him. "I think my son is still smarting from last night, as are you, no doubt. Do not judge him so quickly. I merely ask you give him time to prove himself as worthy."

"Worthy?"

"Of your hand, Miss Carew. Despite your frankness, you have the potential to make a great lady. I shall be watching you to see if my initial impressions bear out." He patted her hand. "I only ask you retain an open mind when it comes to my son."

Lucy Chalcroft fell in beside Portia. "Your Grace, Lady Barrington wonders if you might attend her?"

The duke nodded. "Remember my words, Miss Carew." He stepped off the path and waited for Lady Barrington.

Lucy waited until they were out of earshot of the duke. "What words?"

"To keep an open mind about his son." Portia didn't see the

harm in telling her. She sighed. "Winterton has set his sights on me."

"You don't want him?"

"I'd prefer someone with a little more experience with women. He is a touch uncouth."

"But he is a viscount!"

"I suspect it has more to do with the fact he believes I'm a woman of easy virtue, rather than with his social standing." Portia grimaced at the man's back.

"Oh dear, he has started all wrong with you, hasn't he?" Lucy sighed. "A pity, he's quite handsome."

Portia grinned. "You can have him!"

"He'd not look at me, Portia. I am thoroughly on the shelf."

"Only because your mother makes you wear those ridiculous caps."

"Not all the time."

"Often enough."

Lucy conceded the point. "What did Knightson want earlier?"

Portia shrugged. She didn't dare tell Lucy the truth. "He knows I'm on the market, although he didn't make much of a bid."

"Market!" Lucy giggled. "What a terrible thing to say!"

"But true." She sighed again. "Oh, Lucy, sometimes I wish that I hadn't protested the rumors so vigorously. I could be set up in a cottage somewhere, living quietly, without having to put up with all of this."

The next morning, with the mist still rising from the valleys, Portia walked to the pond. At first, she worried that someone from the house would see her—oh, not her mother or any of the guests, for it was too early for them, but servants did tattle.

Next on her mind—for she refused to think about Knightson, no matter how many times her thoughts returned to the insufferable man—was the improved behavior of young Winterton. He had behaved like a perfect gentleman the previous night, treating her like a desirable angel.

She had allowed it—and why not? Knightson had not said a word to her since the walk to the folly and hadn't even looked her way the entire evening. If Winterton had reformed, why shouldn't she enjoy it?

She entered the woods, the air turning cooler. Sun had yet to reach here, to filter through the dappled leaves and warm the earth. She hastened her step, until she reached the little wooden bridge that crossed the edge of the pond.

Not all of the water was visible at this point, for here it narrowed into the stream that flowed beneath and away from the bridge.

She stood there, irresolute. She saw no sign of Knightson anywhere. Had this been a prank? She didn't want to call, didn't want to seem nervous, uncertain.

Yesterday, they had taken the path leading away from the pond, but Portia saw that another path forked off from that one to follow the line of the pond.

She took it. If this was Knightson's idea of amusing, she would enjoy the stroll and return as if this had been her own idea.

She turned a corner in the path and the parting of ferns revealed a blue plaid blanket laying near the pond. Knightson lay on it, one hand tucked behind his head.

Naked.

"I had thought about a swim," he said, conversationally, "but the water is too cold." His smile flashed, dark and wicked.

Portia folded her arms, her bearing stiff. She didn't want him to see how she took in his delicious, naked body. He reminded her of a living, breathing Greek statue: broad shoulders, slim waist and hips, contoured thighs.

And his cock . . . He stroked it lazily, his large hand skimming up and down his thick shaft. It seemed to be larger and harder now, than the moment she arrived.

She remembered what it was like with that bulk crammed inside her and knew herself to be lost. "What—what is today's lesson?" Her voice shook.

"I have explained the importance of imagery when bringing oneself to release. Today, you shall see another example." His gaze dropped to his cock as if to say you must remember this. This and only this and no other man's cock.

Portia thought she'd easily oblige him in that unspoken command. She moved to settle down on the blanket next to him, but his next words forestalled her.

"Remove your clothing, Portia."

"But if I am to observe . . ."

His eyes glittered. "Observe then, but you shall do it without clothing. This is not the only lesson you'll have today."

She obeyed him with alacrity, stripping off her gown, loosely tied stays and underthings, and tossing them over a branch. Her bare feet squelched in the mossy bank before stepping on the dry blanket. One of many blankets, she realized. She sat by his hips, curling her legs around her, her eyes avidly watching his cock.

He lazily stroked himself. Portia imagined the circle he made with thumb and forefinger mimicked her quim. He entered in, and slid out. She wriggled, not wanting to watch any more.

She looked at his face and found him watching her, his eyes as hungry as she felt. "I think . . ." she started. "I think I would have a much stronger memory, if we . . . if you . . ."

"Say it, Portia," he growled.

"Fuck me." She shifted, rising and straddling him. His cock stood before her parted legs. She ran a fingertip over his balls.

He moaned, his hands falling to her hips.

"Perhaps I should torture you a little first," she purred, even though she wanted nothing more than to impale herself on his hard and ready cock.

He grunted in approval. Moisture dripped from the head of his cock and she smoothed it in a circular motion. Her fingers brushed the velvety silk of his cock, the rock solid muscle beneath. It twitched and strained at her touch.

"Portia," Knightson groaned, grabbing her wrists and rolling so that she lay beneath him.

She wriggled against him. His cock butted her groin, resisting all her attempts to slide him in her.

Knightson still held her wrists and hauled them over her head, imprisoning her with one large hand. Their hands sunk into the mud, cool and sticky.

He bent his head, kissing and biting her nipples until they were swollen, red and burning. Portia thought she might come there and then if he kept that up. The gentle and not-so-gentle tugging of his teeth combined with his wet tongue drove her wild.

She panted and moaned, still wriggling beneath him. He gripped her waist and grains of mud smeared her belly. "Mark . . . Mark, please."

He shifted, reaching for something. He slid up her body, the head of his cock at last nudged into place.

Portia stared up at him, aware of her vulnerable position, hands caught above her head, her arched back making her breasts jut up. The chill of their shaded location seeped into her bones, everywhere but the hot pricks at the tips of her breasts and in the well of her groin.

He reared back, holding a silver cup between them, the sides fogged with condensation. He spilled water drops onto her chest.

Portia moaned, her back arching even further. The cold burned her even more, her nipples hardening into tight, painful nubs.

The fiery ice raced to her belly.

Mark slid into her, his hot cock meeting the cold shiver and dissolving it. He thrust into her hard and fast. Portia didn't know whether she burned or cracked like ice. She sobbed beneath him, wave after wave of blazing release engulfing her.

Relentless, Mark kept driving into her, not giving her a moment's reprieve, keeping her in a state of heightened arousal. The air left her lungs, Portia rendered breathless by the power of her climax.

Mark released her hands, hauling them both into a seated position, Portia in his lap with her legs wrapped around his waist. The change in position caused him to penetrate her even more deeply and he set up a rocking motion like a seesaw, his cock pulsing inside her.

Portia decided to endure Mark until he climaxed, for she was at the point where pleasure faded, but she remembered Mark's words of yesterday to relax.

She tried it, feeling herself open even more to him. A fresh wetness spread along her thighs.

"Yes!" Mark's guttural cry echoed through the trees. He rocked her even harder, until what had felt like pain burst into renewed, nay, doubled, pleasure.

Portia screamed her release with him. The strength of her cry left her almost as shaken as the strength of her coming.

Drained, exhausted, she clung to Mark, her face buried in his neck. She didn't think she could rise even if he commanded it. He smelled of their mingled sexes, of acrid male sweat and a hint of sandalwood. Her cunt muscles convulsed one last time for the sheer joy of breathing him in.

Mark chuckled under his breath, guiding them to lie on the blanket, so that they lay spooned together. His breath puffed hot by her ear, and his arms curled around, covering her breasts with his hands.

She gasped, so sensitive there still. The muddy grit made his touch almost unbearable, but nestled in the palms of his hands, she relaxed. It made her aware of him, just an edge aroused, and strangely secure.

This was the first time, she realized, that he hadn't bid her to dress and go, or dressed and departed himself. Was there more in store for her this morning?

His tongue-tip flicked against her earlobe. "Portia, I have never heard you let yourself go like that. You screamed."

She flushed and considered pushing his hands away. "I—I'm sorry," she stuttered. To her astonishment, she felt tears form in her eyes. Had she disappointed him? And why did she care so much?

"No, do not apologize." His dark burr roughened further. "I had thought perhaps my lessons were in vain, that you would never truly let yourself go, never experience...." He trailed off and kissed her ear. "But you did, my sweet Portia, you did. You are more than I expected, not merely repressed, but a woman of great and deep passion."

His words shook her to the core. She couldn't think of a single intelligent thing to say. "Th—thank you."

He chuckled again. "Have I rendered you speechless, my dear? I tell you, these endearments do not come easily to me."

Endearments? They were more like encouragements to a riot of sex. With him and no one else.

"I—I am dirty." This was the best she could come up with? She struggled to rise. Mark let her go. She didn't turn to look at him, but headed for the water's edge, splashing the icy water over her breasts and belly, washing away the mud.

She wished the cold and cleansing water didn't also wash away Mark's scent, his imprint, as well.

Spotting a dried leaf in her hair, she pulled it free. She dried herself using her sole petticoat. Struggling into her stays, she looked over her shoulder at him. "Will you please help me with my stays?"

He frowned. "Irritating things." He rose, still naked and threaded her stays shut. He retreated while she dressed.

Portia kept her gaze averted. Dressed, she prepared to go.

"Portia."

His one word halted her steps. Still, she did not turn. "Yes?"

"What is it? What disturbs you?"

She faced him then, her breath sucking in at the idle arrangement of his limbs, his softening cock draped across one thigh. How could he look so at ease, so wonderful?

"Nothing disturbs me." It was a lie, but Portia had no coherent reason for her actions.

"That is not true. We should have honesty between us, Portia. Lovers should be honest, if nothing else."

Lovers? Did he say lovers?

"You said . . . You said you would teach me, nothing more. Lovers?" Her voice rose at the end, a tiny hint of hysteria peeking through.

He sat up then, resting his arms on his knees. His eyes narrowed. "If you do not want me, Portia, you only have to say the word." His voice turned cold and hard.

"I—" Not want him? She burned for him. She was beyond wanting, she needed him. Their mornings to her had become as essential as breath, and in such a short time. It scared her. She didn't want this. Losing herself in a man was how she'd been almost ruined in the first place. Would be ruined yet, if she wasn't careful.

The silence had drawn out too long. "Oh!" She stomped her foot, heard a satisfying squelch of mud and hurried off down the path, back toward the house.

Her pace hastened by her anger, her frustration, Portia boiled. She wanted to shriek "How dare you?" and retreat behind maidenly sensibilities, but she'd recognized in an instant the hypocrisy of that. Mark Knightson saw no maiden. He saw a woman, ripe and easily picked, easily devoured, easily tossed away.

Choking back a sob, she hurried on.

Mark Knightson couldn't blame the girl. For all the gossip about her, Portia Carew was no jaded wench. True, she had enough experience with men not to be afraid of whatever sexual challenge he sent her. Her eagerness to learn ought to have disgusted him. Instead, he'd respected, yes, respected, the reasons why.

She wanted freedom from men. She had told him she'd no intent to marry, and he knew from personal experience the depths of her sexual desire. So why not learn to seek independence from a man in that?

His problem clarified: the more that he taught her, the more he wanted to possess her for himself. He knew the feelings well enough, the first flush of physical desire, the attenuated need for the other that could not be ignored, the incessant throb of arousal, only partially assuaged with each encounter.

They would pass. These needs had passed before. They would fade and he would go on to his next conquest. And she? What would happen to Portia?

He vowed that he'd give her something to remember. The idea that it would be to the memory of him, their abandoned couplings, that she would masturbate to almost undid him again, then and there.

He groaned, stuffing his swelling cock into his breeches.

Oh yes, she would remember him. He'd make sure of it.

The women had gathered in the morning room, each absorbed in her own little tasks and engaged in desultory conversation. The Chalcrofts and Mrs. Carew bent over their embroidery and mending. Lady Barrington sat at her little escritoire and dealt with correspondence.

Portia sat in the window seat, legs curled up beneath her and trying to read a book. All she felt, however, was the throbbing in her parts. Her breasts, hours later, had not ceased to ache, the contact of her fine linen chemise abraded her like rough wool.

She closed her eyes, for a moment reliving those wild moments in the sun-dappled shade by the pond. Mark had given her no quarter, taking and demanding more. And she gave it. Without hesitation, without repulsion, although there was little about Knightson that could be labeled repulsive.

She must think of him as Knightson, not Mark. One slip of her tongue, one careless utterance of "Mark" and they would both be undone. She would be banished from this house and sent God knows where. It didn't bear thinking about.

A flash of light outside caught her attention. She looked up from her pretended reading. A carriage approached, drawn by four fine black horses.

Portia turned to the others. "It's a carriage."

Lady Barrington looked up at her. "A carriage? Who could that be I wonder?"

The other ladies tucked away their work and rose in unison with Lady Barrington, straightening their gowns. Who would arrive uninvited?

The women filed into the hall, a large open space laid in large black and white marble tiles, bracketed by a staircase that rose three floors.

Freddy Barrington dashed in, the other gentlemen of the party following more slowly behind. "Sorry, Mother!" He struggled to straighten his cravat. "I invited another friend along. You said I may."

Lady Barrington smiled, all graciousness. "Indeed I did."

Portia shot a glance across the room at Mar—Knightson. The men had been interrupted in some game, for his sleeves remained rolled up and his cravat loosened. He seemed not to have the same urge as young Freddy to tidy himself.

Their gazes met. Knightson's gaze darkened, but he gave no other outward sign. Portia looked away, thinking perhaps she had imagined it, had wanted to see him want her.

The Barrington butler opened the door. The first new arrival, a woman, entered, a vision of the latest fashions. Her shining auburn hair gathered up under a pert little purple bonnet covered in tulle. She wore a steel gray pelisse and her skirt shone in purple satin.

She beamed at the assembled company. "It is so kind of you to welcome me, Lady Barrington."

Lady Barrington seemed at a loss at the sight of this beautiful woman.

For some reason, Portia looked across the hall at Knightson. He seemed chiseled in stone.

One by one, the woman greeted each of the men—or rather, accepted their greetings with a cool grace, totally confident of her beauty and its effect on men.

The only one who did not step forward to welcome her was Knightson.

"Mr. Knightson." The woman turned her devastating smile to Knightson and inclined her head.

"Lady Cecily." Portia heard banked anger in Knightson's flat voice. Why did this woman's arrival make him unhappy? "What are you doing here?"

"I was invited—"

As one, the assembled company turned to Lord and Lady Barrington. Lady Barrington opened her mouth to reply, but the second guest chose that moment to make his entry.

The man dipped his head to remove his hat and looked up at the crowd. "Freddy, so good of you to ask me along. I brought a friend. Hope you don't mind."

The cheerful ringing tones froze Portia in place. All the

blood rushed from her head and puddled somewhere around her feet, possibly even slipping through the cracks in the tile floor.

No, not him. Let it be anybody but him.

Lucy Chalcroft appeared by her side, slipping her arm through Portia's. "Steady," she whispered.

Everyone knew the rumors, and everyone knew who'd spread them.

Lady Barrington's tight smile conveyed her awareness that her house party had just officially become a disaster. "Sir Guy Symon, such an unexpected pleasure."

6

Portia clung to Lucy. Only her support kept her upright. She longed to sink to the floor in a graceful swoon. Any woman of maidenly sensibilities surely would when confronted with her accuser.

She took one deep breath and then another. She glanced at Knightson, whose features seemed to be a mix of fury and concern. The harpy still clung to him.

"I am all right, Lucy." Portia advanced, weaving her way through the group of assembled women and toward Sir Guy Symon jokingly conversing with Lord Freddy Barrington.

A nudge from Freddy made Sir Guy turn. "Portia." He practically purred her name.

Portia straightened her shoulders. "You, sir, are a bounder." She slapped him hard across the face.

The smacking sound echoed through the silent hall. He took the blow, her small palm print a bright red mark on his cheek. He managed a smile, constricted from its previous glory.

Unable to stand to the sight of him any longer, she spun and headed for the staircase.

Sir Guy's drawl stopped her halfway to the first landing. "That's my Portia. Such fire!"

She resumed ascending the stairs, gripping the banister, her steps slower.

"It's why I love her, you see. Why I've come to woo her back."

Portia turned, staring down at him in unmitigated horror. Now she really would faint. She dug her fingernails into the palms of her hand, horribly aware she and Sir Guy had become the focus of every occupant of the room.

"Portia," Sir Guy cajoled.

"Go to hell," she snarled. This time she ran up the stairs, not stopping in her headlong flight until she reached her room. She slammed the door behind her and leaned against it.

Sir Guy wanted her back? Was he mad? Why? Portia hadn't forgotten the sweet emotions centered around him. They had been engaged—and he'd broken it off and used her willingness to be touched by him as the excuse, calling her a slut and a whore and other awful things.

The tears welled in her eyes. She had given herself to him, so certain of their future together. He had rejected her. Why did he want her back?

Or had he come to shame her all over again? She refused to give him that satisfaction.

Some hours later, she heard a soft scratch at the door. "Portia? It's Lucy."

Portia uncurled from her dry-eyed position on her bed and opened the door. Lucy hustled in, closing the door behind her.

"Oh, Portia. Such a terrible shock!"

Portia nodded in agreement.

"He said some more things after you left. Things I thought you should know."

"What things?" Portia sat on the bed and patted the space on the simple cream quilted bedspread beside her.

"That he made a mistake. That he impugned your name because he was the worst of cowards and didn't want to marry anyone, not even you."

"And you believed him?"

Next to her, Lucy tugged her skirt straight, twirled an escaped blond lock of hair. "He seemed very sincere."

Portia sighed. "Sir Guy is charming. Very charming. How else do you think he got all of London's polite society to believe and sympathize with him?"

"What are you going to do?" Lucy murmured, a little furrow marring her brow.

"Assuming Lady Barrington doesn't pack off Mama and me for fear of having her house party tainted with even more scandal? I want nothing to do with him. Nothing."

"You will have to be sociable. . . ."

"I shall not!" proclaimed Portia, feeling her cheeks heat. "I shall give him the cut direct."

"You wouldn't!" Lucy's hand clutched at her throat.

"I would. You don't know what I'm capable of, Lucy." Portia managed a smile. "Do not worry, I won't slap him across the face again. At least, not unless he commits some fresh offense."

Portia twisted the lace at her cuff and asked the question burning inside her with the same heat as her humiliation of Sir Guy's arrival. "Who was that woman?"

"Lady Cecily Lambeth," Lucy supplied, her blue eyes gleaming. "She is a widow and gallivants much about Society."

"Hmm." Portia rose, bending to peer into the vanity's mirror to restore her appearance.

"It is strange that she has come as Sir Guy's guest, and yet he seems intent on pursuing you." Lucy joined her, tucking away a few curls for her.

"There is more to this than it appears," Portia agreed, turning to her friend. "Perhaps she's set her eye on young Freddy and heard about the mini-marriage market out here." Portia didn't believe it for a second, certain that Lady Cecily's connection lay with Mar—Knightson. "Oh, Lucy. This is such a mess, isn't it?"

Lady Barrington had not ordered the Carews to pack their bags following that afternoon's scene, much to Portia's mother's relief.

"How could she?" Mama studied herself in the mirror, adding the final touches to her hair before going down to dinner. "After all, my dearest Portia, she has to countenance that piece Sir Guy brought with him. If he is here to woo you and I will not gainsay you if you wish to encourage his attentions, he has a funny way of doing it, bringing that woman along."

Portia interrupted Mama's flow of chatter when the latter took a breath. "I thought Lady Cecily was a respectable woman?"

"She is a widow," Mama declared. "She has more freedom than you or I."

"Why Mama, I believe you are jealous!"

"Nonsense, child. Why should I be jealous of Society's curiosity? The sooner that woman marries again, the sooner Society will no longer have to wonder if they embrace an asp in their collective bosom."

"An asp!" Portia closed the door behind her and followed her mother along the hall.

"Indeed. Who knows if she is the sort to steal husbands or fiancés. Some of her kind never remarry, and I hesitate to tell you this, my dearest, but they prefer to keep a succession of lovers rather than marry one man. Who is to say Lady Cecily is not of that sort?"

They reached the dining room without incident or more surprisingly, without being overheard. Sir Guy and Lady Cecily's arrival upset the order of precedence at dinner and Portia gained Mr. Knightson as a dinner partner.

"Save me the waltz," Knightson murmured, before he helped her to sit. His grip tightened on her arm. "Promise."

"I will," she whispered, ducking her head so that her lips would not be seen.

Portia found having Mr. Knightson on the right to be most distracting. His elegant attire gave no hint of that morning's wanton nakedness, nor the afternoon's deshabille.

Portia hung on his every word, be it about the weather, politics or the latest Society happenings, finding herself in agreement with him. She watched him eat in sidelong glances. She imagined those hands, which handled the cutlery with such light grace, forcing her beneath him, holding her to the ground as he fucked her.

She shivered and took a quick gulp of wine in case any dared to question the color of her cheeks. Looking up, she saw Sir Guy gazing at her, his pale blue eyes sparking with assessment.

Portia looked down at her plate. He knew. Or he guessed. Sir Guy had seen firsthand how desire affected her. She must think of cool thoughts, of anything but Mar—Knightson. She devoted her attention to the neglected Miss Sophia Chalcroft for the remainder of the meal.

To enliven the evening, Lady Barrington had proposed dancing. She refused to change her plans even after the unexpected additions to the party. They gathered in the ballroom. Miss Lucy Chalcroft had been volunteered by her mother to play the pianoforte, which made the number of couples conveniently even, as Lady Barrington had decided she wished to dance. Lord Barrington, with his gouty foot, sat it out.

"Dear Portia—" began Sir Guy, beating young Winterton and Knightson to her hand.

"Miss Carew to you, Sir Guy. You no longer have the right to use my given name." From the corner of her eye, she saw Knightson direct Winterton in Lady Cecily's direction, while at the same time appearing he hadn't been headed toward Portia after all.

"Miss Carew, if I may have the honor of this dance?" Sir Guy flourished a bow. He straightened, eyeing her, and lowered his voice. "If you refuse, there will be no more dancing for you tonight."

Even though this wasn't a public assembly, Portia knew this to be true. She couldn't miss out on being held in Knightson's arms, no matter how chastely.

Portia accepted his hand and he led her out to join the others on the dance floor. She looked everywhere but at her unwanted partner. Miss Sophia seemed to brim with excitement, at last gaining a partner, no matter how temporary.

"We need to talk," Sir Guy told her.

They stepped toward each other in the first steps of the dance. The Barringtons had set up their ballroom so that the dancers used only the portion nearest the pianoforte. It kept the set close, and private conversation almost impossible.

Portia glanced aside at young Winterton and Lady Cecily who stood next to them. "I do not think we do."

"At least give me the chance to explain—"

"I heard what you said to everyone this afternoon. I do not need to hear more."

"You do." They joined uplifted hands to turn in a circle. "I am sorry, Portia."

Too startled to protest the use of her name again, Portia just stared at him. Did he mean it? Was this sincerity or his charm?

"I made a mistake with you," he continued. He kept his voice low, but it was impossible for him not to be overheard. "Let me speak with you in private, Portia. I would say more."

She retreated behind scorn. "And prove to every person here that I am as loose as you say? I think not."

"Portia . . ." Sir Guy tried his cajoling expression, eyes wide and sad. She'd fallen for it once, never twice.

Portia said nothing, remaining silent for the remainder of the dance. She had no intentions of again succumbing to Sir Guy's charm.

Lucy started the introduction to yet another country dance. Young Winterton approached and claimed Portia from Sir Guy.

"Oh, Miss Carew!" he began, reddening from enthusiasm. "I have never been in more admiration of you than tonight!"

"How so?" she asked coolly. Portia had tired of men's protestations.

"Such fire! Such spirit this afternoon!" Young Winterton took the chance to kiss her hand as they made a turn. "You were quite divine. I would see this side of you more often, Miss Carew."

"Keep this up," Portia retorted, exasperated, "and I will be more than happy to oblige you with a sharp slap." Would every man who insulted her return with cooing praises? Was there not one honest man left?

Winterton pinked further and oohed with delight. Behind them, she heard Knightson choke down a chuckle. She repressed the urge to give Winterton the beating he deserved. Besides, it would quite throw them out of step with the rest of the set.

"I never imagined, no, not even in all of Sir Guy's tales, that you possessed such unknown depths."

"Depths?" Portia flicked an uncertain glance at young Winterton. "Tales?"

He took the opportunity to lean close to her. "The infliction of pain for pleasure, Miss Carew." They moved apart. "You have no idea how much it delights me."

Portia chewed on her lip. Was he suggesting . . . ? "I am not sure I understand you, my lord."

"Oh you do," Winterton fatuously informed her. "You will."

He regaled her with what passed as his wit for the remainder of the country dance.

They finished at the bottom of the set, nearest the pianoforte. Portia met Lucy's envious gaze. "Miss Chalcroft, let me play for a while. Here, my lord, take Miss Chalcroft for the next set. Shall I play a polonaise?"

Before anyone could protest, she'd nudged Lucy off the piano stool and commenced playing. Young Winterton remained where he stood, with Lucy standing awkwardly nearby.

"My lord," Portia directed a glare at him, "if you do not do as I ask, I will have to punish you." She didn't know what made her say it, other than he had practically begged her for it the entire time they'd danced.

Winterton pinked again. "Oh, Miss Carew, how you tempt me. Say you will punish me for dancing with Miss Chalcroft and I shall escort her onto the floor immediately."

She felt ill in her stomach. "Perhaps I might, my lord."

"When I least expect it?" Winterton danced a brief jig. "Come, Miss Chalcroft."

Portia launched into the polonaise, ignoring the glares of both her mother and Mrs. Chalcroft. Why shouldn't Lucy be allowed to enjoy herself a little? A dance or two would not hurt.

Lucy returned at the end, with a winking Winterton. "Miss Carew, I cannot let you sit out another dance." She bent to whisper by Portia's ear. "Mother is furious."

Portia squeezed her hand. "Did you have fun?"

"He is a weird one." Lucy grinned.

Portia laughed. "Play me a waltz, Miss Chalcroft?" She couldn't wait any longer to dance with Knightson.

Lucy's eyes widened at the thought of a playing a dance still considered scandalous in conservative circles. "Curious. Mr. Knightson has also asked me to play one."

Portia smiled, not daring to comment. Winterton still hung about them, but the significance of Miss Chalcroft's words had not registered. Portia hoped he would remain clueless.

Winterton bowed. "A waltz! How delightful! Miss Carew?"

She shook her head. "My apologies, my lord, I have promised this dance to Mr. Knightson."

Knightson appeared on cue, taking her hand and leading her onto the floor. Instead of keeping to one end of the ballroom, he guided her out into the center of the ballroom floor, farther away from the watchers.

Portia noted that the other dancers followed Knightson's lead. At the opening notes, she and Knightson linked arms and clasped hands. They danced as if alone, easily done in such a large space with so few couples.

Stepping forward, Knightson surveyed the others with a quiet smile. "Good," he murmured, watching her pirouette beneath his arm. "Now we can talk."

"About what, Mr. Knightson?" Portia inquired, daring to be pert. His hands held her waist, sending a slight shiver through her.

His voice dropped to that delicious burr that made her burn inside. "I wish to speak of us."

"Us?" Portia slid her hands up to his shoulders, drawing him in closer. They made several turns.

"Us." Facing in different directions, his arm wrapped about her waist, her other hand suspended above their heads by his. Face angled to face, he guided her into a slow turn. Portia's heart pounded, close enough to catch the faint whiff of his sandalwood soap and the darker, more delicious scent of him.

Knightson continued. "About how I have longed to slip that demure gown from your shoulders and kiss your breasts until your little nubs have grown hard, until you ache for me and beg me to take you."

They turned again, still clasped in an intimate embrace. His touch burned through her thin silk gown, reminding her of how else he had touched her. Portia took a shaky breath, gazing nowhere but up at him, her belly burning for him. "You do not need to do any of that. I ache for you now."

She saw the answering fire in his gaze. "I had hoped so. Plead a headache and leave. Wait for me in the drawing room across the hall and I will join you when I can."

The dance forced them to part into a demure promenade. "Across the hall?" Portia lifted her startled gaze to his. "Isn't that close?"

Another step and once more he encircled her waist with both hands. "You like to be quiet, do you not?" he teased, his mouth dipping close to her ear.

She blushed, dipping her head. "I think I may enjoy screaming more."

He laughed and whirled her around in time with the music. "Not tonight. Although I shall do my best to make you cry out."

He drew her into that second, more intimate embrace. Facing him, she saw his desire for her in his expression. She trembled. "If you continue to speak like that, I shall soon be begging you to ravish me here in front of everyone."

He drew her closer, scandalously so. Portia didn't care. Let everyone see. So long as he continued to hold her like that, body pressed against body.

"Ravish? I would do no such thing, my dear. It would be a slow seduction that everyone would see, for I would have you beg me for release. There would be nothing quick about it."

Lucy played the ending chords of the waltz. Portia remembered wanting to ask Knightson about Lady Cecily. But why should she? He had no interest in the woman if he intended to bed Portia again. Perhaps it was a case of simple dislike?

Portia endured another dance with young Winterton, batting off his wandering hands and his bizarre hinting at something that sounded quite distasteful.

That dance ended. Portia begged a headache to her mother and Lady Barrington. Both of them frowned, not approving of her early departure.

"Stay just a moment longer, my dear girl," Portia's mother suggested.

Lucy Chalcroft played the opening of a minuet. The Duke of Winterton strolled toward her from the pianoforte, making a leg. "Miss Carew, I would be honored if you would dance with an old man."

She could hardly refuse. Not daring to even look Knightson's way, she placed her hand in the duke's and allowed him to lead her onto the floor.

"You are not so very old, your grace," she remarked, having completed the opening movements in perfect unison with the duke.

He beamed at her. "You are very kind to say so, my dear."

She darted a small smile at him. Why had the Duke asked her to dance?

"I do hope you forgive me for importuning you in this manner, but you bloomed so delightfully during the waltz, I just had to bask in your youth."

Portia chose that moment to remember the duke was a widower. She swallowed. "The waltz is very invigorating," she hedged when she had the chance to speak with him again.

"And the dance with my son? You glow when you blush, Miss Carew. It is quite becoming."

"If you are not careful, your Grace, you shall make me blush again." She smiled. Why not flirt with the old man a little?

He chuckled. "Is that modesty, Miss Carew, or a challenge?"

The minuet drew to an end and they made their final bows.

"Shall we say 'modesty,' your Grace?" Portia curtseyed again. "If you will excuse me, I will retire. I have lingered overlong as it is."

"It was kind of you to stay longer to dance with me, Miss Carew. Shall I escort you to your rooms?"

"No! No." Portia tried to wipe all traces of haste from her expression. "I do not wish to discommode you."

The Duke of Winterton allowed her to make her escape. She slipped across the hallway and into a drawing room filled with shadows, the colors faded into grays.

She sank into a chair, covering her eyes. What had she become? A woman who so quickly responded to a man's demands and yet blushed in confusion at young Winterton's profane hints.

This couldn't last. In her heart of hearts, Portia knew this. Knightson's offer of a "few" lessons had extended into incredible sex he had not set a bar upon, but he made no promises either.

Indeed, he had made no promises other than declaring he would make her scream with release again.

And why should he? She had told him she didn't want marriage, and he seemed to have taken the hint that this would be her last love affair. In fact, he seemed to prefer the idea she remember him as her last lover, while working herself to a satisfying release.

She squeezed her legs together. It worked. Just the thought of him on her, in her, fucking her was enough to release the heat in her veins, to make her want to touch herself.

Yet she must wait. If Knightson wanted her to scream, he was going to have to work for it. Why should she make it easy?

At last, he entered the room, the door closing with a firm click behind him.

She rose, going to him without a word. Their mouths joined, hungry and searching.

"I am going to ruin your gown," he murmured against her lips.

She nibbled at his lips, the tip of her tongue teasing. "As I recall," she purred, "you are the skilled lover. Can you not come up with something? I have missed you, Mark."

"It has not been that long." His eyebrow quirked.

"True, but you are very good at what you do. What woman wouldn't desire more?"

He set her back, his arms bracing the distance between them. "There is no 'more,' Portia. Take what I offer and enjoy it."

She managed, somehow, to breathe normally. "I meant 'more,' in the sense of some new twist to our fucking. You are quite inventive."

Mark relaxed, drawing her back into him. "Just so long as you understand."

"I understand." Her hand slipped between them and stroked his trapped cock, already hardening. "Let's not waste time in talk. Besides, someone might overhear us."

"Willful wench." He grinned. He glanced about the small room. "Come over here."

He led her to the window, away from the door. Parting the drapes, Portia saw it had a window seat, tumbled with cushions.

"Lean against the wall," he advised.

She did so, folding her hands behind her, arching so her breasts pushed out against the silk fabric of her gown. It was utterly wanton of her, but she wanted him to see her willingness. She liked Mark's expression, his gaze feasting upon her pert breasts, as if he'd forgotten his plans for them.

He smoothed over the visible expanse of her bosom, his fingertip edging the neckline of her bodice. Not far from his touch, her nipples ached for his caresses.

"If you would place your foot on the window seat." He sounded husky with passion.

She obeyed. The action parted her thighs, revealing her most intimate self to the air. This felt wild, decadent. It reminded her of the first time she had touched herself in the library, except this time she had a willing partner.

Unbidden, she smoothed her hands down over her breasts.

She saw him watch the path of her hands and squirmed, almost giddy with the power she seemed to have over him. Her skin felt hot beneath the cool of her silk gown and she pressed the fabric against her belly, dipping lower.

When she reached her groin, Mark caught her gloved hand. He kissed it. "That pleasure will be mine," he advised her. He dropped to his knees, stripping off his white kid gloves.

She shivered, marveling at how this simple act tantalized her beyond words.

His hands smoothed over her stockinged calves, each stroke taking his hands a little higher up her legs. He reached past the backs of her knees, surprisingly sensitive to his touch. Her skirt bunched in the crook of his elbow.

He blew her a kiss and ducked under her skirt and petticoat, shuffling forward until he knelt beneath her. She felt his breath hot at her moist opening.

He peppered kisses against the insides of her thighs. She shifted, spreading her legs farther, granting him more access, encouraging him to come closer. Why must he always tease her?

His finger nudged between her nether lips and she heard Mark moan. She gave a small, secret smile. She'd known she'd been so very ready for him. His reaction to discovering that just made her even wetter.

He wasted no time in slipping a finger inside her. She bent her knees, wanting him in deeper. He moved inside her, searching for that special smooth spot that made her scream before.

She moaned when he found it, reaching down to stroke his hair through the thin silk of her gown. The tiny movements of his finger had her twisting at his teasing touch.

She swallowed her cries. What if someone passed by the door and heard her? They'd be undone. It would all be over, and she didn't want that just yet.

The tip of his tongue flicked over her clit. She gripped him, holding him there. Was it possible to die from this sinful pleasure?

A second finger slid in to join the first, thrusting upward as Portia bore down to meet his mouth. She felt the tiny shudders start, presaging the great release that hovered on the edge of her senses.

She kept her moaning low, longing to give full voice to her needs, but afraid of being overheard. The danger of discovery gave an added edge of deliciousness to it. Would there be enough warning for them to reassemble themselves? Would there be time enough for Mark to make her come?

She urged him on, her hands bunching about fistfuls of his hair and her skirts. Her entire body tensed, a cascade of thrilling shivers rocking her body. She grabbed at the wall behind her, her knees starting to sag, unable to stand.

Somehow, his other hand bore her up, supporting her buttocks while his fingers fucked her fast. His mouth licked and sucked upon her clit, communicating his own urgency.

She wanted that release, grinding against his mouth and hand. Coming hit her out of nowhere. Stuffing her hand into her mouth, she muffled her cries, her hips bucking hard against his face, feeling the juices escape her cunt, trickling down her thighs.

Mark sank back on his heels, escaping the confines of her skirt. He gazed up at her, his face glazed with her juices.

She sagged to sit on the window seat, leaning against the wall, struggling for enough breath. From head to toe, she trembled with the aftershocks of her release.

He licked his lips before retrieving a handkerchief from his coat pocket and wiping his face. Rising, he held the soiled linen to his nose for a moment. "Now I can breathe you in when you are not with me."

His words alone almost made her come again. She craved to have him inside her. Fucking her. Hard and merciless until they both came again.

"And what about you?" She accepted his hand to help her to her feet. She leaned into him, pressing her hand against the prominent bulge in his breeches.

His eyes closed for a moment of bliss before opening again. He placed his hand over hers, stilling her movements. "There are things I would ask of you," he said, almost in a growl, "but I fear we have been too long away as it is. Someone may discover you are not in your room."

Reluctant, she moved away from him, giving him some time to compose himself. She focused on smoothing the new creases in her gown and convincing her shaking legs to function properly.

She didn't want to think about how utterly she'd abandoned herself to him, how she obeyed her body's demands without a second thought. Or if there was a second thought, it had soon been buried beneath excuses.

She gazed at his back, dark and lovely in his evening coat. Mark stood by the window, his palm against the cold glass, staring out at the night. What did he think in order to bring himself back from the brink?

She didn't care she'd used excuses or even faulty reasoning. She'd gone into this with her eyes open, and she wanted him. That was the end of it. She'd deal with the hurt of separation when it came, if it came.

At last, he seemed recovered and turned to face her once more. She glanced down at his crotch to find that his arousal had not fully subsided.

The thought he still wanted her, still needed his own release, made her want to drag him back to the library or to the pond. . . . But he was right, someone might discover her missing and begin to wonder.

7

Mark opened the door to the drawing room, casually strolling out before turning back to beckon her forth. Feeling her slip by him, so close that he caught a whiff of her aroused sex, he watched her hurry down the hallway and ascend the staircase.

He had not planned on retiring for the night, but to return to the dancing. That idea did not appeal.

His closed fist landed against the doorjamb with a muffled thud. What had he been thinking? Why did he frig her with his mouth instead of bending her over the back of the sofa and fucking her mercilessly?

Her soft sounds escaping from her lips . . . The way she had been completely open to him. . . . How had he resisted? What had made him stop?

Mark paced the drawing room floor. How unlike him to be caught up in a woman's softness, even one eager and adventurous like Portia Carew. What then? Why?

Unable to face the answer, Mark stalked from the drawing room, ascending to his own chamber. Whatever the reason, his cock would be assuaged.

He paused outside one of the chamber doors. He heard voices from within, indistinct. Was this Portia's room? Had her mother come to check on her?

He restrained the urge to burst in, reassure the woman—of what? That she hadn't dallied with him?

Shaking his head, he walked on to his room. He waved his valet away after only divesting himself of his jacket and cravat. "I'll finish."

The valet gave a knowing wink. Mark sighed. The front of his breeches strained with his erection. He wasn't about to display it to his body-servant. No doubt the man expected to find a woman in Mark's bed in the morning.

He stripped and slid into bed, clutching his come-drenched handkerchief. He lifted the fine linen fabric to his face and inhaled deeply.

His cock jerked in response. He stroked himself idly, breathing air filled with *her*. In his mind, he relived orally frigging her, but instead of turning to the window and cursing himself for a fool for stopping, his dream self pulled Portia into his arms.

Rubbing his groin against her belly, he plundered her mouth. His hand flattened his cock against his belly, rubbing his shaft.

He groaned aloud. He imagined hoisting Portia's skirts to her waist, turning her and bending her over the low back of the sofa.

He pushed her legs apart, rubbed his cock in her soaking slit. Oh, God, how good she felt: all soft and wet, coating his cock with her come.

His fingers tightened around the handkerchief at his nose. He pumped his cock, imagining the first hard thrust and the second, and the third. He'd start slow, make her wonder when the next thrust would come and then fill her, stretch her in one sharp move. He'd feel her cunt clutch at him, feel her grip him, milk him, keep him inside.

And yet he would pull back and pause before thrusting in again. And again.

Mark gave himself over to pleasure, fucking Portia fast and hard in his mind. Her breasts would bobble in his hands, her hard little nipple nubs grazing his palms.

She'd be screaming, coming and coming around him. He'd rip her bodice, bare her breasts, mash them with his hands, possess her.

His hips moved in a frenzy, his hand pistoning up and down his cock. He was on the verge of spending himself and he imagined his jism shooting into Portia's depths. He imagined pulling out, flipping her around to face him and climaxing all over her bare breasts, his creamy come a strand of sticky pearls upon her fair skin.

He groaned, feeling his balls swell, his jism pushing up through his—

"Why, Mark, if you were that lonely, you should have come to me."

Mark's eyes flew open. At the foot of his bed stood Lady Cecily Lambeth. She'd loosened her bodice, her fingers teasing a pert nipple. How long had she been standing there?

"Get out," he growled.

"Now that's no way to speak to a lady," Lady Cecily purred. She approached him, pulling the bodice off her shoulders. "Especially not a lady who has a convenient little hole to fill."

His balls burned. How could he get rid of her, so he could come?

"I am not interested, Cecily."

"You look very interested to me." She sat by his side, her lily-white fingers stroking his thigh. "You are a magnificent specimen."

Her fingertips trailed up his thigh.

Mark rolled, coming up into a seated position, a pillow clutched before his privates. "Cecily, I did not give you permission to touch me."

"I remember, once, you did. I had no idea you intended to revoke it."

Mark growled in frustration. His cock throbbed into the cool of his pillow. "That was a game, Cecily. Such parties are not the place to form attachments. You know I don't make any sort of commitment. It was one night only, Cecily. I am not interested in you, or fucking you again. Can I make myself any clearer?"

She scowled, and snatched up the handkerchief he had abandoned. "No, but I shall have something to remember you by." She lifted the cloth to her nose. She paused, her eyes widening. "You have a strumpet already, do you? And you've kept her sex odor by you? How unlike the profligate Knightson to keep a souvenir."

"Cecily." He leaned forward and snatched the handkerchief out of her loose grasp.

Cecily laughed. "Who is she? One of the serving girls? One of the guests?" He eyes narrowed. "You are not as masked as you like to think you are, Mark. A guest then. I will guess it is that pretty dark-haired thing that displayed quite a temper this afternoon. The girl you danced with tonight, instead of dancing with me. That was quite rude of you." She paused, loosening the tapes of her gown and letting it drop to the floor. "And I recall, she left early, and you left soon after. For a little tryst? And she left you unsated?" Cecily crawled onto the bed. "Allow me."

"By God, Cecily, if I have to physically haul you from this room half-naked, I will."

She slid off the bed, pulled on her gown. "That would not

suit me, Mark, and you know it. But I will have you. I always get what I want and what I want is you."

"Not this time." Mark folded his arms across his bare chest.

"Not tonight," she agreed. "But you've seen my charms, and we both know that if you're bedding that little chit, it won't last. The duke has his eye on her for his son and he is a man also used to getting his way. She's far better off with the boy Winterton than sticking to a lecher like you, who will abandon her at a moment's notice for a fresh plaything."

He didn't bother wincing at her bitterness. "You knew that's what I was when I had you. I have told you, Cecily, and I don't need to repeat it yet again."

"You don't need to," Cecily flounced toward the door. "But I'm sure a certain young miss would be *very* interested, no matter how much of a whore she actually is."

Cecily closed the door behind her.

Mark sank back onto his heels. He pulled the pillow away and looked down at his limp cock. His senses were still edged with that raw need for release, but his enthusiasm for it had passed.

He crushed the handkerchief in his fist. It had been nice while it lasted. He didn't doubt that Portia would back off once Cecily got her claws into her. No woman, no matter how highly sexed, wanted to be abandoned.

Damn.

Portia opened the door to her room and rocketed to a standstill. Her mouth gaped, shock washing away any residual pleasure from Mark's lovemaking. "What are you doing here?"

Viscount Winterton, unhooked his crossed legs and scrambled from his relaxed position on her bed. "Waiting for you to give my punishment."

"What?"

While she still reeled from his pronouncement, his eyes narrowed in suspicion. "Where have you been?"

"That is none of your concern," Portia snapped.

She remained motionless as he approached her. "No? You look more disheveled than when you left the ballroom tonight."

Portia tossed her head. "I went for a walk."

He bent closer and his lips twisted. "You stink of sex."

She held her breath. If Mark didn't enter her, did that still count as sex? "I haven't," she whispered.

Winterton grabbed her shoulders and pulled her to him. "I have been wrong about you, I see—or should I say, I've been right all along."

"No!" Portia snapped, low-voiced, for she didn't want anyone seeing this meeting and come to the wrong conclusions. "How dare you, sir? If I choose to pleasure myself, that is my choice!"

His head cocked to one side. "Pleasure yourself? When I was waiting for you?"

Portia thought fast. "Your punishment is more than a slap, my lord." She almost laughed at his abrupt, hopeful expression, even though she was in the direst danger. "You shall not taste of me this night."

Winterton bowed his head. "I am disappointed, but it is a rightful punishment. For haven't I been rude to you, my mistress? Haven't I doubted you?" He lifted his head, meeting her gaze. "I will make it up to you, mistress, and receive my reward."

"Only I shall decide if your recompense is enough." Portia breathed easier. Using this man's peccadilloes would get him out of her room.

"Will you spank me now, mistress?" Young Winterton stepped away from her, going down on all fours and presented his behind.

"I should whip you," Portia growled, allowing her anger at him to escape.

"Oh yes!" The finely tailored behind of young Winterton wriggled in excitement.

She rolled her eyes. "Very well." She crossed to her closet and pulled out her riding crop.

She gave his behind a light switch with it. She didn't want to hurt the viscount.

"Harder! Harder!" the viscount begged. "Show no mercy, oh mistress!"

Portia changed her stance, readying herself for a large swing. She figured that if a horse didn't mind her riding crop too much, then neither should Viscount Winterton. Not that she had ever hit an animal as hard as she prepared to now.

At the last moment, she faltered, hitting him harder but not so hard as she had intended.

Winterton gave a yelp. "More! Harder!"

"Very well." Portia summoned up all her strength and laid the riding crop hard across his haunches.

"Yes! Yes!"

She wondered if that had caused a welt. Would the young viscount be able to sit tomorrow? She delivered another sharp slap and another.

"And you will never disrespect me again. Is that understood?"

The air cracked with the force of her blow.

"No, never!" Winterton choked out.

"And you will obey my every wish?"

Whack.

"Every one!" He sobbed. "Every desire! Oh mistress, forgive me, forgive me, please."

Portia halted in her assault.

He looked over his shoulder at her, his face wet with tears. "No, don't stop, mistress. I haven't been punished enough."

She raised an eyebrow in quelling query. "Is that not up to me, Winterton?" Calling him 'my lord' while he assumed that position seemed absurd.

"Yes, yes, of course, mistress." He ducked his head, his body tensing.

Portia obliged him with a quick succession of three stinging slaps. "There. Enough for now." Winterton didn't move. "Winterton, get to your feet. It is time you left."

The young viscount got to his feet, moving a trifle stiffly. He faced her, his tear-streaked face causing her concern.

That is, until her gaze dropped to his raging hard cock that burst through the gape in his breeches. Its swollen, red head dripped semen.

She gasped, averting her eyes and holding up a hand to shield her face. "Winterton! Put yourself away, please!"

Her beatings had caused that? Winterton wanted her to hurt him that much? Something like that gave pleasure? She recalled her own couplings with Mark had come preciously close to pain. But not like this.

Portia heard the rustle of clothing and assumed he had concealed his cock. She dared to look.

Young Winterton fastened the last button on his breeches. "Forgive me, mistress." His face streaked with fresh tears. "I wanted to please you. Are you not pleased?"

Shaken, Portia murmured, "I told you that you would not taste me tonight."

"One kiss," he begged.

She approached and wiped his cheeks with her thumbs. "No, not even a kiss. Be satisfied."

Winterton stepped back, bowed. "Thank you, mistress." He left, the door snicking shut behind him.

Portia sank onto the bed, covering her face. How had she dared to play such a dangerous sex game with him? Without it, he would have asserted himself, taking her unwillingly. Raping her.

She shuddered. She wanted to bed only one man. No matter how Winterton's woebegone face turned her sympathies.

Only one. Mark Knightson's features rose before her, contorted by his restraint in not fucking her. Perhaps she should go to his room and ease his frustration.

But no. Had he not told her once, that the pleasure is sweeter after one has been frustrated? It remained only then to wait until the morrow, until some opportunity offered that sweeter release.

The morning mist swooped down into the valley where Barrington Manor nestled. The mist turned into a light rain, and so the women remained indoors.

Another morning of sewing, reading, and other sedentary tasks. Portia resumed her accustomed position in the drawing room's window seat, reading a tedious, virtuous book, unlike the one secreted in her room upstairs.

To retreat to her room would be unacceptably unsociable, alas.

Through the open door of the drawing room, young Winterton entered, his red hair dripping and plastered flat against his skull. One of the ladies made a cry of dismay, making Portia look up from her book.

The viscount spotted her and hastened in her direction. Her lips quirked to see the muddy prints left in Lady Barrington's expensive rug.

"Miss Carew," he said, getting down on bended knee. The women gasped. He presented a tiny bouquet of violets. "For you, Miss Carew, in recompense for my bad behavior and in hope that you shall forgive me for it."

Portia delicately extracted the posy from his hands and raised them to her nose, sniffing. "You are too kind, my lord."

"Not as kind or as merciful as you, Miss Carew. May I sit with you?"

"I think perhaps you should go and change. You are muddy and dripping wet."

"Of course!" Young Winterton slapped his forehead. "Forgive me, Miss Carew, for so sullying your presence."

He did it a bit too brown. "Lady Barrington would be relieved, my lord," she said, hoping her subtle reminder others were present would rein in his effusions.

He glanced at the other astonished ladies, bowed to Portia and hastily left.

Wearily, Lady Barrington rang for a maid to clean up Winterton's debris.

Portia's mother rose from her place next to Lady Barrington and joined her daughter. "Portia! I never knew you attracted the attentions of the young viscount. Oh, my dear, I was sure he had taken you into dislike."

"Easy to do," grumbled young Sophia. As usual, Mrs. Carew had spoken in ringing tones.

Lady Cecily Lambeth set aside her embroidery, a tiny white handkerchief. "Do tell, Miss Carew. Even though I have scarcely been here a day, I had thought your heart lay with Mr. Knightson."

Mama shot a startled look at Portia. "Mr. Knightson? Portia, what did I tell you—"

"Mama—" Portia's heart pounded. How had Lady Cecily found them out so soon?

"Mrs. Carew, I am glad you spoke of the dangers involving Mr. Knightson." Lady Cecily smiled her approval.

"I said only that he is not ready to settle down. He is no match."

"Mr. Knightson is a gentleman," corrected Lady Barrington.

"On the surface, this is so," Lady Cecily agreed, bobbing her head. "He does all the social niceties. . . ."

Portia's eyes narrowed. "You have experience of his behavior in private setting?"

"My dear, I was a new widow, highly vulnerable. I felt quite lost without a man to guide me."

Unsure the other ladies believed Lady Cecily's simpering, Portia decided to err on the side of caution. "Then he comforted you, as a gentleman might."

Lady Cecily's face sprouted a wicked smirk. "You could say that, my dear. He made his intentions plain, and then he abandoned me. I would be the happiest of women if he settled on me." She sighed dramatically. "But he does rather seem to have his eye on you."

"I have not noticed." Portia hoped she didn't blush.

"How could one not notice a man like Mr. Knightson, all that sexual power—"

"Lady Cecily!" barked Lady Barrington. "Remember yourself. There are unmarried girls present." She smoothed her stern visage in turning to Portia. "My dear, I am sure your mother will agree that the viscount is an excellent catch."

"Indeed he is," weighed in Mrs. Chalcroft, frowning. "But his attentions to my youngest daughter should not go unremarked. Do not get your hopes up, Miss Carew," she advised. "Young Lord Winterton hasn't given his heart yet."

"My hopes are not raised, Mrs. Chalcroft, and neither should yours be, Mama." Portia patted her mother's hand. "What is clear to me is that Lord Winterton has repented of his cruel behavior to me. In fact, he said as much. You do remember how horribly he treated me. He is being no more than a proper gentleman."

She and Lucy exchanged a grin. Portia wanted to take Lucy off and have a private coze about Lord Winterton.

"Do not forget Sir Guy Symon," Sophia put in acidly. "Did he not declare his intentions yesterday morn?"

Portia bristled. "Marry the man who practically ruined me with his cruel, ungentlemanly lies? I would no more marry him than the stablehand!"

The previous subject of their conversation chose to enter. Lord Winterton had changed into a handsome bottle-green coat and breeches that matched, darker by a couple of shades.

He beamed at the assembled women. He bowed to Lady Barrington. "Please forgive the mess I made." The maid had entered during the women's conversation and had cleaned up the worst of the mud, unremarked.

He strolled toward Portia, his confidence revealed in his slight swagger. With one glance, he displaced Mrs. Carew from her place next to Portia on the window seat and took it for himself, settling with his back to the other women.

"Miss Carew, you look even more ravishing than when I last saw you." He took her hand and kissed it.

Portia slipped her hand free. "Thank you, my lord, but I am sure that is not true."

He chuckled. "You are blushing, Miss Carew, that alone adds beauty. What do you read?"

She showed him the book. "Something dull." She glanced over at the other women. All but Miss Sophia had returned to their regular pastimes. Sophia glowered at them, gnawing on her lip.

Portia lowered her voice. "You are not sore?"

"I ache with the memory of it." Winterton's expression transformed from cocky confidence into a puppy dog look. "Is my punishment complete?"

"We shall see." Portia hoped the others didn't take their whispered conversation amiss.

"Please, allow me to sit here and bathe in your beauty. Carry on with whatever you were doing."

"Reading," Portia reminded him, picking up her book and turning back to the current page.

Winterton's close presence disconcerted her, making it impossible to read. He did nothing inappropriate, but his soulful stares only reminded her of the dangerous path she had chosen.

Unable to stand it any longer, she snapped her book closed and rose. "I am going to walk along the gallery. The paintings there are wonderful."

Young Winterton leapt to his feet. "Excellent idea! I shall join you."

Portia turned a despairing glance to Lucy. "Miss Chalcroft, would you like to join us?"

Lucy accepted with alacrity, bundling her mending into her mother's sewing bag. Before anyone protested, the three departed.

Putting Lucy's arm firmly in hers, the trio strolled along the gallery's length. For some reason, the viscount chose to follow a few paces behind.

Halfway through the gallery, Mr. Knightson appeared from the far end. Portia stopped and waited for his approach, only half-listening to Lucy ramble on about the ancient costumes in the family portrait before them.

"Mr. Knightson," Portia acknowledged him with a brief bow of her head. "I am not sure whether or not we should permit you to join us."

"Permit?" Mark Knightson made it sound like he had never been denied anything in his life.

"We have heard less than pleasant things about you." Portia ignored Lucy's quailing beside her. Even young Winterton seemed disinclined to join the group.

"I am not surprised," Knightson declared in quelling tones. "It is probably true."

"You abandoned a poor widow?" Portia's eyes narrowed.

His dark eyebrow rose in an elegant arc. "Hardly. This is not the place to talk of it, Por—Miss Carew. You are shocking poor Miss Chalcroft."

Lucy twittered and dipped her head.

"Is it true or not?"

"Perhaps if I knew exactly what I stand accused of. We shall discuss this later."

Portia frowned. Knightson seemed annoyed at Lady Cecily's indiscreet speech. His gaze flicked over the group. "You have quite the entourage. Winterton, I thought you had given up hanging on to apron strings?"

"I say, old man, that's not fair!" Winterton's chest puffed up. "I am merely admiring the beauties. Not the same thing at all."

Portia turned to face Winterton. "My lord, please do not remark upon us as if we are horseflesh."

Winterton flourished a bow. "You are quite right. Forgive me."

Portia feared she read his hopeful look right and another punishing session awaited her. She tried not to let her shoulders slump, returning her attention to Mark Knightson.

He had stalked off, back the way he'd come.

The weather cleared and more than one person took the clear skies as a chance to wander in the expansive gardens.

Sir Guy Symon caught up with Lady Cecily Lambeth. "Well? Have you made any progress?"

Lady Cecily twirled her parasol. "None. But I am sure my Mr. Knightson has his hooks into your Miss Carew."

"Portia?" His sandy eyebrows disappeared upward. "She wouldn't make the same mistake twice and go with a bounder like him."

"You are just jealous." Cecily tapped his arm with a folded fan. "Besides, if you think that, what makes you believe she'll come back to you?"

"She'll have no choice. I'll shame her to it, if I have to." Sir Guy grimaced. His hands closed into fists. He looked sidelong at her. Lady Cecily seemed the epitome of cool hauteur. "How do you know?"

"I know he's bedding somebody at this estate, and it's not me," Cecily replied frankly. "You saw the way he danced with your Miss Carew and how curious he left shortly after she supposedly retired for the evening."

"Circumstantial," Sir Guy grunted. "To know we'll have to catch them at it."

Lady Cecily choked back a laugh. "And how do you propose we do that?"

"I need to know for sure." The thought that another man had taken Portia suffused his senses with dull anger. She was his, and it was past time she realized it. "It will be something I can hold over her head to get her to submit to me. We shall have to watch them. Get your maid to befriend Portia's. We'll know soon enough."

"In the meantime, we must look for ways to put myself in a compromising position with Mr. Knightson. The censure will surely force his hand to marry me."

Why did Lady Cecily always think of herself? "You forget: you are a widow now, not an untouched maiden. I warned you about that idea. It could well blow up in your face. Seducing him is a sure thing." He cast a long glance at her. "Any man would fall for your charms."

She batted him on the arm. "You are a flirt, Sir Guy. How do you ever plan to keep your hands on your future wife only?"

Sir Guy barked a brief laugh. "I don't."

8

"**P**ortia! Sweeting!" Mama shrieked across the calm gardens. Birds scattered from the hedges into the air.

Portia straightened from smelling the lavender. She waited while Mama bustled toward her. Portia had managed to get rid of the viscount with Lucy's collusion, and the two of them had taken a ramble on the other side of the house, Lucy delivering hints to Winterton on how to win Portia.

She smoothed out her smirk, frowning at the sight of Sir Guy and Lady Cecily deep in conversation. Their paths crossed Mama's. Did Sir Guy really mean his proposal this time? She found it hard to credit.

Mama arrived, panting. She waved a kerchief in her face. "Oh! Oh, my dear. Such news, such news!"

"What news, Mama?" Portia remained still, unable to tell if Mama's gossip was good or bad. Had Lady Barrington decided to turn them out anyway? What could it be?

"The ideal solution, my dearest one, to all our concerns." Still panting, Mama pointed to a bench. "I need to sit." She staggered over to the wooden bench and sunk onto it. "Oh, my dear! My dear!"

Portia didn't like the direction of her mother's news. Whose concerns did this news solve, after all? She settled next to her mother and waited for her to catch her breath.

Mama began at last. "Portia, my dearest, you shall never guess who approached me at breakfast this morning!"

Portia restricted herself to a "Who?"

"Why, the Duke of Winterton, of course! He took me aside and do you know what he asked?"

Why didn't Mama just tell her? Portia shook her head.

"His son has spoken of you to him and he wishes to better make your acquaintance before he gives his blessing. I do agree. Young men can be a bit rash, and young Winterton is very much so."

"But—" Her mother had never heard her beg off marriage before. Portia wanted to restore her reputation, nothing more. She sighed. Then why had she allowed matters with Knightson to continue?

A warm glow within told her why. Sighing again, she listened to her mother's words.

"He is waiting in the blue drawing room. I want you to go upstairs and change into that pretty flocked white muslin before attending him there." Mama wagged her finger. "You will behave with the utmost decorum, my dear girl. Convince him you are the perfect match for the viscount and will make the best viscountess. Mind your manners, be as sweet and pretty as I know you can be when you put your mind to it."

"But Mama, I don't want to—"

Mama's brow furrowed. "I will brook no disobedience! You must do this, Portia dear. Your place in Society will be secured if you please the duke and marry his son. There is none better here than he. Why, I am even willing to give up my hopes of you marrying Freddy for this unlooked for opportunity. Do say you will do as I ask."

Portia rose and curtsied. "Very well, Mama. I will be nice to the duke, but if there is a proposal, I shall refuse."

Mama grinned. "All the better to negotiate terms with, my dear. An excellent suggestion." She fluttered her fan. "I do believe young Winterton is so besotted that he would give anything for you. Imagine such a settlement upon you!"

Portia would rather not. She excused herself and went to change.

About half an hour later, she let herself into the drawing room. The Duke of Winterton stood by the window, his back to her. The sun shone in, turning his hair to blazing silver. He wore it long, tied back with a simple black ribbon.

He turned, a civil smile upon his face. "Miss Carew, do close the door and sit down."

Portia obeyed and sat on the edge of a floral brocade sofa. She clasped her hands in her lap and looked at the Duke with her patented attentive expression.

"I will be frank, Miss Carew. You have captured the affections of my youngest son." He approached, his hands behind his back. He wore a plain black suit, the only relief from the unrelenting black being his snowy white cravat and shirt. A slender man, he filled the room with charisma.

He had a very deliberate way of moving, of drawing the eye. Portia thought he must have been quite the handsome, attractive gentleman once.

"So I have heard, your Grace," Portia replied, her head bowed in modesty.

"Yet I am not convinced that you are at all suitable for my son. You have great spirit, Miss Carew, great spirit, but a temper to match. It is your spirit, Miss Carew, that allows me to think there is hope for you."

Portia looked up at him. "I am sure you will agree, your Grace, that in both circumstances I was much taxed. I fear my only alternative may have been to faint in maidenly horror."

"Ah, yes, and my son tells me you are not the sort to invoke maidenly horror." The duke sat on the edge of the sofa, leaning close.

Portia sucked in her breath. "What has he told you, your Grace? I fear that your son may have received the wrong impression of me."

"I do not think he has. My youngest son has run wild. The women who please him most generally are unacceptable to Society."

Did the duke refer to prostitutes? "Forgive me, your Grace, but did you just insult me?"

The duke barked a laugh. "You know more than a young maiden ought."

"I have been out long enough to hear things, your Grace."

He patted her cheek. "I did not intend an insult, my dear. You appear to have stumbled across my son's particular preferences. I do not doubt that it is a natural instinct in you, in the way you would rather scream than faint."

She frowned up at him in concern. "Do you think so?"

"Given the relish with which you spanked my son—"

Portia yelped and leaped up, almost bumping her head into the duke's. "Your—your Grace, I—"

The duke laughed. "My dear, such the right amount of innocence. An admirable dissemblance!"

"Your Grace, I do not think you understand."

"But, my dear, I do." He rose from his perch on the sofa's arm and approached her. She stood very still while he brushed a curl back from her forehead. "Indeed, I do, and that brings me to the real reason I wanted to meet with you."

"The real reason, your Grace?"

"I have requested that we not be disturbed. Indeed, a footman stands outside that very door."

Portia sucked in her breath. Trapped? But why? "I do not understand."

"Allow me to explain. I gave you a little test, for above all else, it is important to my family, to my title, that all decorum be essential to maintaining the proper gravitas."

His finger drifted down her cheek. He continued, "In private, my dear, we Wintertons are the most passionate of men."

She stepped back. "Your Grace, I do not think—"

He laid a finger across her lips. "Hush, my dear. It is a family tradition that prospective brides are run through the full gamut of, shall we say, tests to ensure they will make able Winterton brides."

Portia drew herself up haughtily. "And if I have no intention of becoming a Winterton bride?"

"Nobody refuses a Winterton."

"Then I may be the first," she snapped and spun on her heel. She made for the door, but the duke, despite his age, was faster.

He grabbed her by the elbow and hauled her back. "I said nobody."

She shoved him in the chest, pulling free. "I said no."

"Come, come, Miss Carew. I expected better of you than that. I assure you that I am quite healthy. I am more than able to keep up." His handsome face twisted into a leer. "Come, my dear."

Portia twisted away. "Again, I must refuse." She beat a retreat, placing the sofa between them.

The duke grinned and strolled in pursuit. "There is nowhere to run."

"I could scream." Portia ducked behind a rickety plant stand holding some unidentifiable green leafy plant.

"Scream and you are ruined forever. Banished from this

house and banished from Society. Even from, I suspect, your family. Young misses do not turn down a duke."

"I am turning down a viscount."

He frowned. "You are turning *me* down."

Portia slipped out of his grasp and took refuge behind the pianoforte. "You are not unattractive, your Grace. It is just that I do not intend to marry."

That surprised a laugh out of him. "Not marry? My girl, you're turning down the chance for your children to be of the aristocracy. You're barely above the level of a mushrooming cit as it is."

"What?" Portia stalked back to him and slapped him hard across the face. "How dare you? My father and mother both belong to gentle stock."

He rubbed his cheek, a deep red against his pale skin. "Do not try your dominance on me, Portia. I am not that type. I prefer to take the lead."

He grabbed her arm and twisted it behind her back. He marched her up against a wall, crowding her behind. "You see, my dear, I may be old but I am still strong."

Portia stayed still, keeping her face turned away from the duke. She bit her lip. She didn't know what to do, beyond all hope of Mark Knightson coming to her rescue.

She had no other choice but to rescue herself.

"Your Grace," she murmured, "I have no desire for your son."

The Duke of Winterton nuzzled the back of her neck, laying kisses across her bared skin. "Loosen your bodice."

"No, your Grace, you do not understand." He'd relaxed his grip on her arm and she turned to face him. Her back against the wall, she discovered that the duke gave her little room to move.

"What is it I do not understand?" The duke bent his head to

kiss his way to the top of her bodice. "You wish me to disrobe you? I would be honored." He fished for the tapes of her bodice.

She covered his hands with her own, hoping to still them. ".No, your Grace. I—I used your son's weakness against him. I swear, I stumbled across his, ahh, interest, accidentally. He would not leave me alone, he wanted to—wanted to bed me, so I—I used that against him, to keep him at arm's length."

The duke buried his face in her cleavage.

She hauled his face up to hers. "I mean it, your Grace. Your son thought I was a whore and this was the only way I could save myself."

"Save yourself?" The duke looked only mildly outraged at her rough handling of his person. He pulled her hands down to her waist. "Sir Guy has confided in me that everything he said was true."

She gaped at him. "He what?"

He captured her mouth in a bruising kiss. It stole her breath away, suffocated her. She wriggled to free herself, but it seemed only to arouse the duke even more.

He pressed against her, squeezing her against the wall, his hands roaming to grasp at her breasts, at her behind, hauling her up against his stiff, trapped cock.

His lips left hers. "He told me everything. How you so easily followed his lead, allowed him to touch you, to fondle you. That he fucked you."

The last he said with a sharp thrust of his bony hips.

"And he wasn't very good at it," she retorted, hiding her incipient hysteria behind bravado.

His white eyebrow rose. "So, Sir Guy was not your only lover? You are perfectly discreet, Portia. You will make a wonderful Winterton."

"That's not it at all." Portia tried to corral his roaming hands. "Sir Guy roused my senses, yes. He made me realize what I had been missing out on. I had truly hoped to marry him, you know. That's the only reason why I let him—" She shook her head, her careful curls falling out of place. "You know."

He laughed. "You need not deal in euphemisms with me."

"My point is, that I learned how to reach that release myself, fully and completely. I do not need a man. I certainly do not need your son."

He paused in his groping, surveying her upturned face. He gazed upon her for a long time, and Portia saw he thought hard about her words. "You are right," he said at last. "You are not at all suited for my son, although you would ideally keep him in check."

"Thank you." Portia heaved a sigh of relief. "I am so glad you understand."

"I understand that your appetites are deeper, more wide-ranging than I even imagined." He cupped her chin in his hand. "My dear, I would be honored to have you to wife."

"*Your* wife!" She shook her head, fighting clear of his grip. "I did not say all that to have you propose. No, your Grace—"

He stroked her cheek, his weight keeping her against the wall. "My dear, I have been lonely. There was nobody quite like my late, lamented wife. She was a real firebrand. Like you, my pet. I will take you places you have never imagined."

She stared at him. Any marriage to the duke would be for a short period, and then she'd be as free as Lady Cecily. It tempted her, a way to reach her goal of being free of attachment to any man. She only had to endure one short marriage.

"I see you are tempted." The duke's green eyes almost glowed.

Portia played out the scene in her mind. The announcement of their betrothal, Knightson's betrayed expression at the news. The very thought of it stabbed her in the gut. She took a steadying breath. "I must decline."

His hand closed about her throat. "I will not hear of it."

She panted for breath, clawing at his hand. "I regret—"

"So will I." His grip tightened. "I am not like my son. I am a duke and will not be so commanded. I am the one who dominates."

"Then we will not suit," Portia gasped.

"Ah, but you will. You are young and malleable." His grip on her throat loosened.

"I have no care to be dominated." Portia rubbed her neck. She tried not to quail under his stare. It wasn't true, of course. Mark only had to growl a word and she scrambled to obey.

"I doubt that." He proceeded to push down her loosened bodice to reveal her breasts.

Portia scrambled for another reason, choosing to fight him with words, rather than with her hands. "What if you can't keep up with me?"

"Not keep up?" He gave one of her nipples a sharp tweak. "I think that's highly unlikely."

She winced. Such an act gave her pleasure only when she herself or Knightson did it, it seemed. "If you believed Sir Guy, then you know I can be wild, very wild. I fear too wild for you."

The Duke of Winterton actually laughed.

She pulled away, covering her breasts. "You would expect your wife to be faithful, would you not?"

"Unless it suited me otherwise," the duke returned darkly, his silver eyebrows hovering into a frown.

"I could never be faithful to you. You are too old and I prefer men with energy, who can keep up with me." With every word, she spoke her ruination, if His Grace deigned to share it with anybody. She had to hope that despite her rejection, he'd keep her secret.

"Trust me, my dear, there will be no difficulty in my keeping up with you."

Desperate, she flung at him: "I have lovers already and I do not intend to give them up."

He surveyed her, and Portia felt her cheeks flush. "No? Who then? My son? I know he has not bedded you yet."

She swallowed. "But another has."

That silver eyebrow arched again. "Who?" His voice lost its casual air, becoming more intense. Was this her way out?

"I am not at liberty to say." She saw the duke's lips purse to suppress new laughter at her sudden prim words. His green eyes sparked with amusement. "But surely you have not been so blind as not to notice that a number of Lady Barrington's gentlemen guests jostle for my attention?"

"Ah, if you mean Sir Guy, you need not fear. I can buy him off. I know you are not taken with him."

Portia folded her arms. "You do not know the games I play."

"I know you talk too much." He leaned in again, his arms outstretched to prevent her escape. She ducked under them and put the sofa between the two of them. She figured he did not have the agility to take the floral brocade sofa in a single leap.

"Please," she begged. "Let me go."

The old duke's grin turned wolfish. "Ah, begging at last. I had suspected you were desperate when you claimed you wouldn't give up your lovers just after telling me you had given up men altogether. Consistency, my dear, consistency." He maneuvered around the sofa.

Portia backed away, stumbling over a wrinkle in the rug. "And you'd want a woman desperate to say anything, who would rather ruin her own reputation before she'd wed you?"

He laughed softly. "I like a challenge."

"Your Grace—" She protested one more time.

"My dear, you have done nothing to prove to me that anything you've said is true. Why should I believe that you do not want me? No woman has ever turned me down before."

"There's always a first time." Portia took a breath, remaining still and sizing him up. "Very well, then let me prove it to you."

She bore toward him and, hands outstretched, pushed him onto the sofa. She followed, hiking her skirts and straddling him. She put all her weight behind her hands, leaning against his shoulders.

To her dismay, the duke's face crinkled in laughter. His hands moved quickly, again loosening the tapes of her bodice. She reared back, the tapes tugging loose and ripped at his cravat. She clawed at it, her nails scraping the fine skin of the duke's neck.

His eyes glowed with an unholy light, a smile playing about his lips. How could she make him see she was not for him? She rent his shirt, baring his chest. She bent over him, biting his nipples, her fingernails digging into his flanks until she drew blood.

He hissed in pain and groaned. She sat upright, out of the reach of his arms. "No, you are right," she said, responding to his amusement. "This is too easy."

She rose and headed for the fireplace. She withdrew a poker from its stand and pointed it at him.

He had risen to follow her and halted, for the first time appearing uncertain.

"Bend over, your Grace. I have something to deliver to you."

The Duke of Winterton held up his hands. "Now, my dear girl . . ."

Portia stepped closer, her poker aimed at his crotch. "Are you begging, your Grace? I'll have my man properly primed before I'll have him. Divest yourself of those breeches, your Grace, and bend over."

The duke fastened his breeches instead. "I will not be buggered. Put that poker down."

"Not on your life." Portia gripped it tighter, holding it now with two hands, like a sword. "If you will not bend over, your Grace, I suggest you quit the room, and we shall forget this conversation ever happened."

"Or?" He stepped closer.

She raised the poker. "Or I will brain you with this and then ram it up your arse, your Grace. Your choice."

The duke gave a weak smile. "A firebrand," he sighed. "There may be time yet to tame you. I fear I have used too heavy a hand." He bowed. "You will forgive me?"

Portia dared to breathe, lowering the poker. "Of course. Passion makes the wisest of men rash."

"Indeed." The Duke of Winterton nodded. "I hope we shall remain cordial to each other, and I ask you to remain open to the idea of wedlock."

There seemed little point in informing him of the notion that she'd never been open to the idea. She gave a short, sharp nod.

"I shall tell my son to keep clear. I would not have him damaged by your fire. You spoke true in one thing at least, Miss Carew, you are too wild indeed. Even for a Winterton."

Portia let the poker's point rest on the carpet. "And what has happened in here . . . ?"

"Stays in here." The duke's smile was rueful. "I still entertain hopes of you, my dear, and a Winterton is always discreet."

He bowed and left the room.

Portia paused only to check her appearance in the mirror. She patted her hair back into place and made sure her bodice once more clung to her form.

Inside her very self rattled at her audacity. Been proposed to by an elderly man? She'd sexually attacked a duke? Had the entire world gone mad?

As she sat for dinner that night, Knightson slipped her a note. She tucked it into her glove, making a play of adjusting it before she unbuttoned it at the wrist and folded the fingers back at her wrist, ready for eating.

Portia found it hard to breathe. What was in the note? Her skin burned where it lay against the soft, smooth inside of her forearm.

Had Knightson decided on another assignation? When? Tomorrow? Tonight?

Even nibbling on the array of food seemed beyond her.

The Duke of Winterton caught her eye. He gave a frown of concern and gestured to his plate with his fork. Did he think her nervous lack of eating was to do with their afternoon encounter? Portia bit back giggles.

He really hadn't believed her about having another lover, a fact which she thought she should be grateful for. A less patient or discreet man would never have allowed such an announcement to pass unchallenged, left unrevealed.

What was in the note? All through dinner, the outline of the paper pressed against her skin, almost burning with the unknown words.

When at last the women retired to allow the men their brandy and cigars, she chose the moment to slip behind a screen in order to relieve herself.

Crouched over the chamber pot, skirts safely lifted out of the way, she used her passing water to conceal the unfolding of Knightson's note.

Await me in my chambers when you retire for the evening. When I arrive, your next lesson will commence.

Portia hastily refolded the note and stuffed it down into her stays. Not a single wrinkle would betray his secret message.

She joined the ladies, choosing to sit beside Lady Cecily Lambeth. She had taken the woman into severe dislike, but refused to let that show.

In turn, Lady Cecily Lambeth had decided to be pleasant,

taking a great deal of interest in Portia's activities during her stay.

Portia replied in an amiable tone, aware of the strong possibility Lady Cecily probed too much in her questions. Did she suspect Portia's affair?

The men joined them at last, but Portia counted the minutes until she could reasonably excuse herself. She almost didn't notice young Winterton draw up a stool at her feet.

"Miss Carew," young Winterton murmured, shooting a glance across the room at his father, who watched them with narrowed eyes. "My father will not permit me to speak to you long—"

"What have you done now, Miss Carew?" drawled Lady Cecily.

Portia shot her an angry glance. "I imagine it is simply that I am not worthy of a viscount's attention. Is that not right, my lord?"

Young Winterton beamed, clearly relieved she'd so easily released him. "Yes, yes, that is it exactly. I hold you in high esteem, Miss Carew, but I regret I cannot continue to pursue my interest in you."

She nodded, her features smooth, masked. "My lord, I hope that at least we may be friends."

Young Winterton rose and delivered a short bow. "If you should ever have need of me, Miss Carew, I am at your service." He left her then, and joined Freddy Barrington in chattering with Miss Sophia Chalcroft.

"A veritable blow, Miss Carew," Lady Cecily murmured.

Portia thought at first to deny it, until she realized Lady Cecily had delivered her a golden opportunity to escape. She bobbed her head. "Yes, yes, you are quite right. Oh, what will Mama say when she finds out?" She wrung her hands, hoping that she didn't overdo her performance. "I think perhaps I better retire before my mother decides to make a scene—you have seen how outspoken she can be."

With that, Portia rose, smoothing out her skirts. Murmuring her excuses to Lady Barrington, she quit the room. Alone, she entered Knightson's quarters unobserved.

She hoped Lady Cecily was not so evil as to dispatch Mama in her direction, for if she were not in her room, she would be lost.

The thought gave her pause. If she had read Lady Cecily's character correctly, that's exactly what she'd do. Sighing, she hastened back to her own room, beating her mother by scarce moments.

Mama's storm rained predictably over her head. With bowed head, Portia pinched herself hard, bringing on the tears she did not feel.

At last the thunder of Mama's rage collapsed under the woman's own tears. "Oh my dearest, dearest chicken! How could I think to heap such wrongs upon your little head? I am sure you did everything you could! I should have known better than to let you aspire so high!"

With another wail, Portia's mother went off to bed.

Portia dried her faked tears and sat on the edge of the bed, waiting just in case Mama returned.

She did not.

Slipping out of her room, she headed back to Knightson's chamber. Why couldn't it be closer? Did he wait for her already?

He did. Knightson stood, his arms folded, and glared at her. "You disobeyed me. You were to await me here."

A swift survey of the room revealed a large four-poster bed draped in dark green velvet and other mahogany furniture. "My mother—"

"Is not even that excessively lugubrious to keep me waiting.

Indeed, I waited a decent interval before coming upstairs. Long enough to have dealt with your mother and await me here."

"You do not know my mother—"

"No, thank God." He ignored her shocked gasp. "Is it done then? Are you to leave here?"

Was that what worried him? She cocked her head to one side, studying him.

"Don't look at me like that."

"Like what? Like you have turned into a madman? You forget, Mr. Knightson. I am not at your beck and call. Indeed, I begin to think the entire male sex must be mad. . . ."

"No, we are quite sane, I thank you. It is woman who is irrational and disobedient."

"You do not own me!" She whirled, heading for the door. She had not come to be insulted.

He grabbed her arm, only holding her in place, not attempting further violence. "A student obeys her teacher."

She slipped free and faced him. "Is this even about that any more?"

Their gazes held for a long moment. She couldn't read him—anger masked any other emotion he might also possess.

"We should proceed with the lesson," he said at last, through gritted teeth.

"And what lesson is that?"

9

Knightson's serious regard didn't flicker. "Patience."

Portia burst out laughing. She clapped her hand over her mouth, her eyes wide. What if someone had heard her? They stood, silent as stone sentinels, waiting for some sort of reaction from the hallway.

Nothing.

"Patience?" Portia allowed amusement and relief to mix in her voice. "Isn't that something you need to learn?"

He snorted. "Perhaps," he acknowledged. "But you rush headlong into release, Portia. You need to tease yourself, allow the rush to come when it will, not push against it."

"Haven't we done this already?" she asked.

"You need to submit."

She rolled her eyes. "The hell I do."

He blinked. "That is not very seemly language."

"You expected more of me?" she jeered. "From a woman who is a known slut? Mr. Knightson, perhaps it is time our lessons ended."

"No." He hauled her against him, daring her to deny the

solid muscle, the power. She tilted her head up to look at him. "No," he repeated. "It cannot end."

Hardly able to breathe, still she contradicted him. "No?"

"No." His mouth covered hers. Without mercy, his tongue pushed past her lips, her teeth. He dragged her into a whirlpool of sensation.

She clung to him, clawing at his jacket. Nothing mattered now: not the lessons, not the command to submit, not anything. She wanted nothing more than to have his naked flesh against hers, his cock pounding inside her.

She wanted it now.

They hauled clothing off themselves and each other. Knightson ripped the cording out of her stays and tore her chemise in half, while she clawed off his cravat.

They tumbled back toward his bed, grasping, kissing, neither willing to cede to the other, both wanting it all. They breathed only when necessary to continue the sensual struggle.

In one swift movement, he took her in his arms and flung her onto the bed. Half a breath behind, he joined her there. He pushed her willing legs apart and gathered her to him.

Her huff of laughter stopped him more than her ineffectual hands against his chest. He shot her a questioning glance.

"Patience?" she gasped between chuckles.

He conceded her a reluctant smile. He bent down to kiss her hard, giving her no room for further laughter. "Shall I show you patience, wench?"

"Is that possible?" she taunted. Inside, panting light filled her, straining already for that incredible release she knew Mark could deliver and thoroughly enjoying the moment, the right now. Their shared heat, his large hands upon her, taking untold liberties—it was all too delicious.

"It is." He slipped from the bed and picked up his ruined cravat. Before she knew it, he had wrapped a swirl of the linen around her wrist and had tied her to the poster behind. The long length of the cravat enabled him to do likewise to her other wrist.

She didn't fight him. She watched his face while he tied her to the bed. Watched his body move, watched his cock bob. He used her stockings to tie her feet wide apart.

She tested the bonds, found them secure. Now that she was tied up, Knightson seemed far more relaxed. "Then teach me patience," she purred. "Why do you delay?"

He laughed, his face transforming into wicked boyishness. "Patience, remember?" he teased.

He grasped his cock, lightly caressing it. Portia became mesmerized by it. He had hold of the thing she wanted from him the most: that velvety silk skin concealing hard power, the bulbous head which even now had started to weep with excitement. With his casual stance, there was something so incredibly powerful about Knightson.

Sure she had flushed pink from head to toe, she squirmed in her bonds. "Are you going to diddle yourself all night?" she challenged.

"If I so please," came his insouciant reply. "You may remember this when you are touching yourself for pleasure."

Portia almost burst from that pleasure right there. The image rose in her mind of her playing with her wet cunt with Mark standing before her, stroking his cock until he came all over her writhing body.

"God, yes," she breathed.

Mark's breath caught. She saw his chest hitch, freeze. He crawled onto the bed, between her spread legs. He sat back on his heels, and resumed playing with his cock. "What did you just imagine?" he asked, his voice low and husky.

She told him in detail and delighted to see him suck in another startled breath.

"God." He abandoned his cock for the moment and bent forward to take her nipple into his mouth. He edged on cruelty, nipping and tugging on her already hard nipple, until her breasts became a roar of heat.

She whimpered, arching her back, pushing her breast into his mouth. Was it possible just to come from this taunting of his mouth upon her breast without him once teasing her cunt?

She moaned soft and low. He tweaked her other nipple, doubling the building ecstasy. She begged him incoherently, if only he would slide into her, she would come, she just knew it. "Please, please . . ."

His cock poked at her thigh, leaving a sticky trail. Had he read her mind? Her movement was too limited to draw him into her already sopping wet, hot cunt.

"Mark . . . oh, Mark . . ." A thick vein of pleasure throbbed from her chest to her cunt. Any moment now. . . . Any moment now.

Mark moved away, kneeling between her legs.

"Wha—You stopped!" Portia didn't know how she found the breath to accuse him.

He held his cock. She noted he didn't stroke it this time and yet it dripped with his jism. "Patience," he whispered. "You must have patience."

She pouted at him, feeling the edge vanish from her arousal, the chance to come fading. Her breathing grew more even. "Is this what you have planned? To tease me all night?"

"As much as possible," he responded agreeably, still stroking his cock. She saw the sharp delineation of every muscle, suggesting his struggle for self-control. "You will see why."

"I better," she muttered, feeling mutinous, scowling when he laughed at her.

He amended his bad behavior by laying his palms over her breasts. She bit her lip, arching her breasts into his hands, hoping this hint will urge him to bring her to release.

His hands slid to her belly. She sighed, half disappointed, half hopeful his hands would keep moving down. His light caresses over her stomach, rising up to encircle her breasts, almost lulled her to sleep.

Except that it made her so much more aware of him, and the gentleness of his touch after his rough teasing sent her into a hazy bliss. The incredible heat diffused into a languorous warmth.

Was this still about sex? Portia, unable to focus on finding an answer to that question, gazed at Mark through slitted eyes.

His face showed nothing but pleasure, intent on warming every part of her body with nothing more than his hands. Such care and consideration . . . Portia's breath hitched. Had Mark Knightson fallen in love with her?

At the very least, if this were truly a lesson, how would she complete such a thorough job without getting into contortions?

This arousing of her senses felt so different from before. Before, he took her with little warning, or pursued her releases like a possessed man, unrelenting in his chosen path.

He smoothed along the insides of her thighs and her pulse started pounding again. Was the delay over, soft and delicious though it was? She kept very still, not wanting to seem over-eager for him.

He'd heard the sharp intake of her breath for he shot her an amused glance. "Your patience improves," he murmured.

"Good," she responded quickly. "Can you finish now?"

He laughed outright, a rich honeyed sound that made the pit of her belly tremble. "Patience, Portia, patience."

Mark Knightson almost laughed again when he saw her squeeze her eyes shut, head pressed back against the pillow as if preparing to undergo torture. The quirk in her lips revealed she only played.

He liked that about her. So willing to play games, so willing to follow where he led. For an unmarried miss, she behaved with the alacrity of a whore. And yet, he knew he'd taken her further than any other man.

God, and her skin was so soft. He distracted himself from his disturbing thoughts about the girl—no, don't think of her as Portia—by paying attention to his self-appointed task.

So soft, so pliable beneath his skimming hands. Her natural perfume rose and filled his nostrils. He longed to bury his face into her quim and inhale deeply, giving her the excitement she wanted.

But he mustn't cave into her unspoken demands just yet. He couldn't say exactly why, but he wanted her to feel the depth and breadth—everything—that there was to sex.

Did he hope to win her to him? Surely not. She'd acquiesced to this meeting and others with an eagerness that suggested she was his already.

At this point, the game should pall, but all he wanted to do was further plumb her depths.

He bent forward to kiss her stomach, weaving an intricate trail along her velvet, white skin. From tiny licks, to kisses, to the barest breath upon her dampened skin, he dipped lower and lower, until he reached the crease of her groin.

Blowing air on her crotch, he saw the first droplets of her arousal.

Not yet, not yet. He repeated the mantra, schooling himself to hold back once more and made his oral journey down her thigh, nibbling on her knee.

He caressed her calf and retraced the path he had made, until he hovered before her spread cunt.

He couldn't help it. He dipped in and gave her clit a quick lick. She squealed and squirmed in an invitation for him to continue.

Not yet, not yet. He wondered if she ever thought of the sweet torture this brought him. He grinned, peppering her other leg with kisses. He decided to tell her so.

"Portia," he murmured, keeping his voice to a low burr, at a pitch guaranteed to excite. "Portia, I want..." He paused to press a kiss against the inside of her knee. "I want to fuck you."

He heard her delighted gasp and continued, "I want to cram myself deep inside you...." More kisses. "Fuck you until you scream."

"Oh, yes," she breathed.

"But first," he whispered against her calf, "I want to taste you...." His teeth grazed her flesh. "I want to sup on your warm juices...."

He reached her thigh once more. "Lick and drink you dry, until I have taken all your sweet juices ... until you are unconscious from coming..."

He'd returned to the awesome sight of her parted cunt lips, all glistening and ready for him.

God, was he ready.

"I want to make you come so many times, Portia." He breathed his promise into her dripping cunt. "So many times that you won't be able to stand when I'm done."

"And then..." He flicked his tongue against her pert clit. Her heat jolted through him as if he were buried inside already. His cock jerked in response, digging into the velvet counterpane, seeking entry. God, he'd fuck the blankets if he had to. "And then I will fuck you...."

"Mark!" she begged in a breathy sigh.

"I'll be in you, on you, breathing with you...." He punctuated each phrase with teasing licks on her clit. "I'll be in your tight little cunt ... pounding you ..."

"And by God, you will feel so good...." He swallowed his next words, swooping his tongue along the length of her wet slit. And again. As he promised, he'd drink her dry.

Her sweet nectar kept coming, her imprisoned hips bucking against his mouth. He slipped his tongue inside, swirling it around her opening.

He let no part of her wet slit remain untouched, keeping his touch light, teasing. Too much and she would climax, or become so sensitized she'd flip from pleasure to pain, he'd have to pause and start over.

He paused, his cheeks and chin tight with a layer of her sex fluids. His lips and nose filled with her scent and every breath and every swallow was a small ecstasy.

A wicked thought occurred to him. "Portia?" He kept his voice light and casual. "Forgive me, but I believe I am too tired—"

Her squawk cut him off. "Don't you dare, Mark Knightson!" His tongue flicked at her cunt and eased one finger inside her. "You are a terrible tease."

"Patience, remember?" he replied, almost groaning with the effort of restraining himself. What he wouldn't give to fuck her senseless now. His cock ached for it.

But not yet, not yet.

With his mouth and tongue, he brought her to the brink, her hard clit now swollen, her cunt lips flushed red. He watched the miniscule flutter, sinking two fingers into her and finding that place.

"Yes!" Portia cried.

He smiled again, still licking at her clit. She must know, must remember the last time he brought her to release. "Come for me," he growled. "Come hard." He wanted his sheets to be soaked with her come, so he could bury his face in it when she was gone.

She groaned, her body stiffening and for his reward, a small gush crossed his lips. He gave a few more tongue laps to her slit and then slid up her body.

He kissed her, immediately deepening the kiss to probe her mouth, to share how she tasted with her. He noticed but a moment's hesitation before she hungrily returned his kiss.

A bold woman. Before he even thought, he slid his cock inside her juicy channel. A groan escaped his lips. That first moment of entry, the clutch of her muscles about him, he loved it, no matter her status: widow or whore.

This, though . . . This . . .

He pulled back and thrust into her pulsing channel, and again, trying to overwhelm the unfamiliar sensation with the sound of their sexes slapping together.

Unable to shake the weird feeling free, he lay inside her. He gathered her in his arms and looked down at her flushed face. Her eyes were closed, lost in the bliss suddenly denied to him.

Her liquid warmth wrapped his cock. He had the strong sensation of melting inside her, that if he withdrew, he'd leave the molten mass of his cock behind.

Unmanned. God, was he unmanned, and by a mere chit of a thing—

Her muscles clenched him. A tremor of relief shook him. He was still intact.

He moved out and back in again to reassure himself. Yes.

He thrust again, held himself inside her, daring her to melt him. Ridiculous that she could. But oh God, she felt good. So good.

He slowly withdrew and inched his way back inside, lost in the sensation of her cunt engulfing him. Lost in everything. Including the strange sensation he felt earlier.

It cast him into a dream state and he moved as if through heavy water. It slowed each movement and each time he lingered longer and longer inside her.

He achieved a state of mind he'd never thought he'd experience. An endless swirl of sensation gripped his cock, cocooned his entire body, and yet it was something more than just sensation. God, it was so sweet he could almost—

Cry. He opened his eyes. Portia looked up at him, silent

tears streaking from the corner of her eyes. He bent to kiss her, to soothe her, blinking back his own tears.

He held still, kissing her with such sweetness, a single tear escaped him and splashed into her fanned hair. He hoped she hadn't felt it.

Rearing up, he reached back and untied her ankles, freeing her to wrap her legs around him. He raised her hips, plunging in deeper, changing the angle and sparking a new heat between them.

It burned away the strange muffling of his lust, whatever the cause of it, and the old wildness rose again. He bucked and thrust, drawing excited cries from the woman writhing beneath him.

Not just any woman. Portia.

He sobbed, spending himself inside her. His hot gush washed back over him, wetting his balls. He pulled out, perhaps too hastily, but even now the last vestiges of that odd feeling clawed at him.

Untying her hands, he rolled off her and lay panting at her side. For a moment, Portia likewise heaved unladylike breaths and then rolled into him, lifting her head to look down at him.

He thumbed away the tracks of her tears with a gentleness that startled him.

"What," she whispered, "was that?"

He pretended ignorance, his heart thudding. She had felt it too? Damnation. "What was what?"

"When you . . ." She trailed off, shaking her head, the last of her curls falling loose of their pins. "I suppose that was the result of patience?"

He hoped not. "Patience is not striving. When you arouse yourself, remember that. Take your time. Stop. It will gently build and build."

"Gently?"

Perhaps he shouldn't have used that word. The gentleness had shaken him, more deeply than he cared to admit. He remembered the thread of conversation. "Portia, it is not all hard and rough. I fear you've had too much of that, and I wanted you to know . . ."

"Thank you." Not a nuance edged her polite words.

What had he said? He sounded like a greensick fool, wanting to cosset his woman, to love her. He knew better than that.

He rolled them both so he lay on top of her. "Sweet Portia, I fear I have taken my pleasure with you and have rather forgot the lesson."

"Patience?" she queried. Something fragile skirted her eyes.

"Ah yes, but I had not planned on teaching you that just yet. You rather drove me to it." His smile echoed faintly on her face.

"What then?"

"You do not deny that you enjoy the feeling of a man inside you?"

Portia remained silent, her expression wary. From what little she'd told him, he knew she'd never admit it. Not yet.

"There are certain . . . items that can be used in place of a man's cock."

Her right eyebrow quirked upward, animation returning to her face. "Are you telling me that you are replaceable?"

"Absolutely. Isn't that what you want?"

Her smile grew wider. "Absolutely."

He sat up, turning away. He rested a moment, hands resting lightly on his knees. She was so determined to be without any man, to be without him.

Well, he had promised to give her the means to do it.

He rose and crossed to the chest of drawers. He ruffled through some items and pulled out a large leather pouch. Returning to the bed, he unraveled the leather straps that held it closed.

"This." He produced a thick rod, carved to look like a man's penis.

Portia covered her mouth, but he still heard her muffled giggle. "You carry one with you?"

"There are other uses than the one I am about to show you." And perhaps he'd show her, at some point, although it did not fall under his aegis as teacher of masturbation. "One of its names is 'dildo.' "

He handed it to her.

She turned it over in her hands, running them along its smooth length. It had been well-oiled, the surface smooth. Mark's cock hardened, just watching her play with the wooden object. "And I use it, just like a—like your—"

"Yes." He bit off the word, draping his arms in an effort to conceal her effect on him.

"But is it not too hard?"

"It is not as large as I." Mark couldn't help but display himself. By God, he was ready to knock her over and plough himself into her again. His cock twitched at the idea.

Portia giggled. "It does not move as you do either."

"No, I'm afraid not. It will not hurt if you are ready for it."

"And so?"

"And so, when you have brought yourself to a close point to release, slide this inside you. You may mimic fucking with it, or let it lie inside for you to grip. It's your choice."

She held it out to him. "Will you show me?"

He took it from her, noting a slight tremble in his hand. He hoped she hadn't noticed. "You know its placement."

Portia lay back, her calves dangling over the edge of the bed. "Show me."

"Portia, you have been much used—"

"I will not take it without instruction."

"I have given you it."

She raised her head. "Mark." She reached out to him, stroked his back. "Do you fear you will be overthrown?"

"Overthrown from what?" he snapped. He kneeled upon the bed, his bobbing, aching cock before her face.

Her gaze fastened upon his cock. She said nothing, licking her lips. "Then perhaps," she murmured, "you may show me one of its other uses."

"What do you mean?" He sucked in his breath.

She reached and took the dildo from him. "I mean this." She closed her lips about the dildo's tip, and she slid it in a little way.

"Portia," he said roughly, his hands fisted in sudden anger. "Where did you—"

The dildo popped from her mouth. "Who else but Sir Guy? It pleased him, he told me. Back then, I would have done anything to make him happy. For all the good it did," she ended bitterly.

He stroked the hair off her forehead. "I am here to bring you pleasure," he murmured. "Give me that and I will show you how to bring pleasure to yourself."

She stared up at him, her eyes wide. The dildo exchanged hands and he found his face framed in her hands. "Kiss me."

He did, his mouth plundering hers.

He trailed the wet tip of the dildo between her breasts and over her belly. He slipped it between her legs, felt it nudge against her opening and slide inside.

Portia gasped into his mouth. He pushed it all the way in, until he reached her clit with his thumb. He brushed her clit and she gasped again. She clutched at his shoulders.

Before long, she writhed in his grip. He kept his mouth upon her, holding her in place with nothing but his mouth and his hand on her crotch.

Her moans vibrated his lips. He felt, more than heard, them coming higher in pitch. She bucked beneath him, once, then twice and went rigid. She bit on his lower lip, her cry muffled and she subsided against him.

He slid the dildo out of her, ended that timeless kiss. He wiped his mouth and saw the streak of blood.

"I'm sorry," she murmured, her fingertips brushing his swelling lip.

"It will mend." He brushed her hand away. "Do not worry about it."

She gave a brief nod and rolled over, concealing her luscious curves, but revealing the sweet rounds of her bottom.

"You will need to clean and dry this after each use. Otherwise it becomes quite nasty smelling." He smiled at her back. "And difficult to hide."

She said nothing, rising to put on the remains of her shift and bending to reach for her stays.

"Portia, how will you hide it?"

Her back still turned, she shrugged. "It is none of your concern."

That put him in his place, reminded him to teach, not to care. He crossed to the wash stand and doused the dildo. He washed it in the water, lamenting that he had not licked it clean. Ah, what would Portia think if she saw that?

His cock ached. The very hope she found that arousing, excited him even more. He sighed. He was a hopeless case.

He dried off the dildo, slipped it back into its pouch and turned to hand it to her. She'd gotten into her dress, trying to fasten tapes and hoist her breasts into the tight bodice. Her stays lay on the floor.

Portia took the pouch. "I don't need the stays just to get back to my room. Could you help—?"

"Of course," He gathered in the tapes to her gown until she was at last somewhat presentable, even though her hair tumbled down her back.

She clutched the pouch and her stays to her chest. "Thank

you," she murmured. "Would you check to see if the hallway's clear?"

He did, and in moments she was gone.

The room seemed empty. Rubbing his head, he shook off that strange notion. He needed sleep, that would solve all ills.

10

Portia closed the door behind her. With some twisting, she managed to unfasten the tapes of her gown. Leaving it and her undergarments in a puddle on the floor, she slipped between the bed sheets.

She lay on her back. The fine cotton, cool against her hot skin, soaked up the heat from her swollen nipples and clung to the jointure of her thighs.

She'd had to get out. She'd had to escape. The last thing she had expected was . . . was that he'd make love to her. How else to describe his sudden gentleness? Those slow, rhythmic thrusts . . .

Portia shuddered. She'd never been on a ship before, but she imagined that the swell of amorphous emotion would be like a little ship rocking on a gentle sea.

The emotion transformed into something real, a warm liquid that buoyed her up—and drowned her. Both heaven and hell, an incredible bliss that suffused her heart and her limbs, dragging her down into—well, she didn't want to know what, although she had never wanted it to end.

Oh God.

She would not, she could not fall in love with this man. It had been nothing more than a temporary arrangement, giving her the skills to please herself. Oh, she knew from the first that Knightson had wanted her, desired her, and she had figured that allowing him to have sex with her would be payment for her knowledge.

But she had not expected *this*.

She flung an arm over her eyes. What to do? Was it really . . . ? Was it really *love*?

And if so, if so, did she return that love? She squeezed her eyes shut. How would she know? What if it were no more than garden variety lust, the same feelings she had for Sir Guy?

But believing herself in love with Sir Guy had not felt like this. Of that, she was certain.

But love? Portia remained unconvinced. Knightson was handsome, delicious, a fantastic fuck. If it were just sex, just sex, she'd let him possess her, own her. But it seemed more than that now.

That hadn't been fucking, that had been making love.

What to do?

Portia didn't know how she got through breakfast. The once-delicious food spread on the sideboard tasted lumpen, wooden. She pushed warm scrambled eggs around her plate, dodging the slice of toast made soggy by butter.

The golden walls of the breakfast room did little to cheer her. She didn't want to stay at Willowhill Hall any more. Flight seemed the best option.

Alas, Mama didn't agree. So she was stuck here until the house party ended or she got engaged—

Got engaged.

Would it be worth accepting an offer of marriage just to escape this place?

She flung down her napkin and collected her parasol. A good long walk might solve her problem.

"Miss Carew?" Lady Cecily's voice halted her as she crossed the hallway. "Would you care for some company?"

Portia debated being rude and pretending not to hear her. On the other hand, Lady Cecily pretended to have former acquaintance with Knightson. Perhaps she might illuminate the mystery of Knightson the man. She stopped and smiled. "Of course."

The house cast its three-story morning shadow across them and the verdant lawn. Partway across the first part of the front lawn, Lady Cecily broke the tense silence. "I did not expect you to be kind, Miss Carew."

"My reputation as a shrew far exceeds itself," Portia remarked, her lips in a bitter twist.

"Perhaps."

Portia glanced sidelong at the thin, prim line of Lady Cecily's mouth. "I thank you for your kindness."

Lady Cecily sniffed.

"I was wondering if you might be more frank about Mr. Knightson."

Lady Cecily's parasol jerked. "Ah. So he does have his hooks into you."

"Is it as bad as that?"

"Worse. I love him still, you know. If you can, wipe him from your heart."

"What is it about him that is so terrible?"

"It is simple really. He beds a woman five times and then moves onto the next. There is no reprieve, no mercy. He is gone. *Finis*."

Portia sucked in her breath. How had she forgotten his warning? She mentally counted the times they'd slept together. Should she count the times he didn't penetrate her? Was last night the fifth time? Was that why he was so gentle? She took a deep breath, twirling her parasol. "What makes him so harsh?"

"I wish I knew. I can only think he's looking for some perfect woman." Lady Cecily stopped, taking Portia's arm and making her face her. "You should know that I believe I am that woman. It is just that this 'five times' had become a bad habit and he doesn't know he's let the right woman slip him by."

"You are?" Portia let her parasol drag on the ground.

"I am." Lady Cecily eyed her up and down. "Will you stand aside?"

Portia surveyed Lady Cecily in turn. The woman seemed to burn with a mixture of determination and desperation. Portia saw it burn in her green eyes, in the tightness of her face. "If what you say is true . . ."

"It is."

"Do you have proof?"

Lady Cecily laughed, a brittle sound. "Miss Carew, haven't you experienced enough of him to know what I say is true?"

"I have not slept with the man," Portia retorted, stung.

"Come, come, we are two women alone. I swear that your confidences will not be repeated. I can see his touch on you."

She managed a laugh. "I hardly think so!"

"Poor Miss Carew. Are you really that naive?" Again, that fragile laugh. "He has marked you more plainly than with a brand."

"If that is so, it does not explain why practically every gentleman has marked attentions toward me. Even the old Duke has proposed!"

"His Grace, the Duke of Winterton does not propose to innocent young misses."

"He proposed to me." Portia spoke quietly. "Do not dare suggest I am anything other than a gentlewoman."

Lady Cecily barked a laugh. "My dear, you are a whore. Sir Guy has made it known to me exactly what passed between the two of you, and believe me, it will be a fast exit from Society if it is revealed that you are still on your back for any man who asks."

Whip-fast, Portia slapped her face. "There is no such thing to reveal, Lady Cecily. I thank you for your conversation, but I find I have had enough of it. Good day."

She stalked back to the house, longing to break into a run. That hadn't helped at all. Lady Cecily would ruin her for her violence.

Maybe she should leave.

Somehow managing to remain unseen, she slipped into the library. Knightson might be within, but for a bit of privacy, she'd risk it.

At least, that's what she repeated to herself. She searched the library, making sure there was no male form hidden in a wing chair, or behind the curtains. She settled in a window seat. It made her visible to the outside, but nobody passed by that side of the house often, if at all.

She wrapped her arms around her knees, making sure her skirts concealed her parts and gazed out the window. What was she going to do?

It had been nothing short of a miracle she had avoided Sir Guy for as long as she had. The sight of him made her shudder, but fortunately he had not progressed in the renewal of his suit to her. And to her relief, nobody else at Willowhill Hall urged her to accept the proposal.

What did she want?

She didn't get a chance to ruminate. She heard the library door open and close. Portia remained still, hoping against hope the curtain concealed her presence, and whoever wanted to use the library would take his or her book and go.

"Portia?" Sir Guy called in a low voice. "I know you are in here."

So much for not being alone with him. Against all hope, she kept still, holding her breath.

"There you are." The curtain twitched back and the blond visage of Sir Guy gazed down at her. "Why are you hiding?"

"I slapped Lady Cecily." The first thing she thought of blurted out of her mouth. She wasn't about to tell him about the bizarre feelings she'd had while she'd fucked Knightson.

Fuck. The word helped a little in alleviating that strange pain in her heart.

Sir Guy's lips suppressed and he let loose a brief chuckle. "She probably deserved that."

"How can you say that? She's your friend!"

Sir Guy sat, uninvited, in the window seat next to her. "She is an acquaintance, nothing more. She needed to be here, I provided the means."

"She's after Mr. Knightson."

Sir Guy nodded. "I saw you dance that waltz. Are you developing a tendré for him? His reputation is not exactly sterling."

"According to Lady Cecily." She meant her tone to dampen the conversation.

"It is commonly known among the gentlemen too." Impeccably turned out, he twitched the cuff of his bottle-green coat over a snow-white cuff. "We know which ones we wouldn't want our sisters to become involved with."

Portia's gaze narrowed. "You don't have a sister."

He waved away the error with florid grace. "That's irrelevant. I might one day have a sister-in-law."

Portia thought of her sister Viola, on the verge of her launch upon Society. "In your dreams."

Sir Guy chuckled and leaned forward. Portia shrank back against the broad window jamb. "I plan to make my dreams a reality."

She held out her hands, fending him off. "No, Sir Guy. How many times must I say it? You were the one who called off the engagement. You were the one who vilified my name. What makes you think I would even consider a new proposal?"

"What can I do, Portia—"

"Miss Carew."

He made a face. "What can I do, Miss Carew, but apologize a thousandfold? I made a mistake. I thought I was ready for marriage, but I was not. I thought I wanted a passionate wife, but was convinced that a virtuous wife was more necessary. You had shown such passion, that I—well, I threw you off.

"It took me a while to realize my error. It took a virtuous miss to realize that's the last thing I want in my bed. You were so eager, so willing, and I'm willing to fix it all, every last bit of it."

"How?"

"By marrying you. Marrying you will wipe away every last horrid word I said about you. It will bring you back firmly into Society. I would rather take the black stain upon myself that in a temper after we quarreled, I tried to destroy your name."

That gave Portia pause. In everything she knew about him, Sir Guy had always been the selfish one. "You would do that?"

"And more. For if you forgive me for my slight, for my abandoning you, by marrying me, we fix everything. We can go back to the way we were."

She regarded him. He seemed utterly sincere. "There is no going back," she murmured. "I am sorry. You will have to deal with the guilt of unfairly blackening my name for the rest of your life. I will not marry you, not even to restore my reputation."

Sir Guy surveyed her with an enviable careless air. "You have taken me into a severe dislike, and I cannot blame you."

"It is not just that. Since you pushed me from the dais of innocent maiden, I have tasted more of that passion I thought we shared. You will not do."

Sir Guy rose, his pale cheeks flaring red. "You are goading me to abandon you. There has not been time for you to form another attachment. Indeed, who would have you in your fallen state?"

"Almost fallen," she corrected. "If I were truly outcast, I would not be here under the Barrington's roof."

"You have been lucky." Sir Guy gripped her chin, hauled it up to meet his sour gaze. "You should not count on that luck. Marry me, Portia."

"No," she murmured. "Remove your hands from my person."

Sir Guy barked incredulous laughter.

"Do as she says."

Portia swiveled toward the door. Mark Knightson stood there, his face twisted with displeasure. Or was it anger? Jealousy? Portia's heart swelled with relief.

Sir Guy backed off. "I was merely speaking to the girl."

Bristling, the two men seemed to sense the other as competition.

"You had your hand upon her. The lady asked you to remove it."

"You do not understand the nature of my relationship with Miss Carew."

Portia settled back against the window jamb, watching the two of them. Asserting herself at this point appeared pointless. The room reeked of male posturing.

"I think it is you who do not understand it. How dare you, sir, accost the woman when she was alone?"

"I did not expect it. I merely made the most of the opportunity."

"Sir, I suggest we end this conversation before I am forced to call you out for your unseemly behavior."

Sir Guy snorted, but shifted away from Portia and toward the door.

Knightson stepped aside and gave him a clear exit. He waited until the door closed behind Sir Guy. He raised a dark eyebrow at Portia. "What were you doing alone with him?"

"It was as he said. I did not expect him. I came here to be alone."

Knightson crossed the room and perched on a sofa arm. "Alone? Or seeking me?"

Both answers were true, Portia realized in a heartbeat. She remained silent.

His brows lowered. "Did he hurt you?"

She shook her head.

"It is as well I found you here."

She met his gaze, calm washing through her. "Yes, I was having little success in getting rid of Sir Guy. So I must thank you, Mr. Knightson."

His face grew still, motionless. "'Mr. Knightson'? Portia, what disturbs you?"

"I am merely trying to retain some perspective," she blurted.

"Ah." The answer seemed to satisfy him, judging by his growing boyish smile. He joined her on the window seat. His knee brushed her thigh, sending a sizzle through her. "I have been giving our situation some thought, also."

She blinked at him, puzzled. Had he felt the same strange emotions she had last night? Was he about to cut her free, or had those sweet sensations brought him to a more respectable conclusion? Was he about to propose?

Did she want to hear this? "How interesting," she said in a hopefully dampening manner. "Is there much more to teach me?"

He swiped a hand over his jaw, not immediately answering her question. "It is not a matter of lessons anymore, Portia. Surely you realize that."

Her chin went up. "I understood it to be payment for services rendered, Mr. Knightson."

He cursed. At length. With a great deal of creativity. Portia didn't know half the words. His black brows snapped together. "Have you thought you were selling your body to me all this time for a few paltry lessons?"

"Wasn't I?" she retorted.

"I had . . . hoped . . . you felt more than that." His shoulders slumped just the tiniest bit.

So he would propose? "Mr. Knightson—Mark—I . . ." What could she tell him? The truth. "I enjoyed it."

The corner of his mouth twitched. "I know you did. I expected no payment. I wanted none."

"I had thought . . ." Portia took a minute to compose herself. "I had thought that because of our intimacy, that my availability was expected. Indeed, I recall a certain moment on the stairs when you commanded me—" Her breath hitched, the vision of her bent over the railing, having the life fucked out of her, made her want it—him—again.

She tried to slow her breathing, bring her heart back to its normal rate. She couldn't lose control now. She laid a calming hand over her bosom.

His gaze followed her hand to her neckline and twitched away. "Damn it, Portia. I lost my temper." His forehead smoothed. "But you must admit, it was good."

She snorted, snatching her hand away from her décolletage. His admission alone crumbled her will to be strong against him. "Must I?"

"You wanted me then, Portia, don't try to deny it. I'll wager if I stuck my hand between your legs right now, you would be ready."

She inhaled shakily. He didn't need to do that. She was ready.

"How large your eyes get, Miss Carew," he purred. He gathered her unprotesting body in his arms, holding her against the hard lines of his body. Her tiptoes rested on the ground.

"Someone will see," she breathed, feasting on his lust-darkened eyes, his kissable lips.

"Let them." He lowered his head, his mouth covering hers. She melted against him. This is what she wanted to feel: the delicious spark of desire fanned into full flames.

With one hand, he switched the curtains closed.

"I thought you didn't care," she taunted breathlessly against his mouth.

"Yours is the wiser head in this." Apparently, her words had remained with him, even though her own mind had blanked at the touch of his lips. "Portia, you have said that you do not want marriage."

She sucked in air. "I do not."

"Does this still hold true?"

"Haven't I just said so?" She willed herself to stay strong. To stay strong even though he held her so close to him.

"That is as well. I thought perhaps after last night . . ." Mark trailed off, shaking his head free of that thought, that remembrance.

"Last night was . . . different," Portia ventured. To make sense of it, she needed to talk to someone about it.

"I believe we went to another level of existence," Mark told her, his voice tight. His body radiated tension and Portia received the impression that the experience had not been a pleasant one for him.

But why? What didn't he tell her? "Is that what it was?"

He gave a curt nod. "I am glad you did not mistake it for being in love. You are wiser than your experience suggests."

She wanted to shrug, but remained still in his arms, his words ringing in her mind. *Being in love.* Is that why he shied away? Or was Mark right in explaining it as an illusion, another step up in their sexual life?

"Which brings me to the reason why I sought you out." He smiled at her widened eyes. "Oh yes, I looked for you, Portia. Before we go any further, matters need to be decided."

"Matters?"

"You do not wish marriage. Well, nor do I."

Portia sank inside. So he did not want her to wife. She shouldn't feel this way. She didn't want that either.

Or did she?

"However . . ." he trailed off, his gaze burning her face. He looked for something in her, but what she didn't know. "Portia, my dear, I fear this may incense you . . ."

"Then you had best get it over with," she snapped. What did he want then?

"What do you know of me?"

"What the gossips say," she replied, avoiding his gaze.

"Which is?" he prompted.

Her gaze snapped to his. "At the kindest level, that you are an unremarkable gentleman, and at the worst, a veritable rake. Do you recall your warning me you will only fuck a woman five times before getting bored with her? It was recently repeated to me."

He bared his clenched teeth. "That came from Lady Cecily."

Portia managed her sweetest smile. "How ever did you guess Lady Cecily repeated it? Did you tell her too?"

"Yes." Knightson got the answer out between gritted teeth.

Portia fought for calm, for carelessness. "Did she exaggerate in what she told me then?"

A long silence followed. Portia watched him war with himself, his hands flexing into fists. "No," he said at last. "But there are reasons for it."

"I am all ears." Portia clasped her hands and assumed an exaggerated attentive pose.

He dismissed the idea with a curt wave. His expression made a signal shift from frustrated anger and embarrassment to an undefinable one that reminded her of last night.

"It doesn't matter now," he purred, "for I am about to break that rule."

No doubt he meant his forthcoming proposal. Portia waited patiently. Would she say yes? To a man who gave her brilliant sex but about whom she knew nothing but gossip?

"Portia, I have thought long and hard about this. Keeping your wishes in mind and our shared desires, I came to only one conclusion."

He paused, his blue eyes darkened and searching her for some sort of response. Portia decided to err on the side of caution.

"You will not ask what it is?"

"I am sure I am soon to hear it." Portia smiled, hoping she didn't look too infatuated, too stupid.

He clasped her hand in both of his. "Portia, you do not know what it costs me to ask you this. What it will cost you. When I think of how your mother will react, and of course, we would have to leave at once—"

"Mark," Portia interrupted his stream of babble, a little frightened by his intensity. "Your conclusion."

He flashed a smile. "Yes, yes, of course. Portia, there can be no denying it. I want you. My ridiculous, self-imposed rule of five times will not stand against these feelings. Oh, I have tried to fight it, tried to tell myself that I would tire of you. But I have not."

He squeezed her hand.

"Portia, I don't know how to even ask you this. I don't want us to be separated once this house party comes to an end. I want you with me." His lip curled in a defensive sneer. "I don't want you to put my lessons to use. I intend to satisfy you, Portia, for a very long time indeed."

"What are you asking?" What a most peculiar proposal. Of course, what else could he speak of except their shared lusts? That's all they had.

"I am asking you to become my mistress."

Her ears roared with some unseen force. Mistress? Mistress?! Anger and want demanded dominance inside her.

"You do not want marriage and nor do I, and I do expect, in time, that we will tire of each other." His forehead creased and he squeezed her hand. Were her emotions that transparent? "Divorce is far too public and humiliating. I will have papers drawn up that ensure you a home and an annuity to live off of. You won't have to rely on any other man after me."

"So very kind of you." Portia bit off each word, slipping her hand free of his.

"Portia, what is wrong?"

"You, sir, propose to ruin me completely and expect me to be happy about it?"

"But you are ruined."

"But nobody else need know it!" Portia rose and stomped away. She swirled and pointed at him. "Everybody will know it if you set me up as a mistress. There will be no question of me being able to see any member of my family again. My mother will have conniptions. . . ."

She trailed off. She stared, wide-eyed, at him. "My God. That's what you meant when you said you thought my mother would react badly. Here I foolishly thought it was merely because she had taken you into dislike!"

Mark folded his arms, the intensity in his face shuttered. "You're turning down my proposition."

Glaring, Portia nodded. "I prefer the original terms."

"Fine. Your lessons are over. Does that make you change your mind?"

Inwardly, she quailed. Her stomach roiled with the threatened loss. She knew enough to satisfy herself, at least so Mark—Mr. Knightson—had insisted.

Had he meant it, or had it been a prelude to his seduction? Far too late to worry about that now.

"Over?" she echoed.

His anger faded, his brow furrowing in concern. The expression in his eyes—Lord, Portia almost preferred it to his lusty leers. "Look, Portia." Mark strode forward and placed his hands on her shoulders. "I recognize that I have asked you to do something quite unconventional, but you are an unconventional woman. You are revolted by the idea now, but give it some time and thought as I have done."

"I could—could do that," Portia allowed. Her voice shook. Could she? Could she really abandon everything for Knightson?

"Meet me tonight on the roof by the balustrades on the right-hand side of the main house." He seemed so sure. "Not the wing, mind," he added.

"Why should I?"

"Give me your final answer then. If it is no, I will test you on what you have learned, and if I am satisfied, then the lessons are over." His gaze darkened. "If you do not accept my proposition, I have no wish to continue the association, Portia, and drag out the pain that comes with the separation a negative answer will force on us."

"You will go away?"

"I have not decided," came his quelling answer. "Perhaps."

Portia raised her chin. "I would not make a fool of myself over you. I will stand by my decision and let you go."

"Decide tonight," Mark repeated, his voice urgent and—did she hear a desperate note? "Do not say any more about what we shall do until then."

"Until tonight, when all have retired." Portia curtsied and

headed for the door. She had to escape, and think, and quite probably sob.

"Do not retire early. We should let no suspicions rise at this late stage."

"Indeed." Portia closed the door behind her. Her throat felt swollen, under the pressure of unshed tears.

Oh damn him, damn him to hell!

She fled.

11

"Portia!" Miss Lucy Chalcroft's sweet, dulcet tones rang out across the great hall.

Portia continued to flee upstairs, hiding her wet face in her hands. Lucy mustn't see her like this: too many questions would be asked.

She heard Lucy run up the stairs behind her, and Portia turned, astonished that Miss Chalcroft would even break into more than a sedate walk.

"What is it?" Lucy asked, grabbing her arm. "What's wrong?"

Mutely, Portia shook her head, watching Lucy's face collapse into concern.

Lucy held out a handkerchief, but Portia refused it. She needed to get to her own room. At least nobody would dare to accost her there.

"Portia," murmured Lucy, tucking Portia's arm firmly into hers. "Let us go for a walk, away from the house. Whatever is bothering you, you need to talk about it. It will make you feel better."

"I doubt it," Portia choked out, but she let Lucy lead her back down the stairs and out the front door.

When they had cut across the front lawn and reached the shelter of the trees, Lucy at last let her go.

"Now tell me what the matter is." Lucy presented the handkerchief once more.

"Oh, I cannot tell you, Lucy." Portia twisted the handkerchief wretchedly. "I cannot tell you. You will not be my friend if I do."

"I cannot be your friend if you keep silence, Portia." Lucy rescued her handkerchief and dabbed Portia's wet cheeks. "There is a log over there. Come, let's sit down and tell me everything."

Seated, Portia looked back toward the house, but saw nothing but a screen of trees and ferns blocking her view. This little area had been "naturalized" by the garden's architect into a deep shady space under the broad beech trees, filling it with ferns and wild garlic and other plants Portia could not name.

She certainly smelled the wild garlic.

Raising her head, she met Lucy's patient gaze. What advice could Miss Chalcroft give? Her sweet manner held not a hint of any corruption.

"I am not sure you would understand," Portia murmured.

"I am willing to guess it involves a man," Lucy returned in an equally low voice. She twisted the ends of her long, lacy scarf.

Who would overhear them in this secluded corner? But some things could not be spoken of aloud.

"Yes," Portia admitted, "but not in the way you think."

"You have said you do not want marriage." Lucy's echo of Mark Knightson's earlier words brought a fresh burst of tears.

Portia dashed them away. "I swear I am not such a waterpot normally. I just do not know what to do!"

"Is it Sir Guy Symon?" Lucy ventured. "Does he continue to pester you?"

Portia's lips twisted. "He does, but that is not it." She sighed, regarding her hands in her lap. How to appear placid when all her world had come apart?

She took a deep breath. "Lucy, you know of my ill-gotten reputation."

"What Sir Guy now claims is all lies," Lucy confirmed.

Portia winced and nodded. "Yes, well, you see, it wasn't quite all lies." She snuck a sidelong look. "Do you want me to continue?"

Lucy patted her hand. "It is all right, Portia. I know you have been much wronged."

"That summarizes the matter well enough. Let us say it was sufficient for me to wish to become completely independent of men."

"As you have told me before, although I do wonder at how you will accomplish this." Lucy's blond hair glinted in the filtered sunlight.

"I wonder about it also," Portia freely admitted with a delicate shrug of her shoulders. "I had thought Mr. Knightson had provided the answer."

"The answer? Him?"

"It is embarrassing to admit it, but he caught me at a, ahh, most awkward moment and offered to teach me—" Portia broke off, shooting a desperate glance at Lucy. "I fear I am going to shock you."

Lucy waved at her to continue. "Shock away. It will make a pleasant change to my dull existence and I will keep every confidence."

Portia swallowed. She should have asked Lucy to be sure of that before proceeding with her tale, even though Lucy had not betrayed a single word about Portia's future plans.

"Thank you." Portia gulped again. "Mr. Knightson offered me the chance to learn how to pleasure myself."

Lucy leaned forward. "Pleasure one's self?"

Gnawing her lip, Portia regarded her friend. "I will teach you, if you like. It evokes the most heavenly sensations."

"As Mama has no plans for me to marry at all, the occasional heavenly sensation would not go astray." Lucy's grin faded. "But Mr. Knightson taught you this?"

Portia nodded. "Oh yes, it was incredibly foolish of me, I know, but who could resist such an offer, and as he had viewed my, er, attempt to do so already, the intimacy barrier had already been irrevocably breached."

"So he taught you ..." Lucy's breath hitched. "And he touched you?"

"Lucy, I swear I don't know what came over me. I could not deny him anything—*anything*! I have never felt like this before: it's like intoxication but with a multitude of awareness rather than oblivion. It's—he's—utterly delicious." She paused for breath. "At least, until now."

"Now what he demands, you must deny?"

Portia nodded, a tear dripping off the end of her nose. "He knows my feelings on the matter of marriage, so he did not propose that."

Reaching out, she grasped Lucy's hands tight. "He wants me to be his mistress," Portia told her, her voice low and rough. "His mistress! He dared ..."

Lucy tilted her head to once side. "But isn't what you are doing now ... isn't that being his mistress?"

Releasing her, Portia shook her head. "We made an agreement: he would give me lessons." She took a deep breath to stop herself from crying again. "The lessons are over, Lucy. He wants to continue the other thing, as if it was more than just aroused lusts."

"Is it?"

Portia sagged, covering her face. "I don't know," she sobbed. "I really don't know." She lifted her wet face and met Lucy's serious gaze. "More than lust is love, isn't it? So if it's love, why won't he offer marriage?"

"Because you do not want it," Lucy advised with a small smile. "Why would a man wish to be so rejected?"

Portia hung her head. "You are right, of course. I may well have refused even a true proposal. I know every part of his body, but the man? The man I know not at all. How can I love a man who is a mystery to me, whom all the gossips say is not to be trusted?"

"Then, it is well that your lessons are over." Lucy tugged on Portia's arm. "You must see that it is so. He is a dangerous man, not the least because he seems to be hellbent on ruining you forever."

Portia made a face. "Lucy, I know you are right, but my heart—or maybe it is my loins—wants to keep seeing him, being with him."

"To the extent of becoming his mistress?"

"I am a hopeless case, I fear." Gazing around at the concealed meadow, the tiny daisies dotting the grass, the bending branches shielding them, Portia wondered if she really ought to be alive at all.

Lucy's arms closed around her and Portia discovered the soothing warmth of her hug. "You need not be so self-destructive. Be strong, Portia."

Portia clung to her friend, the tears rising again. "I will try!" she sobbed. "I am so glad you have not turned from me, Lucy."

"Nor will I ever, for you owe me."

"Owe you?" Portia pulled out of the embrace, blinking away her wretched tears at Lucy's playful tone.

"That small matter of learning how to please myself?" Lucy looked hesitant.

Wiping away the last of her tears, Portia smiled. "Shall I show you now?" She glanced around at their surroundings.

"We will need a blanket and there is something I must get from my room."

Lucy's smile echoed Portia's return to good spirits. "I shall fetch the blanket. If anyone sees me, they shall no doubt think it is for Mother."

"Excellent idea. Meet you back here?"

"As soon as possible."

Breathless, Portia found Lucy waiting for her, sitting on the moss-green plaid blanket spread next to the log. Portia flung down first her bulging reticule, and then herself.

"Where do we begin?" Lucy fiddled with the folds of her gown.

Portia passed her a book she'd borrowed from the Barrington library. "Open it to page five hundred and twenty-three. It shows the female anatomy, our most intimate parts."

Lucy bowed her head over the book. "It looks . . . messy."

"Have you not ever had feelings rise from there?"

"I—I don't think so."

A soft rose colored the diagram, a darker blue marking nearby veins. Portia pointed to the page. "This is the clitoris, or the clit. When touched in the right way, it is the foremost part to gaining pleasure."

"Is that not where I—" Lucy waved her hand, flushing red.

"No, that is farther down." Portia pointed to the urethra. "And here is where the man enters you with his cock. You can use your fingers to mimic that. It's not the same, but there's a place. . . ."

She trailed off, staring at Lucy. Lucy's bosom heaved with short, sharp breaths, her cheeks still stained with a rosy glow. "Lucy, perhaps it is best if I show you." She paused, gnawing her lip. "It would mean seeing your parts, and you seeing mine."

"We should take off our clothes?"

"I think we need only to hitch our skirts to our waist. What

if somebody came along? That way we could easily set ourselves to rights."

Lucy shivered. "Somebody could see us?"

"Not from the house," Portia hastened to reassure her.
Lucy's hands twisted in her lap.

"We don't have to do this if you do not want to," Portia said
gently. "We can talk about it instead."

"No, no." The hem of Lucy's skirt inched upward. "I want
to know." She visibly swallowed. "I want to feel this wonder."
She shifted so the bulk of her skirt now lay behind her, leaving
her pale legs visible. Dark golden curls nestled at the jointure of
her thighs.

Portia hoisted her own skirts. Leaning back, her shoulders
braced against the log, her legs parted, she licked her finger and
touched her clit. At once, warmth spread throughout her groin
and she gave an appreciative sigh.

"I—I don't think it's working. I get flashes, but not . . ."

Portia looked over to see Lucy rubbing at her clit. "I think
you might need a gentler touch. May I touch you?"

Biting her lip, Lucy nodded.

Portia knelt between her friend's legs and parted her cunt
lips. There was but a hint of moisture and the area about Lucy's
clit had reddened. Lucy's thighs trembled, tensed.

"Relax, Lucy. Nothing will happen unless you relax." Leaning
in, Portia gave Lucy's clit a tentative lick.

Lucy squealed, twisting. "Oh! What was that? Do it again!"

Smiling, Portia bent forward and gave Lucy's clit another
lick. She had to grasp onto Lucy's hips to stop her nose from
smashing into Lucy's pelvis.

Lucy babbled something in her moans and cries. Her body
writhed at each flick at her clit and Portia's nostrils filled with
the musky scent of Lucy's arousal. Lucy's booted foot kicked
her in the ribs.

Sitting up, Portia groaned.

Lucy lay panting for a moment before weakly lifting her head. "I was so close," she groaned. "Why did you stop?"

Portia grinned, enjoying her friend's frustration. "I forgot to tell you three things: the first is to remember this, for memories add to pleasuring yourself when you're alone later. Perhaps you should think of me as a man between your legs."

Lucy swallowed. "Perhaps."

Portia's cheeks seemed warmer. "The other thing is that delaying the final release can make it larger. Do not rush onward to get release, not unless you know you've a small amount of time in private."

"I will remember that." Lucy replied, propped up by her elbows.

"The third thing is you best remove your boots!"

Lucy giggled, and bent to the task, looking up to ask: "What is it like? To taste me like that?"

Portia's blush deepened and she ducked her head, using the removal of her boots as an excuse. "It's warm and wet—you are very wet now, you know. The smell is . . . well, it's exciting."

"May I try?" Lucy asked, sitting up and wrapping her arms about her knees. "On you?"

"On me?" Portia's breath caught and she nodded. "Let's see how well you have learned. . . ." She lay back, closing her eyes. She sensed Lucy move between her legs and the puff of warm breath against her dark curls.

"You are very wet," Lucy observed in a tone that was almost cool, but a tremble betrayed her.

Portia squeezed her eyes shut against the first lick, sighing when it came. Lucy must have barely tasted her, so light was her touch.

The next lick came, bolder now, and the next.

"Yes," breathed Portia, "yes, yes. That is it."

The erotic warmth raced through her body, filling her with a building need for her release to come. She sobbed, trying to keep still for Lucy, but failing.

"Oh stop, stop," Portia begged.

Lucy pulled away at once. "What is it? What have I done wrong?"

Portia sat up also. "Nothing," she gasped out. "It is you who needs this release, not I."

She stared at Lucy's chin, shining with her sex fluids. Her eyes widened, and she saw that Lucy had also stopped to stare. Portia leaned forward and kissed Lucy's chin, her lips sliding to cover her mouth.

Lucy kissed back, wrapping her arms around Portia's neck. Portia tasted herself and Lucy mixed together, and felt a surge of want rise from her cunt.

She broke off the kiss. The two sat there, panting. Portia reached out and fumbled with the ties to Lucy's gown, loosening the bodice. She pulled the bodice away, revealing Lucy's small white breasts.

"Another way to pleasure yourself, is to play with your breasts." Portia demonstrated, trying to ignore Lucy's wide-eyed silence. She palmed Lucy's breast, and then drew it away until only her fingers pursed around the nipple. She squeezed, very lightly and gave it a tug. "There," she whispered, "like that. Lie down and touch yourself there. I want to taste more of you."

Uttering a tiny sigh, Lucy obeyed, parting her legs once more. Portia went down between them and laved her tongue against Lucy's swollen little clit.

She dipped lower, sliding her tongue along the length of Lucy's slit and burying her tongue at last inside Lucy's cunt. She swirled her tongue around the flexing entrance and licked her way back up to Lucy's clit.

"Can we not—" Lucy interrupted herself with a little shriek

as Portia drew her tongue across her clit again. "Can we not do this to each other at the same time?"

Portia looked up, saw Lucy's nipples hard and red and pointing up at the sky. Lucy's fingers still worked at them. Portia slid her fingers against Lucy's wet cunt, her fingertip teasing at the entrance. "Our gowns will get in the way."

"Let them," Lucy cried. "Please . . ."

Portia swung around, straddling Lucy, hoisting her skirts out of the way. She pulled at the tapes of her bodice, freeing her hot, heavy breasts to the air. The cool air washed over them, making her nipples even harder.

She lowered herself over Lucy's face, felt Lucy's fingertips dig into her hips and the first tentative flick of her tongue against Portia's clit.

Groaning, Portia bent to her task, licking and suckling on Lucy's clit. Jolts shocked through her, Lucy's ingenious tongue at work, sparing no part of her cunt. Portia did likewise, their cries muffled by the other's cunt.

It was a heaving heaven and Portia felt herself nearing climax. "Lucy," she begged, slipping a finger part way inside her friend. "Lucy, put your finger in me."

She moaned as Lucy inserted one finger with unbearable slowness.

"Another," she begged, "and do this." Portia used two fingers to give little thrusts inside Lucy. She didn't go deep, for she feared to wreck Lucy's virginity.

Lucy complied, but two of her tiny fingers didn't fill her the way Portia wanted. She writhed against Lucy trying to bring herself off.

The release hovered near, tantalizing her, her body so filled with tension, Portia thought she would explode.

Lucy twisted her head away from Portia's cunt and cried out, her body stiff and then writhing beneath Portia. Portia licked and sucked at her clit until Lucy's release subsided.

Portia slipped off her and turned to face her friend. "Did you climax? Did you achieve release?"

Lucy lay, limp, on the blanket. She smiled up at Portia, reaching out to grasp her hand. "Oh yes," she gasped. "It was beautiful, just beautiful."

"I'm glad." Portia bent to kiss her lightly on the cheek. "At least some good has come out of this affair."

"What about you? Did you—" Lucy paused, searching for the word. "Did you climax?"

"No," Portia admitted. "I was very close though." Lucy's downcast expression sent a pang through Portia's heart. "There is one more thing to show you," she said, reaching for her reticule.

Lucy sat up, clutching at her head. "Dizzy," she murmured.

Portia smiled. "That happens." She fished the dildo Mark had given her out of her bag. "Here. It is a replica of a man's cock. You use it just as he would, but it can't make you pregnant."

She handed it to Lucy, who fingered it with awe. "But it is large."

"It fits. Well," amended Portia, "it fits me, for I have lost my virginity. I do not know if it will go all the way inside of you, perhaps just the head." Her fingers encircled the dildo's head.

"Do you . . . do you want me to put it inside you?" Lucy asked.

Portia sucked in her breath. "Would you?"

"After what you have given me, Portia, it is the least I can do." She picked up her light silk scarf that had long ago been discarded and held the dildo to her groin. "What if I wrap it against me, like so?"

It took a few minutes and some awkward wrapping, but it was done.

"Show me," Lucy breathed, "how a man and woman lie together."

"There are many different ways."

Lucy caressed her cheek. "Show me some."

Portia lay down and held out her arms. "Come, lie on top of me and between my legs." Lucy's dildo slid awkwardly between them.

Staring up at Lucy, her face so close, Portia found her breath coming fast. "You have to angle the dildo against me, so it will slip inside."

It took the two of them, but soon it was nestled against her entrance.

"Now, push your hips against mine."

Portia groaned, feeling the dildo sink inside her.

"Does it hurt?" Lucy's face radiated concern.

"No." Portia smiled. "When you lose your virginity it will, for a moment." She sucked in her breath. "Keep going deeper, keep going."

Their hips lay together, their skirts tangled around them.

"Ah yes." Portia's cunt squeezed hard around the immovable object inside of her, but it wasn't enough. "Lucy, remember how you thrust into me with your fingers?"

Lucy required no further prompting. She drew the dildo out, almost all the way and then thrust back in again.

Portia clutched at Lucy's hips, moaning as Lucy filled her again. And again. Portia felt her release grow again, spinning her mind away from all that was outside the two of them, concentrating on the fire in her cunt.

Without warning, Portia hugged Lucy hard and rolled over on top of her.

"Another position?" gasped Lucy.

Portia nodded, her head already tilting back. This way, she buried the dildo deep inside her. This way, she had control. She humped the dildo, rising up and down. She fingered her breasts, plucking them into swollen fire, bouncing against Lucy's slight form and the large dildo buried inside her.

She sobbed, so close, so close.

She looked down at Lucy and saw Lucy had mimicked her movements, her nipples large and dark.

Portia slipped her hand between her legs, felt the dildo pulse in and out of her, and found Lucy's clit. She teased the hard nub, circling her hips to vary the pressure more.

Lucy cried out. "Oh, Portia! That feels. . . ."

She didn't need to say. Portia felt the release pound through her head, exploding her every sense. She bore down on the dildo, squeezing her cunt so hard that it ached.

She screamed, heard Lucy's cry echo faintly and collapsed forward on top of her friend.

Fighting for breath, she slid her body from the hard dildo and rolled to lay by Lucy's side. They clasped hands, gazing up at the dappled light streaking through the beech leaves.

"Portia . . ." Lucy said at last. "I never expected to find release twice!"

Neither had Portia. She quashed the brief surge of jealousy. "I am so glad I taught you, Lucy. What if you had spent the rest of your life not knowing that intensity was yours? Will it be enough for you?"

"Oh yes," Lucy replied, fervor ringing clear in her voice. "This gift will make the passing time seem pleasant."

"Waiting on your mother?" Portia huffed. "I am not sure I would go that far. But I am glad you will find joy in your life." She gave Lucy's hand a squeeze. "We should rise and return to the house before someone comes looking for us."

Lucy sat up, hand to her head. "I feel as weak as a kitten. Dizzy too." She smiled. "Can we not lie here a bit longer?"

"We really should not. You will be all right in a moment." Portia rose, putting her day gown to rights.

Lucy took the hint and came to her assistance, tucking away the last of her tapes. Portia then helped Lucy and by the time they had recovered each other's hairpins and refashioned their hair back into the simple knots they had begun with, their breathing had returned to normal.

Portia surveyed Lucy. "There. A bit wrinkled, but that should pass muster considering we've been traipsing in the woods."

"That's our story?"

Portia nodded.

Lucy stepped in closer, her lips pursing. "One last kiss?"

Taking her by the shoulders, Portia held Lucy at a distance. "We best not. If we become too comfortable in showing affection, the others may wonder."

"Let them," Lucy murmured.

Portia remained silent, begging her to understand. She'd enjoyed the interlude with Lucy, but it had been Mark she thought of, Mark's cock she'd imagined plunging in and out of her.

Lucy sighed. "It's him, isn't it."

Portia nodded, bending to gather up the blanket. "I don't know what's going to happen when I see him tonight."

"You should not go. In my opinion, you have more than passed the test. You have excelled."

Portia grinned, juggling the blanket and the bulging reticule. She'd have to wash and dry the dildo before tonight. "Thank you, but I still have to go."

Taking the blanket from her, Lucy tucked her arm into Portia's. "You love him, don't you."

"I don't know," Portia replied. How could she be anything else but honest with Lucy now? "I do not know if it's love or the sex. He makes me alive, that is all I know."

They left the woods behind, cutting across the broad expanse of green in front of the house.

"I cannot stop you," Lucy said. "But be careful, Portia. I would hate to lose our friendship now."

Portia gave her friend's arm a squeeze. "As would I."

* * *

She refused him?

He would never understand the conundrum of woman. Mark slapped his gloves hard against his thigh, but even the sharp sting did little to quell his anger.

He had presented the obvious solution, had even taken her wretched feelings into account in devising it and *this* was how she repaid him? By refusing him?

She had no desire to marry, he had no wish to either, but by God, couldn't she see how much he wanted her? Every time she drew near, his breath caught at the slightest hint of her scent. Half the time he swore he imagined the smell.

His willpower had been considerably lacking when it came to giving her lessons in self-pleasure. One look at those flushed cheeks, pointy breasts, hearing those sighs and bit-back moans and he was harder than he had ever been in his life.

He knew he affected her the same way. Every time he fucked her, her wet cunt accepted him eagerly, milked him, until he spent himself inside her.

Hell. What if he'd impregnated her? Why hadn't he thought of that since the first time? It was not like him to be so careless.

Mark strolled unseeing through the house and escaped into the park. If he became a father . . .

Would he do the same as his own had done and barely recognize the child? Would seeing Portia pregnant kill any desire he felt for her?

His brilliant, unwanted solution had included setting her up with the independence she desired, once he tired of her, which was bound to happen if she grew with child.

Right?

He gnawed at his lip, listening to his boots crunch across the grass and the faint singing of birds.

The thought of Portia large with child, with his child, twisted in his vitals. His heart fair broke with the pain of it. He wouldn't leave her, abandon her.

Would he?

Having broken his golden rule once, did he truly expect this desire to last more than a few months, whether Portia fell pregnant or not?

He would take good care of her, he decided. Made sure she didn't end up in some poorhouse with an unwanted brat. Any child of his should be loved.

As he was not.

But how to accomplish this?

He scratched at his head, taking a path leading into the pretty woods that edged Willowhill Hall's broad, expansive lawn.

Portia had to say yes, she had to. She had to realize he'd come up with the best solution for them, one which enabled easy parting when the time inevitably came. One which kept her safe.

A soft moan froze him in his tracks. The womanly sigh sounded again with greater urgency.

He crept forward, careful not to let his foot slide on a stick or decaying leaf. The path opened into a small clearing.

Mark crouched, his eyes unbelieving of what he saw.

Portia—his Portia!—cavorted with the elder Chalcroft girl. Skirts around their waists, the two women lay entwined, mouths fastened on the other's twitching cunt.

Good God.

Mark forgot to breathe. Is this why Portia refused him? Because she harbored a tendré for the Chalcroft girl? Could it be possible Portia wanted her more than she wanted him?

He choked, unable to breathe. He had to get out of there.

Backing out, silent as a woodsman, Mark abandoned the woods and strode back to the house, even more deeply disturbed than when he had left it.

12

Very little escaped the Duke of Winterton. He'd witnessed Miss Chalcroft intercept Miss Carew at the head of the stairs. The light pounding of the woman's feet had alerted him to disharmony in the house.

He'd watched, unseen, as Miss Chalcroft had led a tearful Miss Carew away from the house. He admired Miss Chalcroft's discretion. Whatever Miss Carew's secret, she had just ensured he would not overhear it.

An old man has to have his little pleasures.

He let out a slow breath and moved to a window where he saw the women cross the lawn. He'd learn nothing at this rate.

Fresh stamping across the Barrington's fine parquet floor turned his attention back to the house. He caught a glimpse of Mr. Knightson's face, black as thunder, as the man stormed past and out the door.

In the next moment, fresh movement at the edge of the wood alerted him to the women's return.

Whatever Miss Chalcroft had done, Miss Carew seemed

most recovered. Both women seemed excited, even. How curious.

The duke poured himself some tea. He had half a mind to send his youngest son away from Willowhill. The boy threatened to destroy the Winterton reputation, abandon all that he'd drummed into the child about discretion.

He found it difficult to put credence to the boy's threats to abduct Miss Carew. The woman had more than enough gumption to put the boy in his place.

What's this? The duke settled his teacup into its saucer, looking out the window. Miss Chalcroft strode with purpose, laden with a blanket and a few moments later, Miss Carew appeared carrying a well-laden reticule. *How curious.*

He placed Lady Barrington's fine china onto the side table with unconscious grace, his eyes fixed upon the two women. An impromptu picnic—or something else?

At last, Willowhill Hall provided him with some amusement. He gathered up his tall hat, abandoned after his morning walk, and set out after them.

He flicked his black ebony walking stick forward without effort. He noted Mr. Knightson remained abroad, stalking along the far side of the lawn.

By the time he had reached the small clearing where the women had settled upon blankets, they had already begun. His eyes widened. He'd known of Miss Carew's deep wealth of passion, but he'd had no idea about Miss Chalcroft.

He swallowed, casting about for a more comfortable hiding place than the middle of the small path. He spotted a likely trail branching off to the side, and in a few moments, creeping so as not to be heard, he settled his old bones behind a screen of bushes and ferns.

He would have preferred something better than his coat tails to sit on, but the arch of a fern revealed the two cavorting women and he soon forgot his discomfort.

Miss Carew's rear wriggled with excitement while she applied herself to tasting Miss Chalcroft's quim. Then they changed places. *Oh heavens.*

His black breeches growing tight, Winterton chafed his trapped cock with his hand. Miss Carew cried out for Miss Chalcroft to stop. He heard almost every word, his location a prime position for eavesdropping.

The women kissed. Winterton sucked in air, thinking his heart would stop. His gaze didn't shift from the tableau and he feared to touch his cock again in case he burst before this lovemaking session was over.

When Miss Carew drew out the dildo, Winterton unbuttoned his breeches, his cock springing free. He watched the women fashion a harness for the dildo, tying it around Miss Chalcroft's slender hips.

They lay together, Miss Carew moaning while Miss Chalcroft slid the dildo inside. He closed his hand around his cock, stroking it in time with Miss Chalcroft's inexpert thrusts.

When the impertinent Miss Carew rolled Miss Chalcroft beneath her, he matched her quickening pace. *Oh heavens, oh heavens!*

Winterton bit down in his lip, watching his semen fly from his cock. With a shaking hand, he tucked his spent penis away and buttoned up his breeches.

Oh heavens. Would that he could view these women for his personal entertainment whenever he wished. Miss Carew lay beyond his control, but Miss Chalcroft . . .

The women lay spent on the blanket. Winterton overheard them talk, learning of Lucy's coming in quick succession and her unpalatable future as her mother's companion.

Waiting until they were gone, Winterton unbent himself from his cramped position. He groaned with the agony of creaking bones and protesting muscles. He was getting too old for this.

Next time, he planned to watch in comfort.

* * *

Washed and dressed, Portia joined the assembling guests for dinner. Lucy smiled at her from her mother's side, looking very pretty, almost glowing.

Is that what I look like after sex? Portia wondered, sticking to the fringes of the group. With Lucy unable to converse, she didn't want to talk to anybody.

Least of all, her dinner partner, Knightson.

"Miss Carew?" He bowed before her and extended his arm to escort her into dinner. His voice, cool and polite, held all the warmth of a stranger, which is to say, none at all.

They entered the dining room and she glanced up at him. His hard, immobile features held no emotion and even his eyes were ice chips. He smiled not at her, nor anybody else.

Sir Guy echoed Knightson's black mood, glaring at both Knightson and herself. Portia frowned. If Sir Guy had determined a connection, then he would use it to his advantage. That he didn't seem to recognize the stiff coldness between her and Knightson might well be a mixed blessing.

Lady Cecily had eyes for nobody but Knightson and her acuity in body language seemed to far exceed Sir Guy's for she shot Portia a triumphant leer before involving herself in conversation with the people around her.

Freddy Barrington managed to keep up his end of the conversation. He tried to talk past the people between him and draw Miss Sophia into the conversation, longing writ clear on his face.

Sophia blushed and flirted, not seeming to mind the boldness this required in order to transmit her feelings across two couples.

The Duke of Winterton nodded at the conversation at the head of the table, but he seemed not himself, deep in thought. Portia caught his gaze once or twice, receiving a nod of recognition, but no more. His gaze settled often on Miss Chalcroft, but Portia wondered if he really saw Lucy at all, given his absent expression.

Young Winterton stared sullenly into his soup, leaving Portia's mother to fend for herself. Which she ably did, diving into the spirited conversation that Lady Barrington led, no doubt desperate to avoid complete silence falling upon her table.

After an awkward dinner, the women fled to the nearby sitting room. Lady Barrington poured the tea, asking Lucy to pass out the cups.

Lucy took the last two cups and sat beside Portia, near the fireplace. Portia lifted her gaze from the sparking flames and accepted the cup of tea.

"Now that I can think again," Lucy began, keeping her voice low. "I wanted to know why you want Knightson to propose. You don't want to get married."

"I told you I do not know." Portia softened her sharp snapping tones. "I'm sorry, Lucy, but I have been thinking of nothing else. I did not want to marry because I knew I would be used, like Sir Guy used me, and then abandoned to care for the heir and spare, while my husband picked out a new mistress. I would rather be alone, honestly, rather than live with the hypocrisy of that marriage. I don't think there is a man alive who would remain faithful to me, not even Knightson."

"And yet?" Lucy prompted.

"It's foolish, but while he has taken from me, he has given also. Even his proposal for me to become—" Portia's voice lowered further, and she shot a nervous glance over at the other women. Of all of them, only Lady Cecily leaned toward the two women, wanting to overhear their whispered conversation. "Even his proposal for me to become his—his mistress was filled with care. He promised to take care of me when he tired of me."

"Seems like an awful backward way to go about it." Lucy's lips twisted. "Hardly flattering to say: 'I want to bed you but I will leave you.'"

"It's practical," Portia argued. Now, she defended the rogue? "But can you trust that he would do so?"

"He said he would put it all in writing, a legal document."

"And if he reneged?"

Portia stared, wide-eyed, at her friend. "He's a *gentleman*, Lucy! He'd never go back on his word."

Lucy gurgled in laughter. "Oh, Portia. The truth is that you are in love with him."

"No." Portia's low-voiced refusal was sincere.

"I fear it is true." Lucy patted her arm. "You must choose to follow that love and risk everything, or step away from him now. Do not go to him tonight. Save yourself."

Not go to him? "I cannot run away. You are right, I must end this. Better to give him his answer tonight, than to be forced into it at some other place and time not of our choosing." Portia clasped Lucy's hands in turn. "You do understand?"

"You are the soul of discretion." Lucy sighed. "Or a fool."

Portia acknowledged the hit with a smile.

"Lucy!" Mrs. Chalcroft called, beckoning the girl over.

Lucy sighed deeper this time, but she rose, leaving Portia alone in communion with the flames.

Shortly thereafter, the men entered, all of them, with the exception of young Winterton, exceedingly jolly. They mingled with the women at once and Sir Guy took Lucy's place beside Portia.

"My dear, why so gloomy?" His hand fell upon her knee.

Portia twitched her leg away. "It is you who have made me so," she lied.

"Me?" Sir Guy laid his offending hand over his heart. "Are you regretting your refusal of my offer?"

"Hardly." Portia did not look at him, staring at the fire.

"Portia, my sweet. I imagine you were quite taken by Knightson's appearance in the library today. Did that boorish fellow cast you off?"

"Sir Guy, please stop fishing. You could make insinuations against all the men here and I would not tell you." She turned to look at him and found him closer than she liked. She dared not shrink away. "For all you know, my tastes have sunk to enjoying the footmen."

Sir Guy barked a laugh. "Your tastes would never sink that low, my dear."

Portia's lip curled. "Why not? They sank to include you."

He grabbed her upper arm and tugged her toward him. "Minx. Whore," he growled under his breath.

A shadow fell over them. "I say, do not handle Miss Carew so." Young Winterton stood before them, his face suffused with anger.

"Why not?" retorted Sir Guy, not releasing his hold. "I heard you have done worse."

"And repented of it," Young Winterton replied. "I was wrong to do so. Miss Carew is a goddess and I won't see her so abused."

Sir Guy let out the laugh Portia swallowed. "A goddess? You are but a boy if you think so."

Young Winterton puffed out his chest. "I am a man, sir, and if you doubt it, I suggest you meet me on the lawn at sunrise tomorrow. Would pistols suit you?"

Lady Barrington let out a shrill cry that merged with Portia's.

"I will not have it!" Portia got to her feet, shaking off Sir Guy's loosened grip and clutching young Winterton's elbow. She turned to look down at Sir Guy, who still laughed at them. "Sir Guy Symon, you will apologize to us both if you have the slightest shred of decency."

"I second that suggestion." The Duke of Winterton spoke

up, not shifting from his lounging position beside Mrs. Chalcroft. "You have vilified Miss Carew once already, Sir Guy. I do not suggest you do so again, else I shall call you out as well."

"And I," said Freddy, ignoring Miss Sophia's scowl. "Miss Carew is a good egg and Gareth is a jolly fellow."

Under the applied pressure of the group—Knightson muttering something along with the others—Sir Guy had no other recourse but apologize. He bowed prettily to Portia. "My dear, it is your beauty that quite robs me of all delicate speech. Do forgive me."

He delivered a shorter bow. "You also, Winterton."

Without waiting for either of them to accept his apology, Sir Guy stepped toward Lady Barrington and delivered an even more florid bow. "Forgive me, my lady, for disturbing your evening. I fear I must have imbibed too much brandy."

"Then we shall excuse you for this evening," Lady Barrington said, a chill in her voice.

Sir Guy bowed again and quit the room.

The tension lessened at his absence. Portia turned to Gareth Winterton, still clutching at his coat sleeve. "How can I thank you?"

A smiling leer crossed his face. "I can think of many ways," he murmured. The leer vanished. "There is no need to thank me, Miss Carew. Just doing my duty as a gentleman." He gathered up her hand and kissed the back of it. He whispered over it, "Father will not have it."

"I know," she whispered back, giving his hand a sympathetic squeeze. She had no desire to wed young Winterton, nor the elder, but she couldn't help feeling sorry for the fellow.

"Will you join me in a hand of whist?" Young Winterton asked.

"Of course."

She glanced at Knightson, deep in conversation with Lord Barrington, before passing away the rest of the night amidst much merriment. Freddy Barrington and Miss Sophia joined them and a spirited, rowdy game ensued.

She needed that. She laughed at young Winterton's woebegone expression as they lost yet another hand, and crowed in triumph whenever they defeated Freddy and Sophia.

Among the last to leave, with Lucy chaperoning them, they quit the drawing room. Still laughing over their win, Freddy and Sophia ascended the stairs ahead of the others, and when Freddy claimed a kiss at the top of the stairs, Portia cheered in unison with the others.

Young Winterton caught her by the waist, giving her a quick one-armed hug before letting her go.

When they reached the top of the stairs, he gave both Portia and Lucy a formal bow and headed for his rooms without a word.

Despite Lucy's happy chatter, dread settled upon Portia. Did Knightson wait for her now? Was she truly ready to catapult herself into infamy? Abandon that last grasp of respectability?

She shivered beneath Lucy's quick, understanding hug and slipped inside her room.

Her maid undressed her and finally left her in peace. She sat in front of the vanity mirror and stared at herself. How could she change her answer from no?

How could she not? Despite her carefree airs that night, she'd been aware of his brooding presence hovering in the background. She'd done everything to forget he was there, and had almost succeeded.

She wanted him. Portia couldn't deny it. She didn't want this night to be the last with him.

But give up everything?

No closer to an answer, she crept upstairs until the narrowing staircase opened out onto the roof. Had she not been the occasional childhood playmate of Freddy's, she'd never have found it.

She stepped around a chimney and saw Knightson.

He had spread blankets in shades of reds and blues across the flat roof and had lit an assortment of candles, setting the roof aglow.

Knightson wore nothing but a dressing robe, the candlelight picking up its rich crimson hues. The collar was black velvet, and as Portia stepped closer, she itched to stroke her hands along it.

He gestured she sit on the blanket. Wrapping her silk robe even more tightly about herself, she sank to the ground, tucking her legs beneath her.

"Have you reconsidered your answer?" His face mostly in shadow, she saw only the plane of one cheek and his jutting chin.

"I have thought about it, but have not changed my mind." She tried to keep her voice cool and steady, but it wobbled into a tremulo at the end. How else should she answer? Self-preservation came first.

Which is not to say she didn't burn to submit to him now.

He remained still. When he spoke at last, his flat voice chilled her more than the night air. "Then let us see what you have learned."

Portia peeled the robe back, letting it fall off her shoulders. It puddled around her. Beneath she wore a fine lawn nightgown. Translucent, it hinted at her curves, thanks to the candlelight surrounding her.

She straightened her back, meeting his hidden gaze. She knew what she had to do. In a way, her interlude with Lucy that afternoon had been a practice run.

Except this time she was alone.

Pitching her voice low, Portia spoke as she hitched up the hem of her nightgown over her knees. "The first thing you taught me was to use my imagination. So I'm imagining you—"

She shouldn't, it brought fresh dangers to her independence, but she did.

She swallowed. "I'm imagining you as a sultan, lying among your pillows. You're watching me perform. If I please you, I will join your harem. If I do not, you will cast me into the streets."

Ducking her head, she swallowed her tears again. The fantasy had leapt in her mind, unbidden, but it veered too close to her real predicament.

Well, she had made her choice.

"I know you are naked under your robe, ready to ravish me at moment's notice. If you do, I know I will have succeeded."

She lifted her hands to her still-covered breasts. "I imagine your mouth covering my nipples, sucking me through my thin robe."

Closing her eyes, she plucked and teased at her nipples. The last traces of awkwardness faded away beneath the rising heat emanating from her own touch.

She didn't need him.

She pulled at the ribbon that tied the neck of the gown close to her skin. The knot fell free and the folds of the soft linen fell back in two flaps. Her palms concealed her bared bosom, shifting subtly over the hard nubs.

Her breath escaped in a long sigh. She reclined, still fondling her bosom, cushions waiting to support her shoulders and head.

Already her quim slicked with wetness, swollen and ready, ached for her touch. She smoothed down her body, making her nightgown cling to her every curve, her bosom rising farther from its prison.

She sighed at the cold air washing over her breasts, ice to quench the fire, except that her nipples tightened harder, shooting a delicious pain through her.

Palming her breasts again, she hoped to ease some of the tautness. Instead, it roused her further. It didn't help that she sensed Knightson's gaze upon her, devouring her without lifting a finger. Like the sultan.

What does he think? Portia wondered while she stroked her body into a keen edge of arousal. Did he find this as exciting as he had before, or was he too angry to allow desire to intervene?

She sighed, slipping her fingers into her crevice at last. She slid over the slippery fluids, coating her entire quim with the heady liquid.

Brushing her clit, she shivered, a warning that completion hovered near. She touched herself there again and again, the sensitive organ growing beneath her incessant touch.

Her cunt muscles clenched, the first fluttering, the first demand to be crammed full of male muscle.

She stopped her playing to unfasten the ties of the reticule she'd brought with her. The freshly cleaned dildo lay inside. She took her time, a silent reminder to Knightson that one of the lessons had been of patience, to delay the final climax.

He shifted, the first movement he'd made since she'd begun her demonstration. She refused to look at him, to acknowledge his presence.

Despite the romantic setting, the night had turned cold. Better to think him absent, not watching. Better to think of some icy-eyed sultan.

She brought herself back to the edge, plying both breast and quim. The sultan would be bearded, she decided, his bristles burning her quim with its prickles. His long and slender tongue slipped inside her cunt so easily.

She slid two fingers in, writhing on the blanket, not quite yet ready for the dildo. The heat rose from her quim, rising to coat her belly and breasts with its heat.

"And now I know I have won," she gasped. "The sultan commands me to impale myself on his cock." Rising up on her knees, she positioned the dildo between her legs. She sank upon it, her juices so copious it slid right in.

Deep, until the butt of the dildo pressed against her quim. Unyielding, it parted her, nudged at a most sensitive point.

She rubbed herself against it, rising and falling to mimic thrusts. Her breaths came short and sharp. Her head fell back. She was close, so close.

"Stop." Knightson's low-voiced command cut across her senses. Beyond his command, she pushed for her release.

With a growl, Knightson crawled forward, plucking the dildo from her quim.

Wide-eyed with shock at his interruption, Portia swayed. His robe had fallen apart, his cock an eager spear to pierce her. She accepted his offering without a word, sitting in his lap and wrapping her legs around his torso.

He filled her, stretched her, his expansive, pulsing cock out-matching the dildo by far. He crammed inside her until she consumed all of him.

The breath hitched in her throat. She begged him with a single word. "Mark."

He flexed his pelvis, somehow sending him deeper before his muscles relaxed. Mark continued the slow motion, rocking himself in and out of her.

Each short thrust made her gasp, for her clit ended buried and teased in his curls, his cock pushing at some place inside her that wanted more and more of it.

The strange sense of longing and belonging swept over her again, buoyed by the increasing fire of her approaching release. She embraced it, letting the sweet sensations wash over her, clinging to Mark, nails digging into his flesh. Every breath was his breath.

She drew closer and closer to climax, yet it remained out of reach. Portia clawed at his back, her moans begging him to complete her.

At last, with a growl, he hoisted her by her buttocks and bore her beneath him, covering her body.

His hips bucked, pounding her quim with all his vigor.

She clung to him, her senses dissolving into release. All fire and liquid, she drowned in her own coming.

And coming. It seemed to never end, a continuous pulsing and writhing. Limp in his arms, another climax rocked through her, one last wave of fire.

He gripped her tightly, a groan emanating from the depths of his belly. He stiffened and his cock melted inside her, shooting his come until it spilled out of her.

He rested upon his elbows, his face hidden against her shoulder, his torso shuddering.

Portia stared up at the stars, holding Mark in a loose embrace. What did those fiery stars see? Did they remark on their animal coupling? Or the tenderness that followed?

Her heart filled with the strange emotion. She wanted to apologize for every sharp word, to soothe and kiss his sweaty brow until he smiled and kissed her senseless.

She wanted impossible things. Her throat tightened and she willed even breaths to occur. Tears pricked at the corners of her eyes, but she blinked them away.

He could not see her vulnerability. Not here, like this.

Mark raised his head, his features almost invisible from the sputtering candlelight. "You're tense," he murmured.

She tried to relax and met his concern with a shaky smile. "I failed, didn't I?"

"You did very well, too well. I couldn't resist you, Portia. I wanted to join with you." His lips twisted into a grimace. "It was selfish of me to do so, now that I know you prefer your own sex."

She blinked up at him. "My—what?"

"I saw you and Miss Chalcroft in the woods. I saw enough to know you enjoyed it. I understand now why you refused me."

Portia puffed an exasperated laugh. "Lucy has nothing to do with refusing you. I was teaching her as you taught me. She too, has a loveless future ahead of her and it seemed wrong to let her take that journey unequipped." She chuckled. "We did get rather carried away, but it wasn't Lucy's softness, it was imagining your mouth upon me, and your cock in me."

He tilted his head to one side. "You used the dildo?"

"Mm-hm." She licked her lips, summoning up the courage to speak. "I—I seem to need, ahh, something inside me."

He brushed her nose with his lips. "No, you do not. I recall some pretty explosive releases."

She "mmm"-ed again.

Mark seemed disinclined to move, allowing silence to fall. She reveled in his warmth, his closeness, but didn't want to think of what it meant. Most likely, it meant nothing at all.

Imagine lying in his arms every night, sated with their love-making—

Not love. But lust. If it were love, he'd want something more permanent.

"Portia," he murmured, his voice a delicious low burr that sent her toes curling. "We are good together."

"Yes." The affirmation escaped her lips before she even thought about concealing her agreement.

"This is the fifth time I have lain with you and still I want more. If you will not . . . if you will not become my mistress," Mark's voice wavered with uncertainty, "would you consider remaining lovers until it is time to leave here?"

Portia caught her breath. "You tempt me." She reached up and caressed his cheek. "What if we're caught?"

He captured her hand, kissed her palm. "We won't be caught. We have not been yet." His teeth grazed her skin. "Say you will, Portia."

"What happened to the quick ending if I refused you?"

190 / Celia May Hart

Mark reared back, slipping from her, his sex all soft. "You would prefer that?"

"Mark," she chided him, her voice warm with teasing.

"Ah." He took a deep breath. "I thought of nothing else while watching you masturbate. I thought again and again I should leave tomorrow, but I cannot. I cannot resist you. I have not tasted enough of you, Portia. I want more."

Breathless, Portia found her answer. "I want you too, Mark."

A foolhardy acceptance, but then their whole affair had been wild and foolish.

13

Portia awoke, cocooned in warmth. She snuggled her head deeper into the down pillow. Her body ached. They'd made love again—oh very well, she knew she shouldn't call it "making love," but what else should she call their sexual intercourse? It was not some cold, clinical thing, nor was it all hot lust. Their second time had been delicious and tender.

Afterward, he'd doused the candles that were still lit. She'd lain there, watching his muscular form as he padded about the blankets doing this menial task. Portia had thought she'd never be able to move again. All her limbs had turned to jelly.

In darkness, lit only by a half-moon, he picked her up and felt his way downstairs. She'd fallen asleep on the way, rocked by his strong arms and soothed by the pounding of his heart.

Now, her eyes fluttered open, blinking at the unfamiliar sight.

That wasn't her side table. Blue wasn't the color of her walls.

She rolled, the cotton sheets teasing her body into aware life. "Good morning," Mark's familiar voice burred from the foot of the bed. "I have taken the liberty of ordering breakfast for us both."

Portia pushed herself upright in bed, not caring that she revealed her nakedness to him. "Are you mad? I thought we were to be discreet!"

Mark smiled lazily. He sat in a large wing chair, his robe cast loosely about his muscular body. Dark hair sprinkled his chest, leading a line down to where his cock rested, for now.

"We are," he said. "Nobody saw you, my dear Portia. It is early yet. You have time to breakfast and return to your room before anyone stirs."

"Why did you not take me back to my room?" Portia couldn't—wouldn't move from the bed until she'd had her answer. What had he been thinking?

"Come." He gestured with his hand. "Have some tea. The reason why you are not ensconced in your own bed is that I do not know where it is."

She blinked. "You don't?"

"If I had I would have ravished you a thousand times before last night." His feral grin matched the sudden bobbing of his cock.

Heat swooped through her. With just a word, just a look, she was his.

She scrambled out of bed, walking naked toward him. She smiled at the fresh lurch of his cock and casually picked up a cup from the breakfast tray.

She settled onto a low footrest before him, reaching for some toast to nibble. She crunched on the bread, eyes on the carpet.

Unable to explain her sudden shyness, she finished off the small slice of toast and reached for a cup of tea.

"Having second thoughts?" Mark's soft voice cut across her munching.

"No." Her quick response dragged her gaze up to his. "I just wonder what happens next."

His wide, lazy grin gave her more than a few suggestions. She at once imagined his body on hers, surrendering to him and being filled with indescribable bliss, the power of sexual release.

"Dear God," she murmured.

"Amen." Mark's dark eyebrow quirked. "You should see yourself, Portia. You're so full of life, you are glowing with it. A woman of passion, like you, should not be wasted."

She huffed. "I am not being wasted."

"After the house party—"

"No, Mark. I have given you my answer on that and it will not change."

His grin turned wicked, and he leaned toward her. "It might."

She rose, her posture erect, although her breasts sparked with hot leaden desire. She put all the ice in her command into voice. "If you insist on this course of conversation, I shall end this liaison now. Then you don't have to break your silly rule."

"I already have." He sobered, pulling his robe closer about him. "Eat your breakfast," he snapped.

She grinned and surveyed the tray, reaching for a plump sausage. Willowhill Hall made their own sausages. Thin, creamy intestines encased the minced pork and herbs. An inch and a half thick and six inches long, it was certainly not a bite-size morsel.

Her lips closed over the end of the sausage, tasting the salty surface. Before she bit down, Mark had recovered his good humor and flicked open his robe, showing a stiffening cock.

Portia made the connection at once. She smiled, her mouth distorted around the thick sausage. She slipped it from her mouth, resting it upon her lips.

Her stomach rumbled, but she ignored it. "What are you suggesting?"

"Portia love, I have tasted you, why should you not do the same? Show me what you would do." His cock bobbed, daring her.

She didn't need any further urging. Her tongue curled around the sausage's end. She'd already sucked the salt from it, but a strong meaty taste remained.

Did Mark taste like an English breakfast sausage? She swallowed a giggle and extended her tongue, laving the sausage's sides with long, slow licks.

The smooth and firm texture of the sausage felt more like the dildo Mark had gifted her with than the velvety, shifting steel of his cock.

"Suck it." Mark's command halted her licking.

She obeyed, taking the sausage into her mouth partway. Compressing her lips, she sucked, getting a squirt of greasy juice down her throat. She choked, partly on laughter.

She bobbed the sausage in and out of her mouth, imagining her mouth as her cunt, and the sausage, naturally, as his cock. The friction in her mouth transferred to a tingling in her quim.

Moaning softly, she parted her lips, grazing the sausage with her teeth.

Mark echoed her moan, stroking his cock in unison with her sucking of the mock-cock. "Go deeper," he groaned, his skin bunching around his cock head.

Deeper? The sausage slipped free of her mouth. "If I do that, I'll swallow it."

He opened his mouth to protest, she winked at him and he shut it with a snap.

Portia bit off the end of the sausage. Grinning between chews, she swallowed the bite and polished off the remainder. "My apologies," she said, "I was famished." She stepped toward him. "Now," she purred, "let's see how deep I can go."

She slipped to her knees between his parted thighs, bending forward and giving him a view of black hair coursing down her back, brushing her pert buttocks wriggling forward.

Knowing that he gazed upon her nakedness aroused her more, wet heat rising between her legs. She took him into her mouth, letting him slide deep in one long, slow movement until he pressed at the back of her throat.

She inhaled a sharp breath, her nose filled with his musky scent and more than a hint of her own juices, merged with his.

Merged. If it could always be that way.

Portia banished the thought, took another breath and relaxed her throat, letting his head slip into her throat. It had taken a lot of practice with Sir Guy before she'd managed this without gagging, but now, at least, she had this gift to give back to Mark.

He pulsed inside her mouth. Portia nodded, his cock moving in and out of her throat in short thrusts. She slowed, keeping him deep and using her tongue to ply his velvety sheath.

With her fingertips, she teased his balls, there one moment and gone the next.

A feeling of power surged through her. He lay beneath her, responding to her every touch. His hot hands curled in her hair, and yet he didn't force her, didn't shift his hips to pound her throat with his large cock.

He swelled, lengthening and hardening, coming into full arousal. She expected him to lose control then. She felt him tensed, coiled, but somehow he kept it reined in.

Tilting her head, she peeked through the curls fallen over her forehead at him.

His closed eyes squeezed shut, his body a tight rictus of control, every muscle tensed. His face glowed, a strange suffusion of pleasure and . . . and something else.

She looked down again before he caught her watching him. His hands tightened for a moment in her hair. He'd noticed.

She redoubled her efforts in pleasuring him, pumping his cock in and out of her mouth. She gave up the feathery teasing of his balls to stroke and lightly squeeze them.

She would make him come. Make him come so hard. Harder than he'd ever done. She wanted him to feel what she did when she climaxed under his touch.

Maybe then . . .

Her teeth grazed along the full length of his cock until the tip balanced upon her lips. He shuddered beneath her, his hands convulsing in her hair.

Again and again, she drew him in. Her entire body thrummed with the echo of his arousal. She wanted more than anything to have him flip her onto her back and pound her with his cock, fuck her senseless.

But more than that, much more than that, she wanted this pleasure for him. This affair would not last: he had made that patently clear, but she would brand him with her memory— with this.

She'd driven him to the edge. His thighs flexed and he attempted a gentle thrust into her mouth.

Portia let his cock slip free. She licked her lips, looking up at him. "Go on, Mark," she purred. "Fuck me. Fuck my mouth. Let go. Relax."

He broke off a choked laugh that turned into a moan when she took his straining cock into her mouth again.

He waited until he rested deep in her throat. His thrusts stayed gentle but grew in urgency, plowing a silver strand of desire from her mouth to her groin.

She'd not touched herself, but her cunt tingled with the imminent promise of release. She buried her nose into his curls, rising up to take him even deeper, and the first rush of release overtook her.

In shock, she sucked him hard, squeezing him hard. He

groaned and lost all control. He held her head against his groin, fucking her hard while she felt her own come coat her curls.

He came in an explosive burst, filling her with his salty fluid. She let not a single drop escape, swallowing every last bit.

At last, she let his cock escape her mouth and rested her head against his quivering thigh.

Taking long, shuddering breaths, Portia lay there, content to listen to his racing pulse in his thigh. Through half-closed eyes, she watched his cock, wet with saliva and jism, subside into its quiescent length, draped over his balls.

Mark stirred, bending forward to gather her in his arms. He drew her up the length of his body without any apparent effort.

She braced herself on the headrest behind him, gazing down at him, his lap wet and sticky against her buttocks.

He stared up at her. His blue eyes for once had lost their chill. "You are a wonder," he breathed huskily. "I swear I could not stir a muscle."

Portia chuckled, not daring to mention the way he had effortlessly lifted her into his lap. She snuggled close to him. "You are pleased."

"Beyond words." His forefinger traced along her cheekbone to her chin. An expression of wonder on his face, he cupped her neck and drew her in for a kiss.

He must have tasted his own jism, but Portia didn't care, deepening the kiss and plundering his mouth, wanting to crawl inside of him and bask in his heat.

He broke off the kiss, leaving them both panting for air. "You need to dress," he murmured. "The house will be stirring soon." He stroked her hair. "Would that you never needed to leave this room."

Portia heartily agreed. Curled on his lap, the outside world ceased to exist. She almost hated him for reminding her of it.

"When can we—" She trailed off, not sure how to finish the question.

"I will find a way." Despite his pronouncement that she had to leave, he fingered her nipple into sharp prominence. "Tomorrow morning, before dawn, in the stables."

"What about the stable boys?"

"They won't tattle. I'll have my valet drink them into a stupor tonight." His confidence wavered. "You will come?"

"With your help." She grinned, standing. She found her nightgown and pulled it over her head. She freed her head to see him smiling, amused, at her. "It will be difficult. To wait until tomorrow."

His lips twisted. "Perhaps you can give Miss Chalcroft another lesson."

She patted him on the cheek. "Do not be jealous, Mark. You have nothing to fear in that regard." She put on her robe. "But do you have another, ahh, dildo?"

"You imagine I carry a store of them around?"

"I imagine you have many uses for the thing besides what you showed me." She ducked her head shyly. "I would like to learn them."

"The other ways—are not for solo use," he warned, his brows lowering.

He got to his feet, however, and padded over to a chest of drawers. He removed another small bag. "It is smaller, but if Miss Chalcroft has kept her virginity—"

"She has."

"—then she might get more joy from this. Where will you tell her you got it?"

Portia glanced at the expensive rug. "From where I got the first one." She took a deep breath and met his eyes squarely. "She knows about you . . . about us."

She heard Mark suck in air. "You trust her?"

"Would I have taught her what I've learned from you if I

didn't?" Portia knotted the robe's sash about her waist with a sharp tug.

Mark, his face again a mask, handed her the bulging bag. "I left yours on the roof. You shall have to collect it later. Or I could have my valet deliver it to your maid."

Portia hastily shook her head. "No. Tell your man to leave it. I shall fetch it myself."

Surveying the room, she gave Mark one last, long look before fleeing his bed chamber. She didn't know what he saw on her face. She didn't want to know, but hoped she hadn't revealed her longing for him, her wish that they didn't have to mingle in public Society for, well, forever.

Miss Lucy Chalcroft entered the blue salon, hands primly clasped in front of her. She sank into a deep curtsey to the back of the Duke of Winterton.

"Your Grace sent for me?" she said in a clear voice. The duke was older than her mother and in his evening conversations with her mother, Lucy had been made aware of his slight hearing loss.

The Duke, his elbow propped on the fireplace mantel, turned his head to survey her.

She repressed the urge to squirm and bobbed a sketched curtsey. "Is Your Grace in need of something?"

"Indeed, I am." He rolled away from the fireplace and gestured to the cream brocade sofa. "Miss Chalcroft, sit if you please."

Lucy obeyed, settling herself on the sofa's edge. She twisted her upper body slightly to keep him in view.

He strolled around the sofa and stood before her on the rich autumnal carpet. Leaning on his silver-topped cane, he cleared his throat. "I fear I do not know quite where to begin."

A duke, uncertain? Lucy smiled with encouragement up at him. "If I may be at all of service, your Grace."

Winterton harrumphed and took a seat next to her. "Ah, yes. As to that, my dear, I understand you have no expectations of marriage?"

"None." Lucy kept her response calm and steady. Her mother had seemed oddly excited that the duke wished to see her, but Lucy guessed its cause was from receiving ducal notice.

"But there is none who has your heart?" the duke continued, having apparently received the answer he expected. "I wish you to be honest."

Lucy tilted her head, studying him. *What a most peculiar direction for conversation.* "There is no one, your Grace. That is to say, there was one, once, but he has long since married and sired children."

"You are quite sure? No special friends?"

"I wonder at your quizzing me so, your Grace. No, there is nobody."

"I imagine you would not tell me if there were."

She risked much by speaking her mind, but the duke appeared to be asking for frankness. "Indeed, your Grace. It is none of your business."

"That is well." The duke gave her an approving smile. "The Wintertons pride discretion above all else."

Lucy wondered where that left honor and morals. She ought not think such a hypocritical thought: her interlude with Portia called into question her purity and innocence. And yet, Portia's womanhood had prevented her from being despoiled.

Not that it mattered to anyone, or Lucy, doomed to be her mother's helpmeet.

"You are very good at caring for your mother," remarked the duke as if he read her mind.

"Thank you, your Grace." She still wondered what he wanted from her, but didn't dare ask again. At such an aristocratic level as a dukedom, a longwinded request fell under the allowances one made for the upper aristocracy.

"There is nothing quite like the personal care of someone close to you." Winterton fiddled with the glittering top of his cane. "As a widower, I know this."

Lucy didn't quite know what to say. "You miss your wife."

"She was my soul's mate," the duke acknowledged. "There will not be another like her."

His melancholy tones rendered her silent. She waited, watching his fine, aristocratic profile, as still as marble, any emotion frozen.

His smile melted all that. "I know you are curious, Miss Chalcroft, and so I shall explain all, so you may understand. You see, I do know you have a special friend, despite your denials, and you have intrigued me ever since."

Lucy frowned. "Your Grace, I think you may be mistaken."

He gave an impatient shake of his head. "I speak of Miss Carew."

"She is a dear friend," Lucy agreed, perhaps too hastily. "I do not see—"

For an old man, he moved like quicksilver, his forefinger curling under her chin. "But I did see."

Her breath sucked inwards and she stared, panicked, at his amused visage.

Winterton continued in a low, soft voice. "I saw you and Miss Carew cavorting in a most intimate manner in a pretty glade in the woods."

Lucy struggled to breathe. "You saw?"

"Almost all of it." His smile turned ferocious. "I found it most pleasing to me."

"Pleasing." Lucy repeated the foreign-sounding word.

"I already knew Miss Carew to be a woman of great passion," Winterton continued not acknowledging Lucy's blushing confusion. Did anyone not know Portia's secret? "However, I found her not to my tastes. She reminded me much of my late wife, but I am so much older now that I would not properly satisfy her."

He reached out and gathered one of her trembling hands in his. "My dear, you have no expectations of marriage, and nothing but a dull existence ahead of you. Miss Carew, on the other hand, is certain to lead a life of adventure and come to a bad end.

"You, my dear Miss Chalcroft, you need me."

"I need you?" Lucy echoed.

"You do indeed," the duke affirmed, giving her hand a squeeze. "Has not your experience with Miss Carew awakened desires in you?"

Her cheeks burned. "Your Grace, I—"

He patted their joined hands. "My dear, there is no need for you to say anything. My first plan was to simply take you as my mistress." He ignored Lucy's pained intake of breath. "Your mother would rather you a mistress to a great man, than to be discredited as a whore—which you would be, if your session with Miss Carew ever came out."

Struggling to breathe through the tight iron bands of pain about her chest, Lucy grasped at a hopeful straw. "You said . . . you said that was your first plan?"

He chuckled. "So quick to see the way out, Miss Chalcroft. Yes, that was my first plan and then I realized that would not do. As my mistress, other men would become attracted to you and try to win you away from me, my sons not the least of the possible contenders. No, Miss Chalcroft, I decided I must make you mine."

"Yours?" Her suddenly high-pitched voice wobbled.

"Yes, Miss Chalcroft. There is one thing that I must ask of you first before I will offer for you."

"What is that?" Lucy squeaked.

"We must be in accord in the marriage bed, and there is only one way to discover this."

Lucy cringed away. "You want to bed me?"

The duke leaned forward. "I do, Miss Chalcroft," he said, his gaze fastened upon her lips.

"What prevents you then from declaring me a whore if I do not satisfy you?"

The duke slowly shook my head. "You have forgotten the Winterton creed. Discretion above all else. If we do not suit, I will let you go freely."

Lucy frowned. "But ruined."

"You insist on making this difficult, I see." He released her, covering his lips with his fingertips while he surveyed her. "I had hoped you would be more open to this, given my observations."

Lucy's back straightened. "I am sorry to disappoint you, your Grace."

He rose, striding away, leaning heavily upon his cane. Until now, Lucy had thought it a mere affectation. "I will give you a few minutes to consider this, Miss Chalcroft. I have provided you with a great opportunity—"

"Your Grace, I have not declined any opportunity." Lucy swelled with pride at her steady voice. "You may wish to consider that you have overrated the importance of our compatibility in the marriage bed."

He faced her again. "That you speak so calmly, gives me some hope." He studied her and she remained still under his steady gaze. "At worst," he mused aloud, "I would have you as my helpmeet to ease me through my coming old age."

Lucy forbore to mention she thought he was already at that stage.

"You do not compare to my late wife," he continued.

Lucy did her best to keep her expression wooden. If she accepted him, would she be compared to the late duchess for the rest of her life?

"Yet, fortune may smile upon me and you will give me as

much pleasure, if not more than what I received watching you yesterday." His lower lip drooped. "I had hoped you would be pleased at the chance to become a duchess."

"Oh!" The realization struck her. "Oh, I had not thought!" The idea loomed suggestively. Lucy took one steadying breath, and then another.

The Duke of Winterton watched her through all of this. He nodded at some private conclusion. "You are an uncommon woman, Miss Chalcroft."

He returned to her, standing right in front of her. She tilted her head to meet his gaze. "I beg you will forgive my not kneeling, but Miss Chalcroft, I would be honored if you would become my wife."

Lucy stared at him, trying to pierce his mask of respectability. Should she answer yes?

"I assure you, that my word is true. If you accept me, I shall marry you, no matter what happens."

That settled it. Marriage to the duke meant escape from her mother and a chance at last to be what she had always dreamed of but had resigned herself to never coming true: a wife. "Yes, your Grace, I accept your proposition."

"Excellent." He cast himself onto the sofa next to her, his arm going about her shoulders. "Now kiss me."

He said it in tones so low and thrilling that Lucy obeyed him without thought. She knew better than to deliver a chaste kiss. He knew she lacked innocence in that, at least. She pressed her mouth against his, flicking her tongue against his lips.

They parted easily, his tongue storming her mouth, taking possession of her more surely than her simply worded acceptance.

Lucy linked her hands behind his neck, moaning into his mouth. She didn't expect these overwhelming sensations. He didn't taste horrid, or old, but took command of their kiss like a young lover.

He guided her to lie back on the sofa, his body pressing against her, his hands roaming. In moments, he evoked the same sweet sensations that Portia had, coaxing her bosom into hard pinpricks of heat.

His hands slid down along her stays to her thighs. Lucy let go of him to hitch up her skirts, much of the fabric trapped by the duke's lower body.

The duke ended the kiss, tugging her lower lip with his teeth. Her eyes watered from the sharp pain. "Yes," he groaned, his hips already thrusting against her. "We shall do well together, Miss Chalcroft."

Somehow, she managed to catch her breath. "I think, your Grace, that perhaps now you may call me Lucy."

"Lucy." He breathed her name, swooping in for another kiss. "Sweet Lucy, you are mine."

14

Portia hastened to reach the drawing room, where the Barringtons' guests awaited the call to dinner. Every moment separated from Mark Knightson had been torture.

Not just from physical longing for him, but the dread that he would, after all, betray her to the others and have her banished. It was her worst nightmare, losing everyone, even him.

He met her brilliant smile with a cautious one of his own. At once, she dampened down her sudden transparency and turned away from him, joining her mother.

Portia shot a smile at Lucy, who ducked her head. Miss Chalcroft sat between her mother and the Duke of Winterton, with Miss Sophia sulking behind them.

The last of the gentlemen arrived, and the Duke of Winterton rose. "Everyone is here?" He surveyed the assembled guests. Portia felt the heat of his gaze for a moment before he passed onto the next. Was he about to reveal their entanglement?

"Most excellent, for I have an announcement to make," the duke continued.

Portia sucked in her breath and held it.

"It is my pleasure to present to you the next Duchess of Winterton." The duke turned and beamed down at Lucy, holding out his hand. "Miss Chalcroft has done me the honor of agreeing to become my wife."

Watching the blushing Lucy rise, Portia's eyes almost fell out of her head. Lucy? And the duke? Did she know what she let herself in for?

Young Winterton gave voice to her astonishment. "You're making that mouse a Winterton duchess! You deny me my heart's desire and now, now . . ." He waved his hand in the air, his face suffused purple. "Now, *this*!"

The Duke of Winterton stood, still and cold as an icicle. Portia had expected Lucy to cringe behind the duke, but instead she drew closer and shot Portia a brief, beseeching look.

She sighed. She supposed that seeing as young Winterton had submitted to her will once, he might well do so again. She crossed the room and laid an hand on young Winterton's twitching arm. "My lord, you are making a scene."

He shrugged out of her loose touch. "Miss Carew, forgive me for disappointing you. I shall retire." He bowed to Lady and Lord Barrington. "I have disrupted your festivities again. Please, forgive me."

He bowed once more and left, leaving Miss Carew the new focus of the room.

The duke melted slightly. "Thank you, Miss Carew, for your efforts."

Portia smiled and crossed to them. "I am very happy for you both." She looked at Lucy, searching for any sign of coercion but not finding any. She knew the duke's tactics.

The group's felicitations followed in a rush, the butler's declaration of dinner being ready almost going unheard.

Young Winterton's absence upset the order of precedence. That meant Portia lost Knightson's arm and gained the company of the pouting Miss Sophia.

"Are you not happy with your sister's good fortune?"

"Happy? Why should I be happy? She's too old to be married."

"His Grace does not seem to think so."

Miss Sophia sniffed.

Portia smiled. "You have not thought of the connections. You will be sister to a duchess. You might find a duke of your own, or a viscount or marquess."

"Yes, I know."

This news didn't seem to cheer Miss Sophia at all.

Portia gave up and applied herself to dinner.

After dinner, the women gathered around Lucy, repeating their congratulations.

"But how," asked Lady Cecily, "did you manage to attract the attention of a duke?"

Lucy blushed. "He—he noticed the good care I was taking of mother and that appealed to him. Other than that, I cannot say."

The look she sent Portia sent warning hackles up her spine. What did Lucy try to tell her?

Unfortunately, Lucy remained the center of attention all evening. At last Portia caught a moment of privacy with her as the guests dispersed for the night.

They trailed behind the other guests. "Lucy, the duke?" whispered Portia. "I can hardly believe it."

"Thank you," Lucy replied, with an ascerbic toss of her blond head.

"Oh, I did not mean . . ." Portia cursed her hasty tongue. "There was no hint of his interest."

"None until yesterday morning." Lucy swallowed, her blue-eyed gaze darting ahead. "He saw us, Portia."

Portia expelled a sharp gasp. "Oh no."

Lucy nodded. "There is no need to fear. He will not tell."

Portia's mind raced. Had the duke coerced Lucy into marriage? "I cannot let you make this sacrifice. His appetite—"

"I am no martyr. I think . . . I think we will be content." Lucy's shy smile flipped Portia's heart. Is this what love looked like? "It is more than I ever imagined would happen to me." She touched Portia's forearm. "Be happy for me."

Returning the smile, Portia managed to murmur. "I will, so long as you are happy." Her smile turned into an impish grin. "I have a wedding gift for you already."

She winked, and Lucy blushed.

"Then perhaps it is best I collect it now," Lucy managed to say, ending in a giggle.

They grinned with innocence at the women ahead who turned at this sound.

Lucy hurried on to Portia's room and collected her gift, muffled by a scarf. Lucy eyed the large copper bath. "You are bathing in the evening? You will catch a chill."

"I am meeting Mark tomorrow. I thought I would bathe first." Portia blushed, squirming a little at disappointing Lucy.

"Oh, Portia, I wish you wouldn't. You run such danger."

Portia brushed off her concern. "I know what I am doing. I am being very very careful, I promise you."

"I do hope so." Lucy touched her arm once more and bade her good night.

Two housemaids arrived, bearing buckets of hot water. Another arrived with a third bucket of cold water and towels.

Portia dismissed them all and when her own maid had helped her undress, dismissed her also. She wanted to be alone. Utterly alone. An unusual request, but the servants obeyed.

Still dressed in her shift, she sank into the water, now lukewarm. She soaped up, neglecting her hair for she didn't expect it to dry before she retired to bed.

The soap slicked smoothly over her skin, her hand sliding under her shift.

Sinking back against the sides of the tub, Portia closed her eyes. The rim of the tub dug into the base of her skull, preventing her from drifting off to sleep.

The betrothal announcement still echoed in her senses. She'd been shocked by the duke's quick change of heart, even though she'd done her best to turn him from her own self.

A smile drifted onto her face. Mark. The simple thought of him brought a wave of pleasure. She shouldn't give in to it, not even for a moment, but here, secure in her private space, she let herself think of him. To let herself dream of a possible future.

She refused to let Society's restraints cloud her dream. That would come in her waking hours, when again she would refuse Mark's offer of becoming his mistress. She simply could not do that.

She let go the nasty reminder and focused on her memory of Mark's face, recalling the tender expressions of previous couplings.

Recalling his touch, she lifted her hands to her breasts. The thin linen shift clung to her skin, rendered transparent by the water. The material rubbed her sensitive nipples, which swiftly hardened at the thought of Mark touching her.

She tweaked the hardened buds, sending streams of warmth to her belly. Expelling a long, soft sigh, she cupped her breasts, using her thumbs to swipe over her nipples.

One hand slid between her thighs. Parting her legs, she waved water against her slit, feeling the swell lap against her clit.

She wanted more than this naive toying. She brushed her clit, barely touching, teasing. The water tried to cool her heated core.

Instead of imagining Mark so taunting her senses, she imagined him watching her. He would be touching himself also, she decided, embroidering on the fantasy.

She imagined his cock, rising stiff and eager from his robe. His large hand pumping his cock, turning the head into a dark, swollen red.

A droplet would form in the gaping eye of his cock and he would bring it to her, letting her taste. Salty and sour, she'd savor the taste, plunging her fingers inside her in anticipation of receiving Mark's cock.

Portia moaned, very softly, not wanting anyone to hear, squirming against her frotting hand. She thrust her hips up out of the water, splashing the tub's edges.

She bit down on her lip, trying to hold back the gasping sobs.

A hand closed over her pumping hand at her quim.

Eyes wide, Portia squealed, her bottom thumping on the base of the tub. She stared up at her imagination come true, trying to draw in air.

Mark Knightson knelt by the tub, his arm plunged into the water, for he hadn't relinquished his grasp. His drenched, rolled-up shirtsleeve revealed the musculature underneath.

"What are you doing here?" Portia whispered.

His lazy grin would have sent her heart pounding if it hadn't already been going in triple time at his appearance. "I couldn't wait until morning."

He pressed his palm down over her hand. Her hand slipped away, giving him the close access he silently desired. At once, he slid a finger inside, curling up against her vagina walls.

She whimpered, arching up to him.

"Should I make you come now . . . or later?" he growled, his thumb tweaking her clit.

"Now," she gasped. "And later."

He chuckled softly.

"And I want you inside me," she added.

"What exactly do you want inside you?" His finger swirled around the walls of her vagina.

Portia gasped. "More than your finger."

"Tell me," he murmured, his voice a low, vibrating burr.

She took a deep breath. "I want your cock inside me."

"More."

"More?" she gasped.

"More description," he clarified, grinning.

Returning his smile, Portia pitched her voice low. "I want your hot, thick cock inside me. I want you to fuck me until I scream."

"Tell me how you want me to fuck you."

"I want it wild, I want you to fuck me hard and fast, I—"

"What position?" he murmured.

"Any you like—" Her breath caught again at the possibilities. She chewed on her lower lip. "From behind, I want it from behind. I want you to cover me. I want to feel your heat. I want to feel you burn."

"I think," Mark said thickly, "that you better get out of that tub so I may ravish you as you desire."

She rose, the water cascading off her body, her shift clinging to her, revealing every curve and the pointed tips of her arousal.

Mark stood also, bending to apply his hot mouth over the nipples straining against the thin material. She clutched his head to her bosom, her knees weakening.

He scooped her up into his arms, depositing her dripping form onto the rug. With ruthless efficiency, he stripped her shift from her body, tugging it over her head.

He dropped the shift back into the tub. He grabbed a towel and spread it on the floor in front of the bed's baseboard.

"On your knees," he growled.

She fell onto the towel, and turned to look over her shoulder, her damp curls starting to tumble from their pins.

He knelt behind her, snaking his hand along the crack of her rear. She parted for him, bending forward and pushing her buttocks up.

With his fingertips, he parted her wet curls. He slid two fingers inside her quim, making her moan.

Mark bent forward and nipped her shoulder. "Quiet," he murmured. "You don't want to wake your mother." He soothed his bite with a soft kiss.

He shifted to kneel between her calves, covering her breasts with his large hands. In front and behind, his heat encased her, fueling her own desire.

His cock slipped between her buttocks. She gasped when he pressed against her back door. Every muscle tensed. Mark pressed his lips against her shoulder again, murmuring soothing sounds.

He shifted his hips and his cock slid lower. In the next breath, his cock pressed against her quim. She arched her back even more and slowly, ever so slowly, Mark's cock parted her cunt lips.

He tensed against her and his cock slid inside in one long smooth movement, parting her flesh like butter. Her breath expelled in one long sigh.

Mark grasped her hips then. "Hold on," he muttered. He delivered what she had asked: he fucked her hard, his body slamming against hers, sending his cock deep inside her again and again and again.

Each time, she met his thrust, beyond arousal now. Every sense keened with the urgency of her approaching release. Beyond coherent thought, Portia opened herself to him, giving back as fiercely as he gave, squeezing her quim around his thick cock until his low moans mingled with hers.

Her breasts jiggled and despite her braced grip, her head came near to banging against the wooden bed.

Faster and faster, he pounded her quim, his sweat slicking across her dampened back. He curled around her back, sticking and sliding against her.

Heat swirled around their frenzied coupling. Each thrust forced air out of Portia's lungs. She grew dizzy, gripping the bed until her knuckles turned white.

Golden release blossomed in her quim, searing its way

through her belly, exploding in her breasts. She gave a hoarse cry, tensed and trembling.

Mark's fingernails dug deep into her hips, holding her drooping form against his groin. A gut-deep groan burst past his lips. In Portia's battered quim, it felt like his cock swelled to twice its size before expelling his jism, filling her.

He sank upon her, gathering her to him, his hands palming her breasts. Her trembling echoed into him and she felt him shake, and heard him inhale deep gusts of air.

She leaned back against him, daring to luxuriate in his protectiveness.

"Dear sweet God," Mark breathed at last. "I do not think I can move . . ."

Portia covered his hand with one of her own. "Come to bed with me," she murmured. His softening cock still lay gripped inside her.

He kissed along her shoulder blade, pressing her lips against the sweaty shadows of her neck.

Deep in her throat, she moaned appreciatively.

"I dare not stay," he whispered. "If we were caught . . ."

He slipped from her and stood. The icy cool night air slid along Portia's skin. Kneeling upright, she gazed up at him, watching him retrieve his trousers.

He tucked away his wilting cock, his gaze fastened upon her naked form. "I would love to stay, Portia." He took a deep breath. "I will see you before dawn in the stables."

His lopsided smile did little to console her. She gathered up another towel and wrapped it around her shoulders. She nodded once. "Go, then."

His halfsmile melted into a frown, but he turned and left.

Sinking back onto the carpet, Portia wearily rested her head against the bed. For one endless moment, all had been brilliant and warm and alive.

Now, she felt frozen and empty.

* * *

A tap sounded on Lady Cecily's door. She stirred in her bed. A rapping woke her fully.

Frowning, Cecily pulled back the covers and padded to the door. "Who is it?" she whispered.

"Sir Guy," came the response.

Cecily opened the door and stood back to let him in. "What is it?" She rubbed her eyes. "What time is it?"

"A few hours before dawn," Sir Guy told her.

Cecily's lip curled. How could he be so immaculately dressed at this ungodly hour?

"Knightson's valet finally cracked. It took me two bottles of port to do it."

Lady Cecily came fully awake. "And?"

"Knightson has arranged an assignation with Miss Carew in the stables in little more than an hour. Call your maid and dress."

Cecily eyed the knight. "I am not waking my maid at this hour, and I'm certainly not letting her see you in my room. The gossip would be all over the Hall within the day." Her gaze narrowed. "Ruining your chances with the girl."

Sir Guy shrugged. "Then allow me to help you dress."

Playing it cool, which is how Sir Guy seemed to want it, Lady Cecily allowed her robe to slip from her shoulders and puddle to the floor. Standing in nothing but her sheer shift, Cecily ignored his roaming gaze, turning to pull a warm gown from the wardrobe. She laid it out on the bed and retrieved a fresh pair of opaque stockings and her stays.

Sitting on a chair, she pulled on the first stocking.

"Please." Sir Guy moved with surprising swiftness to kneel at her feet. "Allow me."

She chuckled. "I do not think so." She pulled the stocking up over her knee. Sir Guy didn't stir, his gaze burning upon the exposed flesh of her thigh.

Well, she knew him as a lecher. Cooly, she tied a ribbon around the stocking. Her moves grew languorous. She had an hour to dress after all. The second stocking slipped on beneath Sir Guy's hungry eyes.

She stood, crossing to the bed. "I need help with my stays," she murmured.

Cecily slipped the boned garment on like a backwards vest and turned her back to him. She looked over her shoulder at him. "Do you know how?"

Sir Guy got to his feet, grinning. "I assure you I have handled many a corset."

True to his word, he wove the cording through the cotton buttonholes, cinching and tightening along the way.

Feeling his breath hot on the back of her neck, Cecily focused her gaze on the wall before her, being sure to stand straight. The stays held her to her natural form, not nipping in at the waist, but elevating her bosom.

She felt the final tug of a knot being tied and faced him, giving him an eyeful of her swelling bosom. Cecily knew better than to remind him that the one he should be leering at should be none other than Miss Carew.

Men leered. It was a fact of life.

She shimmied into the worsted wool gown and flicked the loose tresses of her auburn hair over her shoulders. "I am ready."

Sir Guy nodded, his leer smoothed into a polite smile.

So he had remembered Miss Carew. She matched his noncommittal smile and gestured that he lead the way.

Sir Guy maintained his silence until they stepped into the rear courtyard. "We will hide up in the loft. Does hay make you sneeze?"

"No."

A few dimming lamps lit the courtyard and a faint gray on the horizon suggested the coming dawn. Cecily almost tripped over an uneven cobblestone but recovered before Sir Guy noticed.

He let her go first up the wooden ladder into the loft, generously holding the folds of her gown.

She knew he couldn't see anything, and even if he did, she didn't care. Scooting to the side of the ladder, she gathered her skirts about her, watching Sir Guy appear through the square hole in the wooden floor.

He ignored her at first, crawling on the floor, his gaze fastened upon the hay strewn boards.

"What are you looking for?" Cecily whispered, making out his shadows in the dark. Warm light spilled from somewhere below through chinks in the boards.

"Knightson has a place set up." Sir Guy didn't turn to speak to her, his attention focused elsewhere. "Ah." He waved at her. Cecily barely saw the movement. "Come over here. You better crawl."

"In skirts?" She sighed and managed to crawl and wriggle her way across to him.

Sir Guy cleared away more straw and light shone up at them. "Look."

Cecily saw a stall, piled with fresh straw. A single lantern secured to a post cast a warm light across the space, a beacon for the two lovers.

"We should have witnesses besides ourselves," Cecily whispered, leaning close to Sir Guy's ear.

"Not yet," Sir Guy murmured in return, his gaze focused on the scene below. "We need to be sure we can rely on the valet's word. How would it look if we dragged Lord Barrington out here and nothing happened?"

"So you dragged me out here instead."

This time he looked at her. "You wanted to be in this together. Go back if—"

Cecily hushed him by placing a hand over his warm lips.

Below, the warning creak Cecily heard revealed Miss Carew, holding a small candle. Miss Carew shielded the light with her hand, making sure no spark would start a fire.

Reaching the stall, Miss Carew doused her flame and set it on the low stable wall. Folding her arms, she surveyed the space, a little frown on her smooth forehead.

Cecily held her breath, watching the silent form of Miss Carew. Had Knightson bamboozled them all?

Miss Carew turned at some noise they couldn't hear from above. A smile broke out on her face, and Cecily mirrored the smile.

Knightson had come.

He strode into the small stall with long strides, gathering up Miss Carew without a single word and drowning her in a passionate kiss that made Cecily burn.

Miss Carew—Portia, Cecily supposed she must think of her, if she were truly about to witness such an explicit act—wrapped her arms around Knightson's neck, bending him over her.

The kiss ended, and a panting Portia hung on while Knightson bent to nuzzle at her neck.

"You prepared all this?" Portia gasped.

Knightson lifted his head. "I did." He looked around at the stall, surveying his valet's work. "It's rather sparse, I know, but I didn't want anyone stumbling over it by accident."

"Very wise." Portia appeared to have recovered her breath.

"Enough talk," Knightson growled in a way that made Cecily's toes curl. His mouth closed over Portia's and her soft moan of desire could be heard up in the loft.

Next to her, Sir Guy shifted. Cecily glanced aside at him. He wiggled his eyebrows at her, managing to leer at the same time.

She rolled her eyes and returned her attention to the scene playing out below.

The two lovers clawed at each other, hungry for more intimacy, even though layers of clothing lay between them. Portia pressed her lips against Knightson's bare throat, cravatless at this hour of the morning.

He held her to him, moaning at the play of her lips against his skin. His head tilted back, eyes closed and Cecily swallowed hard at the sight of open vulnerability on his face.

She'd never seen him so unmasked before. She sucked in her breath. His face was a work of masculine beauty. How unfair that he had fastened his attentions on that Miss Carew. Why couldn't he see that *she*, Lady Cecily Lambeth, was the one?

He bent his head to capture Portia's mouth in another searing kiss. Portia tugged at his coat, trying to pull it off over his shoulders. His arms around her prevented that and so her hands fell away, disappearing between their two bodies.

Their hips ground against each other, until Portia made a little space between them, her hands out of sight, working at something.

Cecily knew. Portia toiled to free his cock from his breeches.

Knightson groaned into her mouth and pushed them apart. He stripped off his coat, his white linen shirt being cast off over his head in short order.

His breeches hung loose over his narrow hips, the flap hanging open. Portia appeared to be feasting on the sight.

Cecily couldn't blame her. His muscles gleamed in the lamplight, the crevices plunged into even deeper shadows.

Knightson pivoted away from Portia in an odd burst of privacy. He didn't know Cecily feasted on the view of him. His cock, hard and ready, rose from the dark shadows of his breeches.

Cecily licked her lips. Her hunger for him grew deep in her belly. How heavenly it would be have him fuck her with that lovely large cock of his. She could almost feel the eager organ thrusting into her hot quim.

He shucked off his boots, so old as to be on the verge of falling apart. His breeches came off next, revealing his every inch of perfect maleness.

Cecily leaned closer, wanting him, wanting to smell his incredible male scent, wanting to lose herself in him.

He faced Portia once more, his hands going quickly to work. Portia had already unbuttoned her pelisse. Her hands were ahead of him, moving to loosen the tapes of her gown.

"Hurry," Portia gasped. "I want you now."

Knightson's groan drowned out Sir Guy's muffled sound. Cecily glanced sidelong at him. The coming dawn gave him form in the faint gray light. Tension lined every inch of him.

Cecily gnawed her lip in worry. Would Sir Guy break from their hiding place and disrupt the lovemaking below?

15

Sir Guy remained in position, all his attention on his Portia and that damnable Knightson pawing his girl.

She didn't have to like it so much. The hussy hadn't even bothered to wear stays. Knightson stripped her lithe form in moments.

Portia's dazzled eyes caused an ache of grief in Sir Guy's heart. She had once looked at him like that. She had once given herself to him with the same abandon.

He eyed the smooth curves of her pale leg, hooking around Knightson's darker thigh. So beautiful. She stood on tiptoe, trying to pull him into her.

Knightson obliged. He lifted her, her legs quickly wrapping around his waist. He drove her back against the wooden wall draped with an old scratchy horse blanket, but less damaging than the wood beneath.

Had he planned even this? Sir Guy admitted to being impressed with the man's foresight.

A moment of adjustment before Knightson rammed inside of her.

Her head tilted, a soft scream breaking through her lips. "Yes!"

His buttocks flexed again and again as Knightson fucked Portia's tight little cunt. Oh, Sir Guy remembered that sweet juiciness very well. It had been his to taste once.

Portia's ecstatic expression flushed dark red, lost in the depths of her lust. Sir Guy felt his crotch tighten, pressing against the wood floor beneath him. God, how he wanted her.

Even Knightson couldn't hold the upright position forever. He stumbled back from the wall, Portia clutched in his arms. Sir Guy admired the tight control Knightson kept, slowly sinking to the hay-strewn floor, until Portia straddled his prone form.

Sir Guy snorted. Giving the woman the dominant position. Was Knightson out of his mind? It was a sure path to matrimony.

It freed Knightson to cover Portia's breasts, teasing and plucking at them like playing some fragile instrument. Portia loved it, her head falling back and her hips grinding against his crotch.

Her flushed, creamy skin glowed with a faint sheen of perspiration. A keening cry started from somewhere deep inside her until her whole body resonated with it.

She slumped forward, her rosy face disappearing over Knightson's shoulder.

Knightson held her, his hands stroking her sweetly bowed back. How unusual that he expressed such tenderness. Had Knightson already fallen into the marriage trap?

Rolling, so that Portia lay beneath him, Knightson pulled out, his shiny cock glistening with her sex juices. His cock still unsatisfied. How had he survived the incredible squeezing of Portia's tight little hole?

Pillowed on a small mound of straw, Portia's languid gaze

fell on all of Knightson. She reached out for him and he came closer until his huge cock hovered before her face.

Her hand moved up and down his slick shaft. Knightson's buttocks flexed with the need to thrust.

Portia let go and licked her fingers, plunging each one past her pursed lips. "Make me come again." Her soft, clear voice held a playful challenge.

Oh God. If only he could, Sir Guy thought. He'd ram her so hard . . .

Knightson delayed, toying once more with Portia's pert breasts. Sir Guy understood the fascination. The way her nipples swelled and hardened was enough to make any man climax.

Sir Guy heard a gasp beside him. He glanced aside at Lady Cecily and stopped to stare. In the pale lemon light of dawn, Lady Cecily had hoisted her bosom out of her stays and toyed with them, the harsh straw tickling them.

From her mouth, she breathed hard. She licked her reddened lips. Hit with the sudden clarity of thought that he could shove his cock down Lady Cecily's throat and she wouldn't even blink almost had him abandon his spying on the scene below.

Well, let her pleasure herself. The way Knightson headed, that would be all she'd be likely to get from that quarter.

With difficulty, he returned to the scene below. Knightson had drawn Portia up on her knees, his hands all over her willing body.

He shuffled around her, keeping her in a swirl of sensation, his hands always on the move, always teasing. He coaxed her to fall forward onto all fours and positioned himself behind her parted legs.

Oh yes. This was what it was all about.

"Yes," hissed Lady Cecily beside him, squirming. Straw fell

through the wide gap in the boards and Sir Guy leaned away, afraid of being seen.

Portia's head shot up, dark hair plastered across her face. "What was that?"

Their gaze tracked the path of falling dust and straw.

"A mouse," Knightson decided. "Maybe a rat."

Portia shuddered beneath him.

"Relax." He smiled down at her. "It is nothing."

She took his comforting smile to heart and bowed her head once more. Just the feeling of him bowed over her body, his cock buried inside her, made her feel secure.

He kept the thrusting slow, languorous, letting that sweet golden tension mount with delicious slowness. She thrust her hips back up at him, wanting more, wanting it faster.

He gripped her hips and kept her steady, no matter how she wiggled at him. She let the rocking motion wash over her, giving herself up utterly to his will. The friction in her quim built a flame of need that spread throughout every inch of her body until she tingled all over.

She moaned. His movement in and out of her felt slick with her juices. She could hardly think: all was sensation and heat and want.

Mark obliged, increasing the speed of his thrusts until one melted into the other. She squeezed around his cock, wanting her release. She moaned in staccato bursts, urging him on faster and faster. She climaxed, a cascading, golden release that obliterated everything else but him.

His fingers dug into her hips and he took one last deep plunge inside her convulsing quim, emptying into her with one long satisfying groan.

They sank to the ground. Hay prickled her naked body but Portia didn't care. She felt exhausted, sated and deliciously alive.

Even the rustling of mice in the loft above didn't bother her.

Not even while they dressed in silence—she hadn't needed Mark's assistance this time. Nor when Mark walked away from the stables without looking back at her, did they bother her.

She followed a few breaths later, wondering why the mice chose the morning to be so active. Weren't they nocturnal creatures?

Shivering at the thought of a mouse falling on top of her, she hurried back to the house.

Knightson knew how to fuck. Lady Cecily squirmed in ecstasy just watching him convey his favors on the lucky Portia. What else could she do but touch herself?

The idea of Knightson's hands on her breasts had her slipping them free from their binds. Her own hands were not nearly as large as Knightson's but she knew how to pretend . . .

She fingered her breasts, her slitted gaze on the lovers beneath her. She tried not to squirm, not wanting to make any noise, but oh, it was so difficult not to.

When Knightson prepared to mount Portia from behind, Cecily melted. Her insides liquified, she hissed, "Yes."

Portia looked up, directly at her, but couldn't pierce the murky loft.

Lady Cecily froze solid, but one thrust of Knightson's hips and she was on fire again. She bit down on her lower lip, her pelvis moving in the same ancient rhythm of Knightson's hips.

Sir Guy stirred beside her, but she paid him no heed, not even when he slipped out of sight. She didn't care if he left, she would see this through to the end. It might not be her beneath Knightson, but her imagination put her right there.

Sudden tension tugged at her skirt hem. Had she caught it on a nail? How?

A brief draft of cold morning air. A warm hand lay on the back of her thigh. Cecily sucked in her breath. Sir Guy hadn't left after all.

His knee nudged at her calves. In one fluid movement, Cecily arched up on all fours, her legs sliding apart. She was hot, wet and ready, and Sir Guy would do just as well as Knightson. Just this once.

Sir Guy's cock was well primed. It nestled in the crack of her rear, pressing for one exciting moment against her anus. She closed her eyes against the sight of the copulating lovers for just one moment.

His cock slid lower, delving between her hairy lips. Her wet quim accepted him with ease. He grabbed her hips and pushed inside her.

His fingernails dug deep into her sides. For one gasping moment, Cecily thought he attempted control. But she didn't care. She wanted sex, she wanted it hard and she wanted it now.

She shoved her buttocks up at him, feeling the buttons of his breeches imprinting her skin. She ground against him, skillfully juicing his slick cock.

He leaned forward and grabbed her hair, tugging it back until her back bent like a bow. The air escaped her in a long silent sigh. She compressed her muscles around him to let him know this pleased her.

Sir Guy accepted the surrender of her body, loosening his grip on her hair. He powered into her, his cock plunging into and dividing her intimate flesh.

She concentrated on breathing, biting back moans, anything that would reveal their presence. She forgot to spy on the pair below, consumed by sensations rivaling those she'd imagined just a brief time ago.

Fiery desire swelled in her head: no thought, just want, *need*. She pulsed under him, meeting each thrust. Lost in sensation, she almost missed Sir Guy's soft words.

"They're gone." He tugged on her hair. "Let go, Cecily. Let me hear you come."

She reacted fast to his command. Her senses turned to liquid mercury, a fire exploding from her in a ragged cry that filled the loft. She subsided to pleasured sobs punctuated by sharp gasps as Sir Guy wildly pounded into her.

He came with a hoarse cry, digging so deep that he drew blood from her flanks. He pulled out of her almost at once and she slumped to the floor, her skirts bunched beneath her.

Their panting filled the air.

Pulling down her skirts to a more demure level, she twisted to look at Sir Guy. Lady Cecily regained her breath first. "Oh my," she whispered.

Sir Guy finished fastening his breeches and crouched on his haunches. "My dear, this changes nothing. I know you thought of *him* while I plowed you."

Lady Cecily didn't deny it. That was how it had started, at least. The rest had been all sensation. All Sir Guy. "You thought of Miss Carew."

He shrugged, not bothering to deny it either. "We must remain focused on our plans. Who could be expected to watch them fuck and not be affected?"

Who indeed? Lady Cecily tucked her breasts back into her dress and into her stays. "What do we do now?"

"The valet will speak again. He will think I kept his first breach of confidence a secret and will trust me now. The next time they meet for sex we will have them." His lip curled. "Everyone should see how Miss Carew lied, blackening *my* name."

Lady Cecily kept very still. So this was about more than him regaining Miss Carew's hand. "I thought you loved her."

Sir Guy wiped at his brow, a sharp gesture. "I do. Marrying her will even out all."

He rose, doubled over because of the low roof, and headed back to the ladder. He descended, and helped Lady Cecily once more with her cumbersome skirts.

If his hands lay upon her thighs, upon her waist, for longer than was really necessary, Lady Cecily forbore to remind him of propriety. After what had just happened to the two of them, to speak of proper behavior seemed absurd.

She followed him outside, squinting against the sudden light of morning. "I should talk to Mr. Knightson."

Sir Guy rounded on her. "To what purpose?"

"The purpose being to have them accede to our demands without having to ruin them. We would be tainted by that also."

"Not you." Sir Guy folded his arms. "Knightson will have no blot on his name after this, and if he does, it will soon be wiped by time."

"And Miss Carew?"

"Will have my name as her honor." He sounded firm.

Lady Cecily gnawed her lip. "If you are quite certain . . ."

"I am." He stepped up to her, using his larger size to dominate her. "You will not speak to Knightson on this matter."

She dared to reach out and straighten his coat. It was a foolish thing to do, to show softness to a man who took charge, but it worked as a delaying tactic.

His Adam's apple bobbed as he swallowed hard. "Cecily," and his voice had lowered, "will Knightson turn to you if you blackmail him into leaving Miss Carew? He will need someone to turn to if his ungentlemanly act is revealed. Society will deny him their virginal misses. Who else will he turn to but you?"

Sir Guy stroked her cheek. "My dear, if he even suspected you were involved with this unveiling, you would never have him."

Lady Cecily shivered and stepped away. "Of course. You are right." She didn't look at him.

He touched her arm and she stilled. "Cecily."

She tilted her head to look up at him. "Guy," she replied, simply. "You have my word."

He gave a brief nod. "Good." He let her go.

Lady Cecily walked into the house in front of him. Thoughts

turmoiled within her, not least of all her still-pounding senses. Sir Guy was right. She had to focus on their goals. On her goal: Mr. Knightson.

Portia sank into a sofa chair next to Lucy. "You look well-rested for a bride-to-be."

Lucy put down her embroidery and gave her a long look. "You do not. You persist in your mad course?"

Glancing around the gilt drawing room to make sure they were not overheard, Portia replied, "I cannot stop this."

"You mean you will not."

A sunny morning had scattered the women. Through the open windows bringing in a fresh breath of air, Portia saw Lady Cecily Lambeth meander through the herb garden alone. Lady Barrington had declared her intent to visit her tenants and Mrs. Carew, Mrs. Chalcroft and Miss Sophia had gone with her. There'd been scarcely enough room for all of Lady Barrington's baskets.

"I know this will not last." Portia picked up the piece of embroidery in her lap and stuck in a needle, but didn't complete the stitch. "I know before this week is over, Mama will want to leave for I have failed to attract anyone of worth."

"She does not have hopes for Sir Guy?"

"Mama is not that cruel." Portia paused, gnawing her lip. "Although she might be that desperate."

"What do you plan to do after your affair is over?"

Portia grinned. "Wear black, wail and rent my hair."

Lucy harrumphed, unamused. "And then?"

"I do not know. I would like to live quietly, perhaps as a companion to someone."

"You would not like it." Lucy spoke with knowledge born of experience.

"I do not have the luxury of affording to travel or retire

230 / Celia May Hart

somewhere as the local eccentric." Portia shrugged. "Mama spends most of her time in Town and Papa is quite undemanding. It shall be pleasant and quiet."

Lucy shuddered. "You? Quiet?"

Portia's grin returned. "I do have newfound knowledge to entertain myself with."

"But—" Lucy interrupted herself, rising and dropping a curtsey. "Your Grace," she said in a soft voice.

Portia rose with alacrity and mimicked Lucy's actions, although not with that softness of voice.

"Miss Chalcroft." The duke said the words like he tasted honey. His voice turned cool. "Miss Carew."

The two women sat, and the duke took his place next to Lucy. He raised her hand to his lips, kissing it. Lucy's embroidery fell unnoticed onto her lap.

He reached for Lucy's other hand, kissing it also and then bent forward to claim a kiss on her lips. It was no polite peck, but a kiss that deepened.

Portia held her breath, familiar sensations swimming in her belly. Not for the duke, but with the idea that Knightson would enter the room like that and kiss her—just like that. Not only with banked passion, but with a sweet tenderness that nearly brought tears to her eyes.

Lucy wrapped her arms around her duke's neck, pressing herself shamelessly against him. His hands wandered to her bosom, thumbing her nipple into erect life.

Portia cleared her throat. She'd considered fleeing but sat rooted to the spot, watching their embrace.

Lucy pulled away from the duke, collecting his caressing hands and bestowing a kiss upon them. "We are embarrassing Miss Carew." Her voice purred with tenderness.

"I doubt that." The duke arched a silver eyebrow at Portia. "It is well that Miss Carew realize what she has lost."

"Oh, that is cruel!" Lucy tapped his chest with her embroidery frame.

"True." The duke turned his attention back to Lucy. "For I have found myself a wonderful prize instead." He leaned forward to kiss her again, but stopped midway.

He shot a look at Portia, one that was filled with desire and love. But not for her. For Lucy. "You are excused, Miss Carew."

Portia grabbed her embroidery and dashed from the room, her ears ringing with the duke's chuckles and Lucy's giggles.

She tossed her embroidery bag on a hallway side table and headed for the outdoors, grabbing a parasol from the umbrella stand along the way.

The whole scene with the duke and Lucy left her unsettled. She didn't want to think about it, she would walk off the feeling and then everything would return to normal.

Her thoughts raced, ignoring her mental edict. Did she regret refusing the duke? No, not for a heartbeat.

What then? Was she not gripped in the midst of exciting passion with Knightson? Shouldn't that be enough? And yet, she wanted Knightson to kiss her in that intimate way. Not as a necessary prelude to sex, but just *because*.

It would never happen. Their affair would end with her departure from Willowhill Hall. With that imminent departure, tenderness had no place in their liaison.

She remembered his soft kiss on her neck after that morning's thrilling lovemaking and the tears rose again. It was useless to believe he meant that tenderness. Useless to think he cared more for her than the cataclysmic sex they shared.

How had she ever thought that she could walk away? Would not a few more weeks and months of this passion be worth a ruined reputation and the quiet retirement she said she longed for?

She dashed away the tears with the back of her hand, walking up the gentle rising hill behind the house. No moping in hothouse gardens for her. She sought true solitude.

If only she had Mark Knightson, the way Lucy had the Duke of Winterton. No, she wanted a relationship deeper than that. More than sex, more than fondness. She wanted love.

The one thing she no longer believed in. She gave a dry laugh at her realization. Her foolish woman's heart betrayed her again.

Knightson wanted pleasure, not a lifetime of living together. It didn't matter that his presence made the air crackle, or that they suited each other. They had not shared confidences, but shared the commonplaces as if they'd done so all their lives.

She expected that level of comfort from Freddy Barrington, who she had known all her life. But not Knightson.

When had the change occurred? It didn't matter. She was trapped with it now. Knightson would never know that her heart had weakened to him, that she wanted more.

He would never know that she . . . that she loved him.

She let out a convulsive gasp. Oh, what a coil! Lucy had been right, so right, about continuing her entanglement, but in reality she'd been lost long before.

She needed to end it, now, before she succumbed to his desire to make her his mistress. Now, before he tired of her and abandoned her, breaking her heart.

She reckoned she could recover from the blow now.

Portia stomped along the dirt path, making a slow circle back to the house. Back to pretending that all she wanted was sex and an experience to live off of for the rest of her life.

How empty that sounded now.

Mark Knightson rode with the other gentlemen. Only the duke had chosen to remain behind, no doubt wishing to remain with his newly betrothed and not jolt his ancient bones on this rough ride.

The men took their horses over fallen tree trunks, fences and low stone walls. The sun glinted between low gray clouds, gilding the green countryside.

Mark welcomed the exertion. His thoughts had swirled too often around Portia Carew and her lovely, lissome body. He needed a break and a good dose of fresh air to clear his head.

And here he was thinking about her again. She entangled in his every thought to the point that he dreaded making the break with her upon her departure from Willowhill Hall.

She intoxicated him. He wanted nothing more than to hold her and never let her go, to have her always there to make love to.

He couldn't remember the last time a woman had so infected him.

It wouldn't happen again. Just because he had never experienced anything like this storm of passion since his first conquest, did not excuse him collapsing before it. The storm would still blow itself out.

Dissipating into nothing. It always had. He'd made sure of it in the past, and would again.

Of course, if he hadn't broken his golden rule of limiting his time with each lovely young woman that became his, this storm may not have gathered sufficient force for him to woolgather like an old woman.

He gritted his teeth. With a hoarse cry, he urged his mount into a gallop, aiming for the nearest fence. Behind him he heard the others give startled shouts and the pounding of hooves against solid earth.

16

Knightson vowed not to touch Portia Carew again that day. Never mind he tortured himself by joining with her in the more mundane activities of the household. Once again he was her dinner partner, young Winterton having abandoned his sulks and rejoining the party.

He didn't like the covetous glances the young man shot at Portia, but any action from him on the matter was impossible.

Beside him, Portia drew Miss Sophia into conversation and before he knew it, he had also joined in, despite the subject matter being nonsense about the various botanical delights in Lady Barrington's garden.

Portia shot him a surprised glance, which he thought unfair. Was he not allowed to be knowledgeable about botany? A smile graced his lips. If there is one thing he did like, it was surprising Portia.

"I spent my early days toddling after the head gardener," he explained in a neutral tone.

Portia's wide eyes just begged for more. Well, he wasn't going to share his entire childhood with the whole dinner table.

"Nearly all my spare time is in my garden!" trilled Sophia.

Lord, was the chit after him now?

No, she beamed a smile toward Freddy Barrington farther up the table. Good. He didn't need the complication of a green miss after him as well.

He nodded and smiled at her declaration and asked after the contents of her garden.

At the end of dinner, the ladies left the men to their own devices. Portia trailed the lightest fingertip across his back, no doubt designed to look like an accident.

He shivered, but pretended not to have felt a thing.

Soon, he had to deal with the good-natured ribbing from the rest of the table about keeping the young ladies entertained.

"Never marked you for a fop," the old duke remarked, his bright eyes glinting through narrow slits.

Mark raised a quelling eyebrow he knew wouldn't work on the old man. "Conquering nature is considered foppish?"

"That's more like it!" boomed Lord Barrington. "Too bad you like to get your hands dirty, Knightson. I prefer to be the general to my soldier-gardeners."

The others chuckled in appreciation.

Mark drank deep of his brandy and gestured for more. Why was he here again?

By the time the gentlemen chose to enter the ladies' domain, liquor fogged Mark's brain. A pleasantly numb sensation, he refused to allow it to draw him toward Portia.

Lady Cecily accosted him instead. Considering that to be currently the lesser of two evils, he delivered a lopsided smile and allowed her to guide him to the window.

The window let in a light breeze of cool air, almost sobering him. Mark didn't bother to flatter Lady Cecily, letting her make the opening conversation gambit.

"Mr. Knightson." Lady Cecily fidgeted at the tassel that dropped from her high-waisted gown of green velvet.

Not so in his cups to realize Lady Cecily had abandoned seduction, he waited for her to continue.

"Mr. Knightson, we only have a few moments—"

Marvelous, she did mean to seduce him then?

"I said I would not but—" She looked right and Mark followed her gaze.

Sir Guy joined them, slipping his arm through Lady Cecily's. "There you are, my dear Lady Cecily. Miss Sophia was just asking about the latest entertainment in London, and I knew you would be just the person to answer her." He smiled at Mark. "I fear I worried that Freddy and I might mention sights not suitable for a young lady. If you will excuse us . . ."

Mark bowed his assent. He watched them stroll away, Sir Guy's head bent close to Lady Cecily's bowed one. Had Sir Guy done him a favor and now pursued Lady Cecily?

Portia drifted past, arm in arm with Miss Chalcroft. A spark of jealousy stirred in Mark. He remembered them clasped in a passionate embrace: two nymphs in a sylvan scene.

His cock stirred, an urge to possess her, reclaim her from Miss Chalcroft, rising. He turned away from them, banking down the primal need.

"Mr. Knightson," said Miss Chalcroft. Portia stood silent next to her, her dark eyes bright.

Mark fixed a smile upon his face. "Ladies." He sketched a short bow. "How may I help?"

"Miss Carew wanted a few words with you." Miss Chalcroft smiled, revealing an impish dimple on her left cheek. "I am her chaperone."

Portia clasped her hands before her, steady where Lady Cecily's had been flighty. Her cheeks colored. "Mr. Knightson, I was wondering about the time of our next assignation?"

Her cool tones washed over him. Not a hint of desire in her voice, but surely the flush of her cheeks hinted at her true feelings.

"Lord Barrington has informed me that there is hunting to be had. Of what, I do not know." He flashed a brief smile. "I am afraid I was not attending. What are the women's plans?"

"It is Lady Barrington's salon," Miss Chalcroft replied when Portia remained silent. "I believe we shall meet a few of her neighbors. The fresh faces will be most welcome."

"Tedious," muttered Portia, earning herself another grin from Mark. He imagined it must be, to sit before a parade of locals eager for the sight of glamorous visitors. He had not thought of it before.

"Indeed," he agreed. "In that case, Portia, I suggest we meet in the billiards room. The men will be abroad and no woman would dare enter a male domain."

"No female but I," she replied, recovering some of her spirit. She stood straighter, meeting his gaze.

"None but you." At her sharp intake of breath, Mark realized not only what he'd said but how he said it. Soft, crooning tones in front of Miss Chalcroft? The women would think he was actually in earnest about Portia.

No. It was a temporary affair. Nothing more. He must keep reminding himself of that.

"At what hour?" Damn it, but her voice trembled. He'd be willing to bet that already her mind was wandering toward love. Have to nip that in the bud.

"An hour after luncheon," he told her, his crisp tones letting her know she ranked with the same consequence as an appointment with his tailor. He delivered a curt bow. "If you ladies will excuse me?"

Pleading a headache, Portia abandoned Lady Barrington's salon precisely an hour after luncheon. Instead of ascending another flight of stairs to her assigned bedroom, she headed down to the main floor.

Knightson's odd behavior last night only served to confirm

her own doubts. Today would be the last time. She would end it now, before she left Willowhill Hall.

She stepped through the open doorway to the billiards room, located at the left wing's far end. She closed the door behind her.

Despite it being early afternoon, the billiards room was cloaked in shadows. Someone—Knightson, she presumed—had closed all the heavy navy blue velvet drapes and had disdained to light any lamps.

The main feature of the room, the billiards table, stood in the center of the room, its green baize top almost glowing in the darkness.

Around it were scattered various sofa chairs where gentlemen could take their ease and a lengthy sideboard where Portia imagined both liquor and delectable tidbits would be served.

This afternoon, a single bottle and two glasses of cut crystal stood on the shining countertop.

Portia stepped toward the wine, scanning the room before her.

"Portia." Knightson's dark, resonant voice came from behind her.

She almost jumped out of her skin. She spun around. "Mark." She hated the breathy quality to her voice. It made her sound like she couldn't wait to be bedded by him.

Never mind the truth of that.

Knightson slipped by her, his dark blue coat almost blending in with the room's shadows. He lifted the bottle of wine and poured into the two glasses.

He held out a glass to her. "To us," he said.

She accepted it, pleased that her hand didn't tremble. "Us?" She wished she could say the same for her voice.

"Portia, I have reached a decision. I know we agreed to continue this liaison until your departure from the Hall . . ."

"You want to end it now." Her flat voice didn't betray her relief and her anguish. "Well, so do I."

He seemed startled by that, the ruby red wine sloshing in his glass. "You do?"

"Each time we meet, it grows more dangerous for us, surely you see that." She'd never tell him that her heart was in danger of breaking.

"Precisely. I also thought that it would be best to end it now, while it was still good. There is nothing more painful than long, drawn out good-byes."

"I quite agree." Certain he lied, she lied blithely back. What was the point in causing a scene? She raised her glass. "To us, then."

They both drank deeply and Mark refilled their glasses. She drank again, enjoying the mellow fruitiness on her tongue. What now? Would they drink and then go their separate ways?

She licked a droplet of wine from her lips. Stronger than the usual ratafia, the wine filled her with a glowing warmth, quite like and yet unlike the sensations Knightson's lovemaking caused.

Oh, she mustn't think of it as lovemaking. It was intercourse, sex, *fucking*. Nothing to do with love.

"Shall we . . . ?" She took a breath and plunged on, her heart racing at the thought of sex. "Mark, one last time?"

He seemed to know of what she spoke. "It would be a fitting conclusion." He drained his glass, replacing it on the mahogany sideboard.

Portia saw the piece of furniture as an ugly thing now, heavily carved vine leaves and other curlicues. She mimicked Mark's move and swallowed the last of her wine, handing the glass to him.

"Now . . ." In a breath, he stood a hair's breadth from her. He cupped her face, his thumbs smoothing across her cheeks as if to make a memory of her soft skin.

He bent and kissed her, his lips tasting of mulberries. At once, she flicked her tongue against his closed mouth. His lips parted, his tongue tangling with hers.

He didn't seem inclined to pursue the kiss to its lurking, deeper passions, and for once, neither did Portia.

This could be the last kiss, she thought, her hands clasping together behind his neck. Its sweetness pricked tears at the corners of her closed eyelids.

The last kiss. The last embrace. The last fuck. Was this really the end? Did she really want this?

Her body molded to his, her every curve aligning with his hard lines. His arousal pricked at her belly, a pressure she welcomed.

She moaned into his mouth, dispelling the sweetness with its darker cousin, desire.

He responded at once, drawing her into an even tighter embrace, lifting her until only her toes brushed the floor. She sank into his embrace, letting herself become overwhelmed by him.

In her world, only he existed. His heat, his hard-bodied strength, the tenderness of his lips . . .

He nibbled along the line of her neck, each kiss soft and tender, the grazing of his teeth the only hint to a deeper desire. Even so, Portia became breathless. She was his to do with as he would, malleable to his every need.

Mark lifted her onto the billiard table. Her legs parted, but the confines of her skirt prevented him from getting as close as she liked.

Portia made do, releasing her hold on him, to unfasten his breeches, his rampant cock springing free. She took it in both hands, marveling at its heat and smoothness. She wondered if she'd ever get over such delicacy sheathed in all that muscle.

Mark's cock pulsed and lengthened under her stroking, a smoky bead spilling from the slitted eye. She met his intense gaze. She read desire in his features, a tightening of the jaw indicated control.

She sent him a slow, sultry smile. He wanted to ravish her and yet held back. She licked her lips and leaned forward. Drawn to her, he met her halfway. Her lips brushed his, her tongue flicking over his lower lip.

Dodging his mouth, she pecked at his cheek, ending the chaste kiss with another tiny lick. She kissed his chin, her lips parting to suckle on the dimple.

He dipped his head but she ducked her chin, his lips connecting with her forehead.

She kissed the corner of his mouth, let him kiss her for just a moment and pulled away again, all the time, stroking his cock into an aching hardness.

"Witch," he murmured into her hair, giving up on capturing her mouth for the time being. He pulled the pins from her hair and fluffed her locks to cascade down her back. "Tease."

She chuckled, low and breathy. "You love it."

He nipped at the base of her neck, mouthing the light bite. He moaned, deep in his throat.

Air brushed Portia's calves. With a soft laugh, she realized Mark had raised her skirts.

"Give yourself to me," he purred. "Surrender to me utterly."

His words made it difficult for her to breathe. She nodded, grabbing his face with her hands and fusing her mouth with his.

He returned the kiss, hungry and insistent. He worked at loosening her bodice, at teasing her breasts to escape from her stays.

He nuzzled her breasts lifted high from their restrictions, guiding her to lie across the green baize of the billiards table. He leaned over her, kissing her, smoothing his hands over her breasts and down her sides.

He tugged a nipple with his teeth, gave it long licks to soothe any pain, deliver more heat.

Portia reached for him, but he straightened, covering her bosom with his hands. She gazed up at him: his dark hair, mussed by her hands; his magnificent square shoulders straining at the broadcloth coat he still wore. While she watched, he shucked it off.

His cravat skewed to the left, concealing the strong column of his neck, hiding his broad chest beneath its snowy white linen. His shirt had come untucked and between the dangling flaps of his breeches, his cock stood rampant.

She sucked in a breath. God, he was marvelous. She wanted to give this up? She banished the thought at once, seeing an echo of her pain flicker across his stern features.

His eyebrow quirked, his lips twisted. "You are mine, Portia. For now."

"For now," she echoed, feeling her heart empty out.

He raised her hips, slid her rumpled skirts beneath her for padding and height. He bent slightly, guiding his cock to press against her.

His cock found her entrance, so slick and ready for him, and slid in. He stopped partway in and she gave a mewling cry of protest.

Mark stepped back, his cock sliding out. He rubbed it up and down the length of her slit, the soft-hard pressure of his cock exciting her pleasure.

He caressed her bared thighs, lifting and guiding them so she lay spread-eagled before him.

Her soft, incoherent cries begged him to stop his teasing. Her arms strained out to him, wanting to gather him in.

He denied her in all but one thing.

Mark thrust in, hard, long and deep. The new angle allowed him to plunge deeper than he ever had before.

Portia let out a shocked, excited cry. In her prone position, she lay at his mercy, her hips little able to do more than twitch at his thrusting cock.

With each stroke, the head of his cock rubbed along the roof of her tunnel, each swipe evoking a shuddering, sensual blow.

She bit her lip, trying not to scream her pleasure.

"There is no one to hear," Mark whispered. "I want to hear you cry out, Portia."

Portia gave herself over utterly. With each thrust, a moan issued from her lips. Beyond any self-control, she sank beneath the rising tide of desire, reaching for the crest of release.

He toyed with her nipples, rolling and pinching them, fucking her until she sobbed for mercy.

A shrill scream pierced the air.

Portia blinked up at Mark, knowing it hadn't come from him. He stared back, for one shocked moment and then looked beyond her.

He reacted at once, hauling her up from the billiards table and holding her against him. The rear hem of her skirts slipped down, concealing her legs.

Portia peeked over her shoulder, through the falling mass of her dark curls. Women filled the space between the double doors to the billiards room.

In the front stood the white-faced Lady Barrington. Miss Lucy Chalcroft clutched at her arm, her face filled with woe for Portia.

Even Lady Cecily seemed somewhat subdued, standing to the left of Lady Barrington.

Thankfully, Portia couldn't see her mother. The others vanished into a blur of tears.

She closed her eyes and pressed her forehead against Mark's chest, all pleasure gone, despite the throbbing of her clit. "Oh God," she whispered.

To her astonishment, Mark thrust her from him, turning to button up his breeches. She leaned her hip against the solid wood of the billiards table. With dazed hands, she concealed her bosom beneath the confines of stays and gown. There didn't seem to be any point in refastening the ties.

Mark pointed at her. "You arranged this."

Portia stared at him, uncomprehending. What had he said? Arranged what? Meeting here had been his idea.

"You wanted to trap me into a marriage. No wonder you were so eager to accede to my wish to end this affair."

Wordlessly, Portia shook her head. His accusations put her beyond words.

"A funny way to end an affair if you ask me," Lady Barrington interrupted, her sharp snap a sign she had recovered from her shock. "I warned you, Miss Carew. You shall pack your bags and leave at once."

Portia gripped the raised cushion of the billiards table. She expected this, she kept telling herself. She expected this.

Taking a breath, she stepped back from her support and walked toward the assembled women. She hated Mrs. Chalcroft, grinning with malevolent delight.

"What is it? What is it?" Portia recognized her mother's piercing voice. The crowd of women, guests and locals, parted for her, bringing her to the forefront. "Portia? What has happened? I was lying down and I was fetched . . ."

Her eyes narrowed at the sight of Portia's disheveled appearance. Mrs. Carew shot a glance at Mark's half-dressed form. "Portia, what have you done?"

What? She had to verbally confess to what everyone else in the room had witnessed? "Mama . . ." she began, her voice trembling.

Lady Barrington turned to her friend and her voice was like ice. "Mrs. Carew, your daughter has been caught fornicating. You are both to leave at once." She paused but for a moment and straightened her shoulders. "I regret that this ends our friendship forever."

"Bitch," Portia muttered under her breath.

A sharp movement from Mark near her suggested that he'd heard her.

Tears streaming down her face, Mrs. Carew turned to Mark. "Mr. Knightson, I beg you to do the honorable thing and wed my daughter!"

Mark's back stiffened. He took an opposite path around the billiards table, not once looking at Portia. "Madam, I regret that I will not."

"You have bedded her, sir! You shall do the right thing by her."

Mark bowed his head for but a moment. "I cannot."

A strangled sob burst from Portia's lips. She clapped her hand over her mouth. He really was deserting her. She was lost, ruined.

Mark strode toward the assembled women and they scattered. He shook off first Mrs. Carew's pleading grasp and then Lucy's, leaving Portia to face the women alone.

Mrs. Carew rubbed her hands together. "Heartless. Utterly heartless." She gestured to Portia. "Come, girl. We must away."

Portia moved forward, her steps stiff and frozen. She hadn't wanted to be trapped in a marriage either, but he hadn't even tried to work out some conciliatory measure with Society.

To deny her made her out as no more than a whore, a streetwalker, too filthy to be given his name.

Portia bit down hard on her lip, refusing to cry in front of all these women, who stood watching her pass in silence. No one touched her, as if her lust were a communicable infection.

She hated them all.

To her surprise, her mother said not a word once they reached their chambers, going into her own to pack, expecting Portia to do the same.

Her maid had already started. Gossip must have already spread through the entire house. Soon, every soul would know. When the men returned. . . .

Sinking onto a stool, Portia stared sightlessly at the floor. When the men returned, Sir Guy would learn of her disgrace, come to claim her, and she'd be faced with a life of misery with him.

She'd much rather be miserable alone.

Would Mama force her to marry him if he offered? And why not? Had she not just proven that every vile thing that Sir Guy had said was true?

She buried her head in her hands, but still did not cry.

After revealing the lovers, the local women guessed that their visit had reached its most exciting moment and took their leave. Lady Barrington's house guests took refuge in the blue drawing room, speaking of the incident in hushed, shocked whispers.

Lady Cecily noted that Miss Lucy Chalcroft said nothing, taking Portia's isolated seat in the bay window. Lucy looked out, no doubt searching for the men's return. Lady Cecily would want the security of her fiancé at a time like this too.

She slipped from the room and hastened upstairs. She'd bet, even though he hadn't been asked, Mark Knightson had also packed his bags.

Staying meant facing the wrath of young Winterton at the very least, and Sir Guy might be forced to give a "show" in defending poor Miss Carew's reviled honor.

She guessed right. She entered, catching his valet strapping shut Knightson's trunk.

"I didn't expect you to fly so quickly," Lady Cecily said.

Knightson turned from where he examined his cravat in his shaving mirror. "It seems my valet got a whiff of the disaster before I did." He paused. "David, you're fired."

His valet stumbled back. "Sir?"

"I do not keep betrayers on my staff." Knightson glared at him. "Get out of my sight and do not expect a reference."

Lady Cecily stepped aside while the valet hastened out. She met Knightson's angry gaze with calm concern. "Is there anything I can do?"

"I have a raging hard prick that would satisfy itself in your cunt, but that would be a disaster."

His bluntness didn't shock her. It made her wet. "How so?" Lady Cecily sashayed toward him. "I carry no disease." That she knew of, she amended to herself.

"I have no need for clinging limpets, Cecily, and you are one of the worst. Your insidious grasp suffocated your husband. I will not be another of your victims."

She froze. "I loved him." The moment of surprise passed and she raised her arm to smack him.

He grabbed her arm. "Like it rough, do you? I can oblige." He hauled her to the bed, grabbing her waist and tossing her onto the bed. "Coming, ready or not!"

Cecily grappled with him, trying to fend him off. His harsh actions excited her. "Mark!"

He shoved off her, a repelled sneer on his face. "Like I said, a mistake. Get out, Cecily."

She sat up, propping her weight on her hands behind her. It showed off her breasts to nice advantage. "It won't be a mistake," she cooed. "I'll make you forget her."

"Not likely," he snapped. He strode to the door and flung it open. "I suggest you leave before someone sees you spread so wantonly across my bed. I have no desire to ruin two women in one day."

Sighing, she rose, brushing down her skirts. She headed for the exit, but paused when exactly opposite him. "Why did you ruin her, Mark? Passion may be excused if it is bound by wedlock. You could have saved her. She'll be cast out from Society now."

At least he winced. "None of your damned business. Now, get out."

She did and jumped when the door slammed behind her.

So much for her great plan to take Portia's place.

Lady Cecily returned downstairs, joining Miss Lucy Chalcroft at the window, waiting for the men.

17

Portia sat by her packed bags, waiting for her mother to appear and give the signal that it was time to leave. She had not moved in the hour it had taken her maid to complete the packing.

At some point, Portia had accepted a blanket from her and had wrapped it tight around her shoulders. Her very bones felt chilled.

And empty, so empty.

A discreet scratching sounded at the door. Portia rose. Time to leave. "Enter."

She sucked in a breath. Young Winterton stood in her doorway, a hangdog expression on his face.

"You should have stuck with me." He looked down at his hands. "I would have taken you to wife."

"Gareth." Portia had never spoken his given name before and it sounded strange to her ears. "Is that why you have come to see me?"

"No." His hands twisted once. He shot her a beseeching look. "Why not me, Portia? Why? I cannot take another man's leavings, but I ache for you."

"Your feelings run deep," said Portia, thinking she might never feel again.

He stepped into her room, gathering up her hands. "Let me take you from here. I fear what will happen to you when you leave this place. I cannot marry you, but become my mistress. I would forever be your slave and keep you safe."

Her brows crouched into a frown. "I refused to be Knightson's mistress, and your father's. What makes you think I would accept you?"

He started back, as if she had stung him. "You cannot afford to be cruel, Portia. Let me save you."

Behind him, Portia's mother cleared her throat. "Your plea is useless, my lord. There is no way His Grace will allow you to marry my daughter. He forbade it before, he will triply do so now."

"What do you intend to do with her?" the young viscount dared to ask.

"That is none of your business, my lord." Mrs. Carew folded her arms over her expansive bosom and stepped aside to let young Winterton depart.

He bowed over Portia's hand, kissing it. "Portia."

"Thank you for deigning to say good-bye to me," she whispered.

The door closed behind him, leaving her with her mother and her maid.

"How many have you slept with in this house?" her mother snapped. "Harlot!"

Portia took a breath. She had been expecting the storm to break and every accusation she deserved. "One other." She met her mother's wide-eyed gaze with an infuriating calm.

"Whore!" The breath blew out of Mama. "We shall discuss this later. At this moment, His Grace and his bride await you in my chambers. Go to him and be meek and humble, you tart."

"Yes, Mama." Portia cast off the blanket from her shoulders and made an effort to tidy herself further.

"No. You are no daughter of mine." Mrs. Carew shook Portia's arm and let her go.

Rubbing her bicep, Portia entered her mother's bedchamber. She closed the door behind her. None should be privy to this interview.

"Oh, Portia!" Lucy flew into her arms, hugging the breath out of her. "I begged His Grace to let me see you before you go, but he would only let me if he were with me."

Portia nodded at the duke over Lucy's shoulder. "That was very proper of him, Lucy."

Lucy stepped back, taking Portia by the shoulders and examining her face. "Oh, Portia, my dear, I did warn you!"

Patting Lucy's arm, Portia agreed. "There is nothing to be done about it now." She clasped Lucy's hand. "I shall treasure the memories of our friendship, for I know I shall not see you again."

The duke cleared his throat over his fiancée's sobs. "I am glad of this chance to thank you for your wedding gift to my Lucy." His arm went about Lucy's shaking shoulders. "It shows a tenderness of thought I had not expected of you."

"I see my womanly mysteries are becoming all too few," Portia quipped, disengaging from Lucy. "I trust you shall use it wisely."

"And diligently, my dear girl," added the duke.

Lucy looked up at her duke. Portia recognized the beseeching expression on her face. Would everyone attempt to intercede on her behalf?

Stroking Lucy's golden hair, the duke turned his attention to Portia. "My dear Lucy reminds me of the other reason we are here." He took a deep breath. "Let us send for you when we are married."

"Send for me?" Portia repeated, dully. "Your Grace will want nothing to do with me."

"It will be at my country estate, Portia, away from the city and the gossips. In the country, we can do as we please."

Portia struggled with this sudden generosity. "Under what capacity?"

"Pardon?"

"Under what capacity do you wish me to stay at your home?" Portia got the words out with difficulty, grief and anger mingling into a hard ball in her chest.

"As our honored guest." Lucy reached out, but dropped her arm at Portia's harsh frown.

"Your Grace?" Portia's direct gaze pinned down the duke.

"I am not used to being spoken to in such an uncouth manner, young lady." His irritation snapped out his offer. "As our guest of course, but also as a playmate for my wife. Do not think I am unaware of the high regard she has for you."

Lucy colored, but said nothing.

"And for yourself?" The duke's hauteur no longer cowed her.

"I hope you will learn to be fond of me also, and to allow me to watch you two at play. I shan't join in unless you wish it."

Portia sucked in her breath, the anger dissipating at the generous offer. "You must allow me to think this over," she got out, her throat choking with unshed tears. "I do not wish to raise your hopes. I do not know if I can. . . ."

"That is why we will not send for you at once," Lucy explained. "We thought you would need time to recover from . . . from Mr. Knightson's cruelty."

Pasting a smile on her face, Portia took another breath. Why did it take so much conscious effort to do even the simplest thing? "I shall be all right. Whatever happens."

"He won't come for you, you know," the duke told her, his smile small and uncertain. "He has left Willowhill already. You cannot allow yourself to hope that your situation may change, that he might come for you."

A sob burst from Portia's lips. She clapped a hand over her mouth, trying to muffle her cries.

Lucy gathered her into another embrace, the duke standing back. "Hush, hush now. All will be well."

It never would. "Oh God, oh God. I have been such a fool!"

At last, the crying jag ended and she squirreled out of Lucy's soothing arms. In her heart, she knew she'd never be able to accept their proposal. She just didn't feel the same way as they did. To give herself over to them, to mimic that desire would be a recipe for disaster.

Portia dried her tears with the back of her hand. "Thank you, thank you both. Send word when you are ready to receive me. I will let you know my decision then."

"Very wise." The duke dropped a kiss on her forehead, stepping past. "Come, my dear."

Portia returned to her own bedchamber where her mother waited. Not her mother. Not any more. Sniffling, Portia decided to refer to her as Mrs. Carew from now on.

"I am ready." Portia slipped on her pelisse, avoiding use of any name.

She descended to the grand entrance hall, with each step fearing to be further reviled. She had come here, hoping to bide her time until Mrs. Carew gave up on trying to marry her off.

Now, she would receive the very retreat from Society she had craved, sans reputation and sans any family support.

Lord Barrington and Sir Guy waited for them by the large front doors. Sir Guy stepped forward. "Miss Carew, my commiserations on this disastrous turn of affairs."

Out of the corner of her eye, Portia spotted Lady Cecily lurking in the shadows of the grand staircase. "Very kind of you to come and see me off," Portia said, all ice and calm. Hiding her emotion kept her safe from further ridicule.

"On the contrary, Miss Carew. I hoped I could make you stay."

"Stay? I could never stay here." She bobbed a brief curtsey. "Your pardon, Lord Barrington."

He acknowledged her apology. "Quite understandable, Miss Carew."

Bet he's glad to be rid of me too, Portia thought, wanting to leave right now. Why did Sir Guy insist on drawing this out?

"Stay as my wife." Sir Guy didn't bother to kneel. "I have a special license already."

Portia stared at him. "You were that sure of me?"

"Absolument." Sir Guy's easy smile of conquest turned Portia's stomach. "I had you first, Portia. By rights, you are mine."

This set Mrs. Carew off into another hail of sobs.

"I am not, nor will ever be, yours." Portia kept her voice level. She stood, straight and alone in the center of the giant marble floor.

Lord Barrington interceded. "Portia, please reconsider. This entire affair has been most lamentable, but Sir Guy offers you a way out of perdition."

"It would wash my hands of you." Mrs. Carew dabbed at her eyes with a lacy handkerchief. "Once, I believed your innocence, but you have wronged me and you have wronged this man. Submit to him, girl, if you know what is good for you."

Another word and Portia felt that she would snap in two. Sir Guy's triumphant grin sank her even deeper into despair.

Her voice cut through the large space like a knife. "Mrs. Carew, I would prefer any horror you have waiting for me than to marry him." She directed a hateful glare at Sir Guy. "Where is your special license, then? Let me see it."

Sir Guy produced it from an inner coat pocket, showing it to her.

Portia snatched it out of his grasp and tore it in two. She

flung the pieces onto the ground and spat on them. "There's that to your stupid license. I'll not have you, Sir Guy. You disgust me."

Sir Guy's expression turned to stone. "You, woman, are shameless. Your beauty masks an ugliness no man will ever want unless he pays for the doubtful pleasure of fucking you."

He ignored Mrs. Carew's shocked gasp and strode from the hall.

Portia turned to her mother—Mrs. Carew. "I think we can leave now."

She left Willowhill Hall, head held high. She was stripped, debased, destroyed, but no one would know it to look at her.

Lady Cecily stepped out of her hiding place in the shadows of Willowhill Hill's great staircase and pursued Sir Guy. He stalked along the hallway, fists clenched at his side.

"Sir Guy." She pitched her call low.

He stopped, turning to glare at her. "What do you want?"

"I am sorry your plans did not work out." Lady Cecily forbore to tell him she feared just a thing might happen. Portia Carew didn't seem like the type of woman to easily cave to threats. "Is there anything I can do?"

His glare didn't diminish, but his fair brows scrunched together. "Why are you still here? Knightson left hours ago. You were supposed to be with him."

"Matters didn't proceed as I had hoped either." Lady Cecily approached him and touched his arm at the elbow. "So much for plans."

His forehead relaxed, the glare lessened. "The bitch will deserve all she gets. I'll wager she'll end up a streetwalker."

Lady Cecily winced. "Don't think of her." She sighed at his renewed frown. "We made such a good team. Why didn't this work?"

He shook his head, distracted, shrugged his shoulders. "I need a drink."

"May I join you?" Lady Cecily kept her request soft, undemanding.

"Why not? Barrington has a stash in the dining room." He cocked an eyebrow at her. "That is, if you can handle stronger liquor."

She nodded once. "Of course."

Lady Cecily followed him into the dining room. Sir Guy crossed to the sideboard, opening one of the paneled doors. He retrieved a decanter and two crystal glasses, the two glasses clinking as he held them in one hand.

Watching him pour, she stood beside him. She accepted the glass from him, her fingertips lingering over his before she gripped the glass.

He didn't appear to notice, lifting his own glass and downing its contents in one long gulp. He slammed the glass back onto the sideboard so hard, Lady Cecily felt sure it would shatter.

It did not and he poured himself another drink. He paused in lifting his glass to his lips. "You have not drunk anything."

Obedient, she lifted the glass to her mouth, tilted it and let the liquor slide down her throat. The fiery liquid burned, but she'd drunk it before. She took her time, but didn't lower her glass until it was all gone.

Licking her lips, she placed the glass next to the decanter. "Pour."

Sir Guy obliged and this time they drank together. Lady Cecily watched him watch her as they drank. A roiling hot mist rose up from her stomach, his intense stare sparking awareness in her breasts and belly.

He did want her.

She held out her empty glass, her hand steady. "Another."

Again, Sir Guy did the honors.

Lady Cecily raised her glass. "To us."

"Us?" A sharp look of suspicion narrowed his gaze.

"Who have fought and lost," Lady Cecily clarified.

"To us." Sir Guy echoed the toast and tossed back the liquor. Lady Cecily followed suit. His skin flushed and the anger melted from his features. "*Damme*, but you drink like a fish."

"A widow's weeds allows many privileges." Lady Cecily leaned toward him. The dining room, the shining mahogany table and the blue striped walls went out of focus.

"The brandy has gone to your head." Sir Guy steadied her, hands upon her upper arms.

"Mmm," she agreed. She swayed forward and Sir Guy caught her in his arms. Blinking, she gazed up at him. "Take me to bed."

He nodded. "You should sleep this off before you embarrass Lady Barrington."

"No." She shook her head, dislodging a few auburn curls. "Don't mean that. Bed me."

He regarded her, and it shook her out of her hazy state. "You cannot be serious."

"Have me," she blurted, her brain too stubborn to give up this idea. "Why not? Can't have her. I can't have him. Why not?" Her fingers crept up the breadth of his waistcoat, reaching his chin. "We were *good* together."

His cock poked the thin material of her gown.

"Anything you want to do. You do want me."

His grip tightened around her. "Anything? You'll submit to me utterly?"

"More than that chit ever did, I'll wager." Her upper lip curled for a moment. "Yes, utterly."

"I had to hold myself back with her. Didn't want to scare the brat." Sir Guy stroked her face.

She blinked up at him. "You don't scare me. You excite me."

His mouth crushed down upon hers, demanding and possessing. Lady Cecily melted into him, returning his kiss with the same ferocity.

He ended the kiss, tugging on her lower lip. "Your chambers or mine?"

"Yours," she breathed.

He swept her up in his arms, kicked open the dining room door and to the astonishment of a scurrying servant, he carried her upstairs to his chamber.

Less happy events surrounded Portia. The entire journey home occurred in silence, her mother saying not a word to her.

On their arrival home—their country abode, not the house they rented in the City—Portia's mother disappeared into Mr. Carew's study. Shrill and angry cries emanated from behind the door, along with the barely heard bass tones of Portia's father.

Portia crept upstairs. A maid had already opened her luggage and had started to pull out clothing.

"You had best put that all back, Bessie," Portia murmured, sitting on the end of her narrow bed. "I do not think I shall be remaining here much longer."

"Yes, ma'am." Bessie's sad curtsey indicated the staff already knew the events at Willowhill Hall.

Which left only her younger siblings in the dark.

The elder of the two, Viola, stuck her head around the open door. Viola winced at a particularly loud shriek from downstairs. Beside her the youngest, Bianca, peeked from behind Viola's skirts.

"What did you do?" whispered Viola, her eyes wide. "Mama isn't even crying, not like last time."

The last time Portia's name and reputation had been besmirched, her mother had believed in her. She gazed down at her gloved fingers. She hadn't even taken off her pelisse. "Viola,

I have fallen from grace." She glanced up at them. "You should not be caught talking to me."

Viola's eyes grew even rounder. "Are you going to be sent away?"

Portia nodded. "I suspect so." She held open her arms. "Quick—one last hug and then you must go."

Little Bianca flew into her arms, her young face full of confusion. "Why?"

Viola, only three years younger than Portia and ready to make her debut upon Society, exchanged a sorrowful look with Portia and hugged her shoulders roughly. "I'll explain it to you, little Bee." She pulled Bianca out of Portia's arms, and with one last sympathetic look over her shoulder, ushered Bianca out of the room.

Her mother's maid ascended the steps. Portia heard the heavy clump of the maid's arthritic tread. She didn't even bob the smallest curtsey. "Your father will see you in his study."

Portia nodded, dismissing the maid and descending the stairs. A weight lay in her heart. Her time had come. Banishment lay ahead. All that remained was the generosity of her father, who might mitigate her exile somewhat.

If she were lucky.

She tapped on the study door and stepped inside. Thankfully, her mother had left, leaving her father sitting behind his expansive desk, a wall of books behind him, his hands steepled over his plump belly.

"Well, daughter. What do you have to say for yourself?" A deep frown marred his round face.

Portia sucked in her breath. She got a hearing? She shook her head. "I am sure that all my mother has said is true, at least at the core. I was caught in an indelicate position with another guest of Willowhill Hall and that is why we are returned home."

Her father took off his glasses and rubbed the bridge of his nose, squinting myopically at her. "Had you no thought for your family? For your sister, Viola? She will be carrying your scar when she makes her debut next year."

Wincing, Portia ducked her head. "I had not planned for it to come out. We kept everything secret, so that my reputation would not suffer."

"The man refused to do the honorable thing, Portia. How could you associate with such a man, let alone succumb to such a liaison?"

Her father's cold voice washed over her. How could she explain herself in a way that wouldn't revolt her father's sensibilities? She settled for the short answer. "That surprised me too," she admitted.

A band tightened around her chest. No, she would not cry. Not for one unworthy of the tears. "I was a trusting fool, Papa," she said, her voice full of tears.

"Why, Portia, my girl, why?" He echoed her pain.

She lifted her shoulders and let them fall. "After Sir Guy's accusations, I never planned to marry. I didn't want to go through that again. He had given me a taste, though"—she swallowed at her father's wince—"and well, Mr. Knightson taught me how to—to please myself without a man."

Mr. Carew covered his eyes. "That's not what it looked like."

"Matters spiraled beyond that," Portia confirmed.

"Foolish child," he murmured, his voice choked with emotion and tenderness. He rose from his seat. "You know we have to send you away. For Viola's sake, you understand. It will help mitigate this disaster heaped upon us."

Portia nodded. "I understand."

"I need a few days to find a place for you. I will send you north to my sister. You shall not show your face until you have reached your final destination. I shall write to your Aunt Maria and explain all. I cannot afford to keep in you in luxury, Portia. It will be the meagerest of subsistences, no maid, and you will have to grow much of your own food."

At least he hadn't thrown her out upon the street. Stumbling over her thanks, Portia remained frozen in place. Her father gave no gesture that he would welcome her embrace.

At the last, she backed out, running up the stairs, tears streaming down her face.

18

Two months later.

Portia knelt in the black loam, her old woolen skirt not preventing the dampness from seeping through. Her tiny cottage, some old shepherd's hut, built of stone, reflected the warm sun upon her back.

She planted another row of seeds, a gift from her aunt, and glanced over at the dirt-strewn book to her right. The battered gardener's manual had saved her from many a disaster thus far, but even so, she worried if she would have food enough to last her through the winter.

She eked out her provisions as a result, relieved that she had least learned how to preserve foods in her mother's kitchen.

Her mother. She straightened, kinking out her lower back. Mrs. Carew had not said another word to her. No word, no letters from her family since then either.

She'd wanted this life, hadn't she? A life alone.

A movement caught her eye farther down the green valley.

She shielded her eyes and discerned a sole rider making his way along the riverbank.

She dismissed him, returning to her chores. Nobody came to her cottage, not even the local minister. She patted dirt over her precious seeds and sprinkled water over them. She rose and shifted to another row, where seedlings sprouted in glorious confusion.

Consulting the manual once more, she flipped the pages until she found the page on weeds. She compared the illustration to the seedlings and dared to pluck one from the earth.

A throat cleared.

Portia shot to her feet, the book tumbling face down into the black dirt. She should bolt. She should—*oh God. Knightson.*

"Excuse me, but I am looking for a young woman. Keeps to herself. She has a cottage near—" Knightson bent forward from the saddle, squinting. "My God. Portia? Is that you?"

She emitted a squeal and ran for the cottage. She slammed the door, shunting the bolt home. Leaning against the door, she panted, reviewing the situation.

Only the chest-high wooden fence slowed his progress to her front door, enabling her to escape. She expected him to hammer on the door at any moment. He would not give up so easily.

What was he doing here?

Knightson pounded on the door. "Portia! Let me in."

She closed her eyes, feeling a tear trickle through the grime on her face. Her palm flattened against the sturdy door as if she could feel his warmth through it.

"Portia!" The pounding on the door made her head ache.

"Go away!" she yelled, hitting the door with her fist. "How dare you come here!"

"Portia, I have been searching for you." His voice, still that same delicious dark burr, wheedled and cajoled her to open the door.

To do that would be disaster. "To make me your mistress? I think not. I am doing very well here, thank you."

"To make you my wife."

"You lie!" she shot through the door.

"Portia, can you not at least open the door so we may stop shouting like fishwives?" His voice dropped lower, until she hardly heard it through the vastness of the door. "I have no desire to let the whole valley learn of your circumstances. Open the door. I will not leave until you have done so."

With trembling hands, she unlatched the door, pulling the bolt back and opening the door. She placed herself firmly in his way, folding her arms. No chance would she invite him in.

She gazed up at him. Stern and lovely as ever, fresh lines marked his cheekbones and his glorious black hair had been ruffled by his ride.

"It really is you," he breathed. He stared at her in disbelief.

Portia patted at her hair, covered by an old piece of striped linen. "I know I look a sight, Mr. Knightson. There is no need to look as if I have sprouted another head."

His lips twisted in wry amusement. "Is this how you planned it, Portia? To live like a serf in such a Godforsaken place as this?"

She tilted her head and regarded him. "It has turned out well enough."

He shook his head. "How can you—?" He stepped forward and placed hands upon her shoulders. "You are to marry me, Portia."

"The hell I am." She shook off his grasp, stepping back. "Why should I marry you? You had your chance—you abandoned me."

"Not one of my better moments." His suntanned skin darkened. "Your parents have given me permission."

"If that is so, why did you spend so long searching for me?"

"Portia—"

"You have said enough, sir. I have no interest in being forced to marry you, any more than you are interested in marrying me. You needn't worry—there is no child resulting from our liaison." A fact she had cried tears over, but he didn't need to know that.

"But I am interested in marrying you." He even looked sincere.

"You had your chance." She slammed the door between them again and slid the bolt home.

To her surprise, he didn't rap on the door and demand she concede to him.

She busied herself in the kitchen, preparing her evening meal. After settling the pot over the fire, she peeked outside the tiny window into her front yard.

Knightson had gone.

Portia slid to the floor and cried, huge sobs that racked her frame.

Damn him, damn him for coming back.

She rose with the sun. She dared not waste an hour in the chores that kept her little cottage in fighting trim.

Taking the wooden bucket from its hook by the door, Portia stepped out into the dawn light. Mist rose from the river below, casting a faint green glow over the valley floor.

She opened the rickety gate that kept most of the wildlife out of her garden and stopped short.

Knightson lay asleep next to the fence, sleeping in a roll of blankets. At the creaking sound of the gate, he awoke, sitting up.

Portia's heart thumped painfully hard and she stared at the bared, dark column of his throat and the darker bristles of his unshaven cheeks. "You didn't leave," she murmured.

"No," he returned, his voice low.

She held out the bucket. "Then you may make yourself useful and fetch me water."

She turned on her heel and strode back into the cottage, leaving the door open. At least he spared her one trip of hauling water from the river below.

She attempted to tidy her hair in his absence and splashed the last of yesterday's water onto her face. She'd fallen asleep in the midst of her tears. *I must look a wreck.*

Turning her attention to breakfast, she started cooking eggs and some bacon she'd bought from a neighbor with her precious, dwindling funds.

Knightson reappeared, putting down the bucket at her direction and sitting at her tiny battered kitchen table. He said nothing, folding his arms and watching her work.

She served him breakfast on chipped china (a gift from her aunt) and sat opposite him. Portia ate, ignoring the approving sounds coming from the other side of the table.

"You can cook," Knightson said at last. "You are a veritable prize."

She looked up at him, her eyes narrowing. "I will not marry you."

He pushed his plate away. "Why not? We were good together."

Portia's lip curled. "Sex isn't everything." She bit down on her lower lip before continuing, "You abused me and abandoned me, yet you expect me to take you back?"

"You really want to live like this?" His arms swept the tiny cottage.

"Haven't I said so all along?" she shot back.

"Portia, be reasonable."

"I will be reasonable when you apologize, when you explain your horrid actions to me, sir. And they are inexcusable!"

He sighed, running a hand through his hair, pulling out a piece of dried grass and discarding it. "I had thought you had trapped me."

"Yes, your words then made that very clear." Portia couldn't stand to look at him anymore. She rose and started dealing with the dirty dishes in the chipped white porcelain sink.

"I was an idiot." He sounded frustrated. "I didn't want marriage and I knew you didn't want it, so why should we be forced into it? That was how I reasoned."

"Reasoned? You were incensed at being trapped." Portia scrubbed the pan harder.

"I was," he allowed. "That's the idiotic part."

She heard his chair scrape, the muffled clunk of his boots on the stone floor. He stood behind her, his breath hot on her neck.

"I tried forgetting about you, Portia. I have not been able to shake you from my mind, or my heart."

He embraced her from behind, but she remained stiff in his arms, gazing up at the exposed roof beams. "I need more than a little flattery, Mark."

His lips pressed against the back of her neck. "It's not flattery. Portia, I have searched all over looking for you. Does that not tell you how much I need you?"

She turned in his loose embrace, her hands pressed against his chest. "How can I be sure of that? Is it not possible that this is a spur of the moment thing for you?"

"I asked everywhere." His blue gaze bored into her. "I know you even refused the Duke of Winterton and his new bride."

Portia sucked in her breath. "You know about that?" The duke and his new duchess had come looking for her, finding her at her aunt's in York. She'd been tearful, but firm.

"I do. I convinced the new duchess of the sincerity of my intentions toward you. That's how I found your aunt."

"She did not tell you."

Portia adored the wry smile that crossed his features and fought to hide it.

"Indeed, she gave me a great ear-wigging over my bad behavior. I almost preferred it to your father's quiet disappointment."

"You saw my father?" Portia recalled him mentioning her parents yesterday but she'd been too angry to stop for news. In her eagerness to hear of him, she leaned forward, closing the distance between them.

"I did. He seemed well." He brushed a loose curl off her cheek. "Had I seen your mother, I am sure I would not have escaped alive."

Portia made a snort of amusement. "No more than your just desserts."

"Portia, my love, how can you stand there smiling at me and tell me so?"

She pushed him away, replacing her smile with a frown. "That smile was for my father, not you."

"So you say." Knightson perched himself on the edge of her kitchen table. "You love me, admit it."

"You arrogant oaf! I shall do no such thing." She folded her arms over her woolen gown and glared at him.

"Portia, what can I do to convince you that I am in earnest?"

She bit back what she wanted to say. She wanted to say: how about proposing to me, rather than declaring we are to be married? "And what can I do to convince you that it is too late? You had your chance, Mark."

"Give me another chance, Portia. How could you be so cruel?" He approached her again. "Please?"

"There is nothing you can do that will make me change my mind. I suggest you leave."

"What about this?" Knightson embraced her, held her tight. She opened her mouth to protest only to find it covered by his. He plundered her senses, robbed her of any words of protest and she sank into him, arms curling behind his neck.

Heaven help her, she kissed him back, giving him all her loneliness over the past couple of months.

He moaned into her mouth, his large hands curving around her buttocks, pulling her to him. "Tell me you won't miss this."

She gazed up at him, her eyebrows quirking. "I'm sure I could find a nice shepherd boy to train," she drawled. "Once I tire of what you have taught me."

"Wench, you are provoking." He grinned down at her. "You cannot deny you want me. You have just shown me you do."

"I want you, yes." Her voice went hoarse. "But do I need you?"

"I need you." Mark kissed her again, a long breathtaking kiss. "Let me show you how much I need you."

She acquiesced with a sigh. When had she ever denied him?

He peppered her throat with kisses. "I am sorry, I am sorry," he whispered in quiet agony against her damp skin.

Portia closed her eyes against incipient tears and held on to him. She wanted to forgive him, but not yet. Not yet.

He lifted her up, swiveling to place her on the kitchen table. He stood back and stared at her. Just stared.

She shifted, uncomfortably aware of the sad state of her appearance.

Stepping in, he cupped her face. "I *missed* you," he murmured. He claimed another kiss before she could reply. "I missed seeing you, talking with you, and yes, bedding you. By God, Portia, it was as if someone had ripped a part of me away. I am so sorry that I didn't realize it sooner."

"Why didn't you?" she whispered.

"Too angry. Angry at being betrayed, manipulated. Angry at my valet when I found out it was he who betrayed us. I turned him off, by the way." He took a deep breath. His hands warmed her cheeks. "Angry at myself. And then there was nobody to be angry at.

"I missed you and came looking for you." He stroked her cheek with the back of his forefinger, his intense blue-eyed gaze riveting her to the spot.

Her heart filled with emotion she'd long thought banished. Her only option had been to bury her feelings for him, forget him, for she'd believed he'd never come for her, having so soundly rejected her in public once already.

And yet, here he stood.

Portia leaned forward, almost slipping off the table to kiss him. In her heart of hearts, she had accepted him, but she refused to tell him so. Not yet.

"Why?" she whispered. "Why did you shame me in front of everyone?"

He blanched, a wince squeezing shut his eyes. "It is not something I am proud of," he murmured. "I thought you had tricked me—stupid, I know—but in my experience that is what women did."

"You should have associated with better women."

He shrugged, his mouth in a pained twist. "After the first betrayal, I chose to associate with women I could trust to walk away at the end of the affair."

She stiffened in his grasp. "The first betrayal."

"I was young." He swallowed. "I fell in love with her, and I thought she fell in love with me, but she manipulated me right out of her arms and into that of her niece's. It is why I have put a limit on my affairs: five consummations gives insufficient time for plotting."

"We've exceeded those five times." She frowned up at him, worried that he might disappear and leave her heartbroken once more.

"You are different." Mark kissed her brow, but she caught the glint of his tears. "I cannot be without you, Portia. I love you."

She drew his head down to hers, their foreheads bumping. "Convince me," she whispered against his lips.

His lips curved into a smile against hers. "With pleasure."

He enraptured her with his kisses, long, slow explorations

of her lips and mouth, both teasing and sparking her desire for him. While he kissed her, his hands skimmed over her woolen-stockinged calves to the back of her knees, bringing her skirts up with him.

With gentle care, he folded the skirts back over her thighs, revealing her soft, pale skin.

Mark broke away from her eager mouth and crouched before her, pressing openmouthed kisses against the tender flesh of her inner thigh.

Portia leaned back, supporting herself on her hands splayed behind her, while Mark's kisses inched closer to her quim. She tried to keep her breathing steady but she wanted his mouth on her cunt *NOW*.

It had been so long—months—that even bringing herself to pleasure seemed a shadow besides Mark's skillful lovemaking.

She reclined all the way, lying across her kitchen table, her head dangerously close to falling off the table lip. Her parted legs dangled over the table's edge.

Mark hooked her legs over his shoulders. His breath puffed hot on her wet slit. Had she been wet for him since the moment she'd seen him again? Certainly, his confession had wrung it from her.

She waited, shivering, for his first lick, his first caress. She heard him breathe deeply. Why didn't he touch her? Her heartbeat quickened in fear, that somehow she had ruined herself, that confronted with the sight of her quim, Mark had realized his mistake, and searched for a way to politely disengage.

He had no need for politeness to her, being so low now on the social scale.

His first tentative lick came without warning and she bucked under him, a relieved yelp escaping her.

He chuckled and dove in for another taste, a long lick from top to bottom, parting her swollen outer lips. His tongue circled around her hole, absorbing the sex fluids she released.

She was ready. More than ready.

Still, Mark took his time, kissing and licking her cunt. He had not shaved that morning, and his beard grazed her sensitive skin. She twitched at his stabbing bristles and he backed off from burying his face completely against her wet quim.

He paid particular gentle attention to her erect clit, coaxing it into a throbbing button. Just his breath across her clit made her sigh.

Portia wriggled beneath him, clenching her skirts as the need for release grew greater and greater. She sobbed and gasped, wanting him closer, wanting him in her, and yet he kept his distance, aware of his bruising beard.

"Mark!" she gasped. "Please!"

He rose from his crouch, bending over her until Portia felt his erection, trapped by his trousers, press against her aching quim.

The lower part of his face glistened with her juices. "I want to feel your release while I'm inside you. Where is your bedroom?"

She gestured behind her. "Next room." There were only two.

He scooped her up, carrying her effortlessly to the next room. He halted in the doorway.

Wincing, Portia closed her eyes, imagining how this room must appear to him. A single, narrow bed, the thin mattress supported by sagging ropes. She kept clean linens on the bed, though, not wanting to eschew that comfort.

Candle smoke and time had done its damage to the walls, leaving them dingy and beige as opposed to the pure white of the kitchen. The only furniture consisted of a chest and a narrow shelf. Portia did all her correspondence at the kitchen table, although she had yet to receive a reply.

Mark kissed her hair. "Oh, Portia, my love." He kissed her hair and carried her into the room, setting her down. His look of sympathy vanished to be replaced by a quite lecherous grin. "I want to see you naked," he said.

The thrill of his aroused gaze excited Portia even further. "And I you," she returned breathlessly.

He barked a laugh and stripped off his coat, his shirt soon following. He worked at unbuttoning his breeches and glanced up at her. "Well, woman, why aren't you undressing?"

Portia grinned at him, her fingers going to loosen the tapes of her gown while she watched him continue to undress, his cock magnificently rampant while he struggled to remove his boots.

"Damn it," he said, snarling at the black leather. "I think I need your help." His expression softened into a speculative one. "Finish undressing first."

Smiling, Portia divested herself of her gown and the shift underneath.

"No stays?"

"No one to help me with them." She had yet to work out a suitable alternative. That her gowns hung loose on her now seemed to make the matter moot. Who cared if she wore stays or not?

Portia crossed to him, and straddled his out-thrust leg, grabbing the boot firmly by the sole and heel. "Ready?"

He planted his other booted foot against her rear. "Ready."

Mark almost knocked her forward with the force of his shove, but she held steady and the boot slipped off. She straddled his other leg without comment, her bottom stinging slightly, the sense of his booted imprint burning her skin.

His boots removed, Portia retreated to the bed, rubbing her rear, much to Mark's amusement.

She watched him finish undressing. His skintight breeches allowed for a little movement, given that he'd ridden in them, so they came off with little fuss.

He stood before her, beautifully naked, a primal force con-

274 / Celia May Hart

tained in flesh and bone. Dark curly hair pooled around his hard cock and ran in a narrow line up his belly.

Mark distracted her from feasting her eyes on him by stroking his cock. Already hard, his pumping seemed to make the bulbous head push out farther.

He strode forward, a tiny bead forming in the eye of his cock. She reached out, taking over the stroking of his shaft, bringing his cock to her mouth.

She licked the promise of more jism off him and then swirled her tongue around the head, thoroughly wetting him with her saliva. She compressed her lips about his cock, sucking him until he groaned.

He put a hand on her forehead, urging her away. "I want to climax inside you and I am close to bursting, my dear Portia. It has been far too long."

She released him from her mouth, gazing up at him, eyes wide. He had not had another woman since he'd left her?

"I wanted no other but you," he purred. His hands rested on her shoulders and he pushed her down onto the bed.

Parting her legs, she felt his cock press against her cunt and she wriggled, delighting in his moans.

"Keep still, wench, or I shall come all over you," he growled through gritted teeth.

He kissed her hard, his tongue plunging into her mouth at the same time as he entered her. She moaned around his swirling tongue, feeling him part her swollen flesh until he buried himself to the hilt.

A sob choking in her throat, Portia kissed him back, her quim squeezing around his cock. It felt good, right, perfect.

He shifted inside her and Portia felt the first wave of tension crest. She cried out, clinging to Mark, her nails clawing his back.

Another slight shift and she hovered on the brink, release just a thrust away.

"Portia," Mark groaned. "I cannot hold out."

"Fuck me, Mark," Portia begged between her gasping cries. "Make me come."

Gathering her into his arms and gripping her shoulders, Mark thrust into her. Again and again and . . .

Lost in the sudden propulsion of release, Portia tensed and bore down hard, squeezing Mark tight with all her strength. She wanted him to stay inside her, to never ever leave.

Through the roaring in her ears, she heard Mark cry out, the last battering a delicious coda to her ecstatic release.

He subsided in her arms, kissing her damp brow, his panting breath hot against her skin. Regaining his breath, he gazed down at her, his eyes filled with something unfathomable.

"Portia, now will you marry me?"

She wiped the sweat that trickled down the side of his face. "Seeing as you have asked so nicely, yes I will."

His embrace tightened convulsively about her. "You are in my blood, Portia. I don't know what I would do if you had said no."

She grinned up at him. "Fucked me until I said yes, I suppose." She made a moue with her lips. "I guess I gave in too soon."

He laughed then, kissing her brow, her nose and finally her mouth. She responded to his kiss, giving him as much as he gave. "There is always celebratory sex."

"Wonderful," she murmured, focused on kissing his chin.

"But I think we should wait until after we're married."

She pushed him away, although he didn't budge much, and stared up at him. "But that could take weeks!"

He chuckled. "Not if we have a special license, which I do. It's in my coat pocket. We merely need to dress and head for the nearest church."

Portia squealed and hugged him tight. "Yes, yes! Yes!"

Take a sneak peek at PURE SEX, starring three hot new authors of contemporary erotica: Lucinda Betts, Bonnie Edwards, and Sasha White. Available in July 2006 from Aphrodisia . . .

Alone below, Teri took in how sumptuous the boat was. The Web site hadn't done it justice. Pleased, she noted an extra long cream-colored leather sofa along one side. A couple of armchairs completed the furnishings while a plasma screen television was set on the wall. Light wood cabinets kept the cooking area from being dark. She marveled at the ingenious use of space and opened every cupboard she saw.

The bathroom off the master cabin was small but well appointed with a shower set in a tiny tub. She opened the medicine chest over the sink to check out what it was that Jared had put away. A variety pack of condoms: glow in the dark, flavored and ribbed for her pleasure.

Extra large.

She snorted. Philip should be so lucky.

Back in the master cabin she checked out the drawer in the night table. The DVDS Jared had put away were X-rated. She popped one into the player, propped herself on the bed and skipped through the beginning to find couples enjoying strong,

healthy, powerful sex. Great sex. Friendly sex. Even affection-
ate sex.

Philip's pious expression when he'd explained the concept
of revirginizing swam in front of her mind's screen. He wanted
them to remember their wedding night as special, he'd said.
She'd been amazingly agreeable. It had been so easy to give up
sleeping with him; she should have seen the signs of a dying relationship.

But by then the wedding had taken on a life of its own, a
juggernaut, there was no stopping it. His mother, her mother,
the caterer, the church, the dress!

None of the energetic sex she saw on the portable bedroom
television had ever happened with Philip. She sighed, wandered
out to the little kitchen, retrieved the champagne from the
fridge, opened it and poured herself a tumbler full. She considered digging out the flutes Jared had put away but the tumbler
held more. And Teri wanted lots.

When she settled back onto the bed a couple onscreen were
enjoying a fabulously decadent *soixante-neuf*. The actor's tongue-
work looked enthusiastic. The actress looked happy.

Teri watched closely, amused at first. The moaning and sex
talk were obviously dubbed in afterward. No one really said
things like that, no one felt things strongly as the actors pretended.

She changed positions on the bed, lying on her belly with
her head at the foot so she could see the action up close. And up
close was what she got.

The camera closed in on his tongue so Teri could see the
moisture, the red, full clit he was licking and sucking gently between his lips.

Her own body reacted to the visual stimulus and moistened
as the actress widened her legs and the actor slid his tongue
deep into her. She thrashed on the bed in a stunning display of
sexual hysteria that had never, ever overcome Teri.

Teri was jealous. Did people react this strongly to oral sex? She never had. But, then, Philip was so fastidious she doubted he'd ever been as deeply involved as the actor was. Even an actor who was being paid to fake it was more turned on that Philip had been the few times she'd insisted.

Teri knew what she wanted, knew what she liked, knew what would get her off like a rocket, but Philip had issues.

She'd always hoped he'd warm up more. Get hotter, get horny. For her. But he hadn't. Wouldn't. Not ever.

The onscreen couple switched positions and the actress performed fellatio until the man bucked and howled with his orgasm. The couple tumbled onto the sofa, sated.

Teri clicked off the TV, took another long drink and rolled onto her back. Her legs slid open and she felt herself, moist and heavy with need.

The bedroom door was open and from here she could see through the living area and up the stairs to one small rectangular patch of sky. She wondered what would happen if Jared were to peer down the hatch and see her here with her legs splayed and her hand on her wet slit.

Would the pirate on the deck come down to the master cabin and grab her ankles like the actor had? She closed her eyes and let her fantasy play out. It was better than any porn flick because she could control every movement, every word and all of her responses. She could tell Jared what to do and he'd do it.

She could tell him to lick her breasts and lift her hips to bring her closer to his mouth. He could trail his scratchy chin delicately along her inner thigh until he got close enough that she could feel his hot breath on her hotter pussy. She slid her other hand to a nipple and plucked it while she opened to her questing fingertip.

She would tell him to linger there, just far enough away from her that he'd be able to see her wet lips, smell her aroused flesh, feel her need. Sliding a fingertip into herself, familiar tension built while she worked to bring herself to orgasm. He would kiss her there where she was hottest, moist and achy. He'd do whatever she told him to and like it.

She wasn't wired for abstinence, hadn't wanted to go along with Philip's crazy idea, but—oh, yes, it was building to a peak now and soon she'd be over the—on a weak sigh, her orgasm pulsed through her lower body in a poor imitation of what she'd witnessed onscreen.

She opened her eyes on the wish that Jared had seen her, that he was right now on his way to ravish her like the pirate he was. But no, he'd been a gentleman and left her to herself.

Her unsatisfied self.

She'd taken the edge off, but it had been far too long since she'd had a truly good orgasm. And she deserved one. Or three.

Or a week full of them. She smiled and rose to wash her hands. In the mirror, she faced herself.

Philip was gone. She was here. Jared was here.

And Jared was hot, hot, hot.

She decided to unpack her lingerie after all.

Her carryon bag sat on the floor beside the bed, tagged and zipped and bulging. A couple of sharp points threatened to poke holes through the sides, but still, she couldn't bring herself to open it.

She took another drink of champagne instead.

The bag was full of shoes. Stilettos, each and every pair. Toes pointed enough to cripple—Philip always wanted her to wear them. If he'd wanted a tall, lanky, long-limbed wife why had he asked her out in the first place? She would never have that look, no matter how high her heels were. She was lean, yes, but her muscle tone was obvious.

Some men liked her athletic build. The pirate above decks for one, she realized as she poured and drank another tumbler of champagne. She sat on the edge of the bed, one toe on the floor for balance, the other heel tucked into her crotch. She bent over toward the night table to grab the bottle again, but nearly fell off the bed.

She was tipsy. Well and truly feeling no pain. She giggled.

Oh, hell, who cared? There was no one here to judge her. No one to tell her she'd had too much and had to mind herself.

No one to tell her to keep her hands to herself and off Jared MacKay.

"Step away from the pirate," she intoned in a dramatic imitation of Philip's most commanding tone. Then she laughed harder.

Philip had no say in anything she did anymore. He'd given up the right to chastise her, instruct her or humiliate her when he'd dashed out of the church this morning.

She stood, still laughing, curiously aware of an incredible sense of freedom. She set aside her carry-on bag. She'd open it later. Right now she wanted her bathing suit and sarong.

There was a sunset waiting for her.

A sunset and a pirate who needed taming.